Ghosts & Phantoms II

A Rollie Kemp Novel

WILLIAM BYRON HILLMAN

APPRECIATION

Thank all the brave men who work at home, and more so to all the women homemakers who put up with men like me 24/7. Your tolerance goes beyond reason.

I want to thank my friends who work as legitimate lawyers striving to help others, my buddies with the FBI, CIA, Secret Service and Homeland Security and others in law enforcement that opened hearts and minds and shared so much with me. Your time and efforts are appreciated as is your protection and the risks you take in protecting all of us. You are the true sense of what Pay Forward stands for.

Most of all I want to thank and acknowledge and select group of my friends and colleagues, and you know whom you are that have been blessed with financial wealth. The art of giving, sharing and helping those in need is immensely appreciated and you're remaining anonymous makes the gift all the more special. You are the engine that quietly keeps hope alive. May I thank you for those who do not know whom you are?

Always For

My Dianne.

Contents

OTHER WORKS

By

William Byron Hillman

BOOKS

Zebra's Rock and Me

Ghosts and Phantoms I

The Hard Way – A Memoir

Ghosts and Phantoms II

Veronique and Murray

April

Let's Sue 'Em

Quigley's Christmas Adventure

MOTION PICTURES

Quigley

The Adventures of Ragtime

Double Exposure

The Man From Clover Grove

Ragin Cajun

Lovelines

Mr. Toy

The Photographer

i

PROLOGUE

Rollie Kemp and Drake Fargo were still alive. Both had survived what should have been a fatal accident. He'd waited long enough.

It had been five months since he ordered everyone to pull back. He had a loathing for failure, and it gnawed constantly in his gut, reminding him of her mistake. She had never failed before, and he knew he should have had her chopped into little pieces and dumped into the ocean as shark food. Any man who failed him would be dead, so why had he spared her? The New York fiasco wasn't her fault. She didn't know that Richie Pataglia looked like Anthony's twin, and it was his fault for not telling her.

He didn't know why he was in hiding. No one knew he was the designer of trying to take out the Pataglia family. It was better, however, to be safe than sorry. Two months in Vancouver and three in San Francisco gave everyone the impression he was dead. He had to make a play, and he had to get even. The deal was too powerful not to work. In the next year of operation, he'd be making tens of millions of dollars. Time to show the families how to do business in the current climate. The Pataglia's had gone too legit. Their time was up.

She called herself The Watcher. He knew where she was, what she wore and whom she hung out with. He knew her favorite restaurants and clubs and where she exercised. She tossed men around like they were in garbage bags and had no personal friends. She was all about business, trying to make up for her mistakes. He was tired of having her followed.

She had a pedigree for success, and right off, on her biggest job he'd given her, she screwed it up. The bitch should be dead. She owed him and begged for another chance. He relented. They spent a week in Hawaii together. She wasn't the best he'd ever had. He knew she was faking it, but the effort she put into the scam made it fun. She knew he'd have her followed, when he sent her away. She had the guts to do a job right under his nose to prove The Watcher was as good as advertised. Her extraordinary flamboyance is what made her attractive and why she was still alive. Even in failure she carried confidence, and he liked that. A beautiful woman who snuffed life with no more thought than stepping on a bug was impressive.

He stood on the edge of the pool and glared down at the ocean. San Francisco was cold year round. Once in a while the weather let up, and the sun would bake mid-day only to tease for a mild evening that never came. What they got instead was crisp icy air that spread over everything in sight the moment the sun set. The blanket of unconscious, cold-blooded arctic wind, cut through the skin and demanded bones of the body to suffer for daring to enjoy. He pulled the jacket together and zipped it up to his neck. That's why most sporting

2

goods stores in the area sold down-insulated jackets year round.

It was time. Five months were long enough to wait. No one would be expecting a second visit, not Rollie Kemp or the Pataglia's. If she failed him again, well, he didn't want to think about that. She was a pro, an ambitious girl who knew the business she was in. Failure wasn't an option.

Inside, he peeled off the thick winter jacket and hung it up. It was ironic trying to enjoy a summer evening in the middle of June when San Francisco obviously paid little attention to the calendar. He opened a briefcase and removed one of several prepaid cell phones. He powered the phone up as he moved to the small desk against the wall. He checked the calendar to make sure it was a Thursday. Rollie Kemp and Drake Fargo were creatures of habit. They had dinner every other Thursday at the same dumpy seafood restaurant in Westwood. He wouldn't put it past them to ordered the same thing on every visit. He punched in a number.

"Yeah, it's me. Are they at the restaurant yet?"

The voice on the other end was a man with a raspy sound. "They just arrived."

"What about our friend?"

"She's at the gym trying to work off the drinks she had with that tennis instructor she likes to tease."

"How much did she have to drink?"

The raspy voice hesitated. "Not sure."

"Let's try a different question. Does she look drunk?"

"No," The raspy voice answered, "but she's a drinker who can put the stuff away. Apparently she can still walk and drive."

"Where are the Pataglia's?"

"Still in the Florida Keys."

"Okay."

"Does okay mean what I think it does?" The raspy voice asked.

"Yeah, let's do this."

The Watcher was in the middle of an exercise class. Her hair was red with yellow, purple and dark blue strands hangin over her shoulders. She wore thick black-framed glasses that changed her facial appearance dramatically. The Watcher did the same exercises as the other twenty women in the room and hated every movement. Most were out of breath and covered in sweat. The Watcher didn't sweat and wasn't out of breath. She did the routine faster and better than the instructor even with a few drinks in her system. The buzz was minor. Having that fourth Scotch and water put her one over the limit and why she turned Mr. Handsome down. He was tempting but too cute for her tastes. She liked rough men, guys who enjoyed pushing women around, and he wasn't one of them. Her cell phone rang, and everyone looked at her purse. It stopped ringing after two rings. A frown settled on her face as her lips curled in a singularly unpleasant position. It was a call she wasn't expecting and had hoped wouldn't come anytime soon. She knew that was wishful thinking. They promised to come back and collect. She owed them, and they never forgot a debt. No one else had the number to that cell phone, so there was no doubt who was calling her. It was time to pay for her mistake, and the only way to stay alive was to honor whatever was asked of her.

Casually she left the aerobics class, grabbed a towel and headed into the dressing room. She checked all toilet stalls to make sure no one was there, and then made the call. She glanced at her reflection in the mirror and smiled. She looked like hell, exactly how she wanted to appear.

"I don't like to wait." His voice was sharp.

"Sorry, I was in an exercise class."

"Are you drunk?" Obviously he had someone watching.

"No," she answered. Damn them, they were still watching her every move. He knew where she was around the clock.

"It's time," he said softly.

"You want me to call you back?" She brushed her hair back and then reached into her purse for lipstick. As she applied it, she listened.

"No, I want you to get in your car and do what you did five months and four days ago. The only difference is your second effort will have different results. You'll need to get out of your car and make sure this time."

The Watcher over-coated her lips and quickly wiped them clean with a paper towel. Her mind started to race. The last time she ran Rollie Kemp and Drake Fargo off the road they survived. She didn't stick around because there were too many cars and witnesses around.

"When?" She asked.

"Tonight. They're having dinner right off Wilshire in Westwood. The place is called Fishy Stuff and More. You know where it is?"

"I know where it is." She kept her emotions in check.

"Good, how far away are you?"

"Twenty minutes." She answered while her mind danced with issues. She was driving her favorite Mercedes convertible. It was a good thing she hadn't registered it yet. She always bought her cars from private parties, and always paid cash. Damn, the car was unique and distinctive, and now it had to go. She glanced back to the mirror and gestured with a shrug that her look was okay and easy to change later. No one would know whom she was even if they got a good look at her.

"Do you need to know what they're eating?" His sarcastic ring was burning.

"What I need to know is where they are going?" She was under his thumb and knew it.

"Malibu. This is Thursday. They have dinner every Thursday, and then they go home. Real creatures of habit they are. Should be easy this time."

"Nothing is easy." She almost laughed. The guy on the other end of the line probably killed or had killed a dozen or more men. He knew how dangerous it was, and even if she disagreed with him there was nothing she could do. "Are they at the restaurant now?"

"They just arrived, so you have time. Behind the dumpster in the back of the restaurant is a box, gas can and canvas bag. Torch the wreckage."

"Why don't I just shoot them?" Her voice sounded cold and methodical.

"Because that's not how we did it last time." He snapped.

"Can I ask you something?" She tried not to purr. He wasn't like most of the guys she dated. He wasn't into purring.

"Make it quick."

"Why don't your guys just take 'em out?"

"That's what I paid you to do. I own you lady and the only way your debts will get settled are after I verify Rollie Kemp is dead. You understand me?"

"I understand."

"Don't try to run on me." He said it with laughter on his tongue.

"You trying to scare me?" She asked while remaining calm.

"No, but we've been watching you. Right now you're in a restroom. You're wearing black tights, a neon yellow skin-tight top and cute little pink tennis shoes."

The Watcher glanced around the room, her eyes drifting back to the mirror to verify they had someone in the gym watching her. The chill she felt inching down her spine was a reminder of whom she was dealing with.

"I never run, and you know that. Both men were lucky last time."

"Yeah, maybe so, but not this time right?"

"I'll make sure."

"Terminate him."

"I'm on my way."

He hung up on her. She threw the phone in her bag and walked out of the restroom.

She drove a few blocks and pulled into a grocery story parking lot. She parked on the side where no one was and striped out of the gym clothes. She put on an all black sweat suit, changed wigs, one with long red hair, and glassed with dark lenses. In the trunk, she kept a package of towels and cleaner. She put on a pair of thin black leather gloves and spent a few minutes wiping the car down. She sprayed the doors, handles, trunk and edges and then moved inside the vehicle where she sprayed and wiped everything in site. She was sweating, and she hated to perspire. Two things could go wrong. Wiping the car down eliminated one of them but she still had to hit their car and still be able to drive away. That was tricky. If she hit them too hard, she'd do too much damage and might not be able to drive away. Getting stuck at the scene would not be good. If she made it, she'd torch the Mercedes closer to her apartment.

The fourth drink was still hanging around, and she hated to be buzzed while working. She got back behind the wheel and thought about Rollie Kemp. Damn him. Why didn't he die the first time she ran him off the road? She had never done a job the same way before and hated the idea of repeating the same act that failed the first time.

She drove west on Santa Monica Boulevard, cut over Venice to Wilshire and drove by the restaurant. She was more than aware that having four drinks could alter her actions. She assumed her blood alcohol level was off the charts even though she felt sharp. She stayed right at the speed limit and even passed a cop without raising a flag.

The Watcher pulled onto the side street next to the restaurant and parked. Behind the seafood diner she found the dumpster right where he said it would be, only a vagrant was standing inside the bin in search of God knows what. She stayed in the shadows and decided to look inside to make sure Rollie was still there. He was sitting with another man in a corner booth, chatting and stuffing their faces. From the looks of things, they were taking their final bites and would be leaving soon. They waved off refills of their drinks and gestured to the waitress for the check.

When The Watcher returned to the dumpster, the street person was out of the bin and exploring the box and bag left for her.

As the tattered man examined the gas can, she came up behind him. He heard footsteps and spun around to confront her. The Watcher paused. The man was late thirties or older, and obviously had been on the street a long time. He was alert to sounds and that made him dangerous. His face was covered with a ragged beard, and he hadn't had a haircut in months. His eyes darted nervously while his hands gathered his trophies and drew them closer. His clothes were filthy, and his body had a stagnant odor that was repulsive.

When she stepped forward, he pulled out a knife and waved it at her. She put up her hands indicating she didn't want trouble. The bum pointed the knife at her.

"Mine! I got here first, so back off."

"What if what you have there is my stuff?" The Watcher asked while her eyes checked behind him. Her peripheral vision said they were alone.

"You have proof?" The bum asked still pointing the knife at her.

She didn't have time to mess with this idiot. She moved to her left, kept her eyes on the knife and watched how fast he reacted. The guy was quicker than she thought he would be.

"I left it here earlier," The Watcher said while moving back to her right.

The bum followed her movement and shook his head. "Mine, finders keepers."

"Then I'm going to have to take it away from you."

He waved the knife at her, and that was his mistake. She lunged forward, grabbed his wrist and in one twisting movement brought his arm up and then down. The blade plunged into his belly. His hand jerked away from the knife and reached for her. That was his last mistake. The Watcher danced behind him in a blur and snapped his neck. His body crumbled to the ground. She straightened up, looked around and then pulled his body behind the dumpster. She grabbed the bag, box, and gas can in one swift movement and ran back to her car.

The moment she pulled to the corner, Rollie and his partner Drake Fargo drove by, and turned north on Bundy. She casually pulled out and followed. Rollie sat in the passenger seat while his hulking partner drove. Drake Fargo appeared to be bigger than the car and acutely uncomfortable. She drove by them when they turned west on Sunset, and sped up so she could reach the canyon before they did. She would wait in the same dark driveway as before, right across from the drop off. She pulled off Sunset and backed into the driveway. The Watcher checked the gasoline, the rags and her lighter. This time, she would make sure both died as they should have five months ago. Damn that fourth drink.

CHAPTER 1

Rollie called his agent, Mildred Wanamaker, the only agent in Hollywood crazy enough to represent the hot-tempered wannabe actor.

"What?" Mildred snapped into the phone the moment she realized it was Rollie calling.

"I'm fine, Mildred, thanks for asking." Rollie wanted to pout. Didn't anyone love him anymore?

"I didn't know you were sick." She didn't beat around the bushes. Rollie imagined her sitting at her cluttered desk, pulling one strand of hair out to look at it. Mildred was one of a kind, in the worst case scenario. She had a handful of studio connections, and most casting directors hated her, and yet she got work for her clients. He was afraid to ask how old she was, but guessed she was around in the silent film era if he had to guess. Depending on the day and how thick the makeup was applied, Mildred could be as young as fifty or old as eighty.

"Mildred…" Rollie hesitated.

"You're wasting time here, Rollie Kemp. No one wants to hire you this week if that's why you're calling me."

"I'm going out of town," Rollie spat out quickly before he could get cut off again.

"And I'm supposed to care?" Mildred said.

"Yeah, well, never mind about that. I just thought you would make a few calls and see if there was any work down south?" Rollie was sorry he called her.

"South, you mean in San Diego?" Mildred started laughing.

"I was thinking more like South Carolina, Georgia or Florida," Rollie added.

"You taking your cell phone with you?" Mildred asked.

"Sure," Rollie said.

"I'll call you," Mildred gushed out and then hung up.

Rollie looked at the phone in repentance and then dialed another number.

"Grandma?"

"You're not coming are you?" Millie Jackson's voice sounded angry, like she always did when he had to disappoint her.

"On the contrary smarty pants. We're on our way to the airport right now. Is your friend still picking us up?"

"Yes we'll be at the airport waiting for you. Why aren't you flying on a commercial airline?"

"This is better. A friend of Drake's offered his plane, and we accepted."

"Private jet?" Millie was huffing and puffing with suspicion. She knew something was wrong.

"Yeah, it's a cute little jet." Rollie tried to hide his anxiety. If she knew both he and Drake were coming to visit as damaged goods, she'd kill him. It would be better for her if he didn't tell her about the body damage until they got there. Seeing him alive would overcome the wounds.

"I bet it's cute. Does this mean you are really coming?" Rollie had to cancel more trips than he could remember and every time he did it, it broke her heart. This time it was different. She didn't know it yet, but he needed her, and so did Drake.

"Too late to cancel and besides I have no place I'd rather go than to visit you, even though I will be bringing Drake with me. That is okay with you, isn't it?" Rollie knew he could bring an army, and she wouldn't care.

"Turn on your video phone," Millie demanded.

"It's, ah," he had to think fast. It could be harmful to her health if she saw the bruises and bandages. "It's not working right now." He lied.

"That's because you haven't turned it on. I'm not hanging up until I see you."

He hesitated, but knew better than to argue with her. She always knew when he was lying. He turned on the video feed to his phone and sat like a dummy in front of the tiny camera. The color screen slowly warmed, and then Millie's imaged filled it. Millie was staring to show her age, mid-fifties, graying black hair, large brown eyes and what Rollie referred to as a light-skinned black lady. Her face had few wrinkles, her skin smooth and eyebrows drawn down tight in anger. She glared at the screen and then shook her head.

"No, wonder you didn't want me to see you. Is Drake worse or about the same?"

"Worse," Rollie mumbled.

"Then he must be near death, right?" Millie was in no mood for humor or sarcasm.

"No, he'll survive." He smiled. "He needs some love and tender care."

"And what do you need?"

"I need a hug." Rollie's eyes stung as tears flooded over and trickles down his cheek.

"That's all?" She said, but the edge on her voice was slipping.

"No ma'am, I need your love and some of your southern cooking."

"Are you going to tell me what happened?" Her voice cracked when she took a breath.

"When I get there. You aren't upset that I'm bringing Drake are you?"

"No, I'm not and you know better than that young man. By the way, what time is it?" Millie waited.

Rollie couldn't lift his arm, so he glanced down at his lifeless limb and the wristwatch he never seemed to take off. Millie's husband loved that watch, and when he died Millie gave it to Rollie. It's what her Clarence would've wanted her to do.

"It's time for me to go to the airport. I'll see you in a couple of hours." Rollie didn't wait for her smart remark. He whispered, "I love you grandma," and hung up.

The Lear Jet made the trip seem shorter than it was. Drake asked a million questions about Millie, and Rollie tried to answer them all.

"Okay, so you beat two thugs up who were robbing Clarence, Millie's late husband, and they just what, adopted you?" Drake didn't understand how a black family could bond with a teenaged white boy.

"When my mom got cancer, Millie started making meals for her."

"Wait a minute. How did they know each other?" Drake asked.

"They lived right down the street. When it got too hot, I mowed their lawn, so Clarence didn't have to suffer in the heat. They never had kids, and I guess I filled a void in their lives."

"Yeah, I can't see it, but go on." Drake didn't understand the relationship.

"When my mom died, Uncle Charlie wanted me to go back to New York with him. I knew they hated my dad for what he did, and I didn't want to live that kind of life. Millie suggested I stay with them for a while, and Uncle Charlie just took off and left me there."

"You moved in with Millie and her husband?" Drake asked incredulously.

"Yeah," Rollie smiled at the memory that suddenly drifted into his head. "They were great. They were also the first black people I'd ever met, but that didn't matter. Nothing did. Millie gave me love I'd never experienced, and Clarence taught me to be a man and how to study. I started getting straight A's in school, and that's how I got my scholarship to law school."

Drake groaned in pain as he shifted his weight from one hip to the other. They were silent for a while, and then Drake raised a finger.

"What do you need?" Rollie asked.

"When you did all that investment stuff and made a bunch of dough you said you bought her a little condo on the beach. How little is little?" Drake raised one eyebrow in anticipation of receiving a stupid answer Rollie hadn't thought about.

"Well, by some standards it's cozy. She has three bedrooms, three baths, a two car garage she never uses, and a nice open layout. You'll like it. I made sure it had a great kitchen because Millie loves to cook for anyone in need of a meal."

"So it's sort of a mansion?" Drake quizzed.

"No," Rollie laughed. "But it's nice. You'll see."

"Maybe I should arrange to stay in a hotel or..."

"No way," Rollie stated firmly. "You can't do squat by yourself and Millie will love pampering your big ass. Just lay back and enjoy a moment you'll never forget."

The Lear touched down on a bed of feathers and came to an equally gentle stop on the tarmac. Two large male nurses Drake's buddy had hired, materialized and helped lower both men down to the runway. Millie was standing in front of a pearl white Rolls Royce, pacing until they were in front of her. She ran to Rollie and threw her arms around his neck. He winced in pain trying not to show the discomfort. Millie didn't care. He rubbed his cheek, kisses him and then turned her attention to Drake, who didn't know what to expect.

"So you're the famous Drake Fargo." Millie stated.

"That's me," Drake said dryly.

"You look terrible." Millie said as she examined him.

"How am I supposed to look? I was in a fiery accident."

"And I bet you caused it, didn't you?" Millie glared, waiting for an answer.

"Grandma!" Rollie made a feeble attempt to control her without luck.

"A whole bunch of people don't like the way I do things," Drake added.

"Mmmm, and you're a tough guy. Should I shudder in fear?"

"Grandma?" Rollie's voice found some volume.

"You might when I can stand up," Drake snapped angrily.

"Well, until then, you are my prisoner and you will behave accordingly."

Millie didn't wait for his argument. She sauntered over to a middle-aged white guy and together they climbed into the front seat of the Rolls. Rollie and Drake were helped into the back seat, and the footing of their visit was established.

Sullivan's Island, South Carolina was located on one of the most incredibly perfect chunks of land anywhere in the world. It was private, well kept, clean and protected. Millie's condo was on the oceanfront and had a spectacular view of Charleston's Harbor. The warm sun felt like hot fingers dancing over their wounded bodies, and Rollie was thankful Rader had suggested getting out of town. Drake had both feet planted on the ground and was nearly forced, or dragged as he would put it later, to the airport. He was angry all the way there and up and until Millie's male companion, Frankie Bean picked them up in a Rolls Royce. It was one of the rare occasions Rollie had witnessed a befuddled Drake to be silent.

It took a week for Millie to stop being mother hen to both men. At first she was horrified seeing all the wounds, bandages and bruises. She also got over Drake Fargo's sharp tongue. Drake knew all about Millie except for the fact she was Black and hated people saying she was African American. She had never set foot in Africa and neither had her parents or grandparents. When she hugged Drake, he literally melted into her caring hands. There was an instant bond, and Rollie was proud of his partner and his lack of being even slightly prejudice. It didn't take long to realize Millie's closest friend was

Frankie Bean. She called him Beanie. He was from Florida, or so he said. Rather than have a chauffeur drive them everywhere they went, Beanie drove the old Rolls Royce by himself. Beanie was a white guy who adored the ground Millie walked on. They were about the same age, and he held her hand as often as she allowed, which was quite a bit. He reminded Rollie of Clarence. His concern over Millie was genuine.

After three, weeks, Drake discovered he and Beanie had many acquaintances and knew people who ran in similar circles. They shared war stories, but avoided getting into intimate details. Beanie's only child, referred to as Bean, was also a private detective in Miami and had offered to help in any way they might need. When both Drake and Rollie were up and about without assistance, Beanie insisted they move into his condo. He would take Millie's spare bedroom until they were ready to return to California. The more they were around Beanie Rollie started thinking he was an old mob guy. He resembled Uncle Charlie in habits, tastes, sayings, and results. Beanie was a no-nonsense kind of guy, and Rollie was sure Beanie would give up his life if it meant saving Millie's. The guy was where the material comes from that creates illustrious characters.

Drake spent lots of time talking to Erinn in California. Erinn was rapidly becoming the love of his life, but he'd never admit it. He became a little boy when he talked to her, a boy with a huge crush. He was, on the other hand, macho-man, and he had to keep up his image so it wouldn't create a conflict between the man he wanted to be and the tough guy everyone thought and came to know he was. Whenever Drake walked into a room, his massive size and always present scowl alone put everyone on edge. Rollie was starting to know the real guy, and he liked that man a whole lot more than the one living up to the legend. There was no doubt in anyone's mind that Drake Fargo had become legendary and could become lethal in a split second. Few men standing six-feet eight, weighing over two hundred and seventy pounds move with the meticulousness of a cat on the prowl. Drake could scare the skin off a beast, albeit a shithead thief or a desperate killer. Erinn was the only person Rollie had met who could tame Drake Fargo.

Rollie didn't hear from his agent Mildred until they had been in South Carolina for almost four months. Most of his cuts and bruises had healed. All the stitches were gone, but from head to toe the body still ached. When the phone rang, Rollie was in the middle of telling a story. No one knew if the story was true or not, and it didn't matter.

"... and the special effects guy wheeled this long dolly of toilet stalls to the stage. He placed them behind a false wall, and they looked like the real deal. Six johns in a row with stalls, doors and everything. This young actor is dancing and turning in circles, so my stuntman buddy asked him what was wrong. The kid said he had to go and was afraid to leave the set. My buddy said he didn't have to leave, there were toilets set up just for the cast and crew right over there. He pointed to a large portable set that had been rolled out. The kid dashed into one of the stalls and relieved himself with all the normal human sound effects that accompany taking a dump. A crowd gathered. Cameras were ready, and when the kid came out everyone applauded and took his picture. The young actor wanted to die right there on the spot, and then the special effects' guy insisted the wannabe actor clean up the mess. You should have seen the look on the kids face." Drake joined Beanie and Millie in wild hysterical laughter. On the third ring, Rollie answered. "Who is this?"

"Who do you think it is big shot?" Mildred's voice couldn't be mistaken.

"Hi Mildred, what's up?" Rollie said it loud enough for everyone to hear.

"Can you be in Miami tomorrow morning?" Mildred asked in her usual impatient voice.

"Can I be in Miami tomorrow morning? What 's in Miami?"

"A commercial. I sent them your picture and reel." Mildred added.

"Hold on, Mildred," Rollie said.

"Make it quick," she snapped.

Rollie looked at all the faces in the room.

"What do you need, kid?" Beanie asked.

"My agent has a commercial for me, but I have to be in Miami tomorrow morning."

"No problem. I'll fly you down there in my plane." Beanie said.

"It's a nice one," Millie added.

"You've been on his plane?" Rollie asked. "You wouldn't fly out to California because you're afraid to fly, and you've been up in his plane?"

"You better answer your agent," Millie said with a glimmer in her eye.

"Do I have the job Mildred, or is this a cattle call for any actor in the vicinity?" Rollie barked into the phone in a tone even Mildred had not heard before.

"They faxed me back a signed contract. For an unknown like you, I got a huge payday, and it comes with great residuals if you make a good commercial. So are you going or what?"

"Where do I go?" Rollie asked.

"I'll send you a text, but I'm telling you right now, don't be late. It's a national spot for the new Ford Mustang." The line went dead.

"Wow," Rollie mumbled. "I got a national commercial."

"Great," Beanie announced, "we'll all go and be your cheering section.

"This is exciting," Millie added, "let's pack our bags."

"Wait a minute," Rollie protested, "let talk about your flying around."

"Don't spoil this, Rollie," Millie said and walked out of the room.

CHAPTER 2

Rollie called his agent, Mildred Wanamaker, the only agent in Hollywood crazy enough to represent the hot-tempered wannabe actor.

"What?" Mildred snapped into the phone the moment she realized it was Rollie calling.

"I'm fine, Mildred, thanks for asking." Rollie wanted to pout. Didn't anyone love him anymore?

"I didn't know you were sick." She didn't beat around the bushes. Rollie imagined her sitting at her cluttered desk, pulling one strand of hair out to look at it. Mildred was one of a kind, in the worst case scenario. She had a handful of studio connections, and most casting directors hated her, and yet she got work for her clients. He was afraid to ask how old she was, but guessed she was around in the silent film era if he had to guess. Depending on the day and how thick the makeup was applied, Mildred could be as young as fifty or old as eighty.

"Mildred..." Rollie hesitated.

"You're wasting time here, Rollie Kemp. No one wants to hire you this week if that's why you're calling me."

"I'm going out of town," Rollie spat out quickly before he could get cut off again.

"And I'm supposed to care?" Mildred said.

"Yeah, well, never mind about that. I just thought you would make a few calls and see if there was any work down south?" Rollie was sorry he called her.

"South, you mean in San Diego?" Mildred started laughing.

"I was thinking more like South Carolina, Georgia or Florida," Rollie added.

"You taking your cell phone with you?" Mildred asked.

"Sure," Rollie said.

"I'll call you," Mildred gushed out and then hung up.

Rollie looked at the phone in repentance and then dialed another number.

"Grandma?"

"You're not coming are you?" Millie Jackson's voice sounded angry, like she always did when he had to disappoint her.

"On the contrary smarty pants. We're on our way to the airport right now. Is your friend still picking us up?"

"Yes we'll be at the airport waiting for you. Why aren't you flying on a commercial airline?"

"This is better. A friend of Drake's offered his plane, and we accepted."

"Private jet?" Millie was huffing and puffing with suspicion. She knew something was wrong.

"Yeah, it's a cute little jet." Rollie tried to hide his anxiety. If she knew both he and Drake were coming to

23

visit as damaged goods, she'd kill him. It would be better for her if he didn't tell her about the body damage until they got there. Seeing him alive would overcome the wounds.

"I bet it's cute. Does this mean you are really coming?" Rollie had to cancel more trips than he could remember and every time he did it, it broke her heart. This time it was different. She didn't know it yet, but he needed her, and so did Drake.

"Too late to cancel and besides I have no place I'd rather go than to visit you, even though I will be bringing Drake with me. That is okay with you, isn't it?" Rollie knew he could bring an army, and she wouldn't care.

"Turn on your video phone," Millie demanded.

"It's, ah," he had to think fast. It could be harmful to her health if she saw the bruises and bandages. "It's not working right now." He lied.

"That's because you haven't turned it on. I'm not hanging up until I see you."

He hesitated, but knew better than to argue with her. She always knew when he was lying. He turned on the video feed to his phone and sat like a dummy in front of the tiny camera. The color screen slowly warmed, and then Millie's imaged filled it. Millie was stating to show her age, mid fifties, graying black hair, large brown eyes and what Rollie referred to as a light-skinned black lady. Her face had few wrinkles, her skin smooth and eyebrows drawn down tight in anger. She glared at the screen and then shook her head.

"No, wonder you didn't want me to see you. Is Drake worse or about the same?"

"Worse," Rollie mumbled.

"Then he must be near death, right?" Millie was in no mood for humor or sarcasm.

"No, he'll survive." He smiled. "He needs some love and tender care."

"And what do you need?"

"I need a hug." Rollie's eyes stung as tears flooded over and trickles down his cheek.

"That's all?" She said, but the edge on her voice was slipping.

"No ma'am, I need your love and some of your southern cooking."

"Are you going to tell me what happened?" Her voice cracked when she took a breath.

"When I get there. You aren't upset that I'm bringing Drake are you?"

"No, I'm not and you know better than that young man. By the way, what time is it?" Millie waited.

Rollie couldn't lift his arm, so he glanced down at his lifeless limb and the wristwatch he never seemed to take off. Millie's husband loved that watch, and when he died Millie gave it to Rollie. It's what her Clarence would've wanted her to do.

"It's time for me to go to the airport. I'll see you in a couple of hours." Rollie didn't wait for her smart remark. He whispered, "I love you grandma," and hung up.

The Lear Jet made the trip seem shorter than it was. Drake asked a million questions about Millie, and Rollie tried to answer them all.

"Okay, so you beat two thugs up who were robbing Clarence, Millie's late husband, and they just what, adopted you?" Drake didn't understand how a black family could bond with a teenaged white boy.

"When my mom got cancer, Millie started making meals for her."

"Wait a minute. How did they know each other?" Drake asked.

"They lived right down the street. When it got too hot, I mowed their lawn, so Clarence didn't have to suffer in the heat. They never had kids, and I guess I filled a void in their lives."

"Yeah, I can't see it, but go on." Drake didn't understand the relationship.

"When my mom died, Uncle Charlie wanted me to go back to New York with him. I knew they hated my dad for what he did, and I didn't want to live that kind of life. Millie suggested I stay with them for a while, and Uncle Charlie just took off and left me there."

"You moved in with Millie and her husband?" Drake asked incredulously.

"Yeah," Rollie smiled at the memory that suddenly drifted into his head. "They were great. They were also the first black people I'd ever met, but that didn't matter. Nothing did. Millie gave me love I'd never experienced, and Clarence taught me to be a man and how to study. I started getting straight A's in school, and that's how I got my scholarship to law school."

Drake groaned in pain as he shifted his weight from one hip to the other. They were silent for a while, and then Drake raised a finger.

"What do you need?" Rollie asked.

"When you did all that investment stuff and made a bunch of dough you said you bought her a little condo on the beach. How little is little?" Drake raised one eyebrow in anticipation of receiving a stupid answer Rollie hadn't thought about.

"Well, by some standards it's cozy. She has three bedrooms, three baths, a two car garage she never uses, and a nice open layout. You'll like it. I made sure it had a great kitchen because Millie loves to cook for anyone in need of a meal."

"So it's sort of a mansion?" Drake quizzed.

"No," Rollie laughed. "But it's nice. You'll see."

"Maybe I should arrange to stay in a hotel or…"

"No way," Rollie stated firmly. "You can't do squat by yourself and Millie will love pampering your big ass. Just lay back and enjoy a moment you'll never forget."

The Lear touched down on a bed of feathers and came to an equally gentle stop on the tarmac. Two large male nurses Drake's buddy had hired, materialized and helped lower both men down to the runway. Millie was standing in front of a pearl white Rolls Royce, pacing until they were in front of her. She ran to Rollie and threw her arms around his neck. He winced in pain trying not to show the discomfort. Millie didn't care. He rubbed his cheek, kisses him and then turned her attention to Drake, who didn't know what to expect.

"So you're the famous Drake Fargo." Millie stated.

"That's me," Drake said dryly.

"You look terrible." Millie said as she examined him.

"How am I supposed to look? I was in a fiery accident."

"And I bet you caused it, didn't you?" Millie glared, waiting for an answer.

"Grandma!" Rollie made a feeble attempt to control her without luck.

"A whole bunch of people don't like the way I do things," Drake added.

"Mmmm, and you're a tough guy. Should I shudder in fear?"

"Grandma?" Rollie's voice found some volume.

"You might when I can stand up," Drake snapped angrily.

"Well, until then, you are my prisoner and you will behave accordingly."

Millie didn't wait for his argument. She sauntered over to a middle-aged white guy and together they climbed into the front seat of the Rolls. Rollie and Drake were helped into the back seat, and the footing of their visit was established.

Sullivan's Island, South Carolina was located on one of the most incredibly perfect chunks of land anywhere in the world. It was private, well kept, clean and protected. Millie's condo was on the oceanfront and had a spectacular view of Charleston's Harbor. The warm sun felt like hot fingers dancing over their wounded bodies, and Rollie was thankful Rader had suggested getting out of town. Drake had both feet planted on the ground and was nearly forced, or dragged as he would put it later, to the airport. He was angry all the way there and up and until Millie's male companion, Frankie Bean picked them up in a Rolls Royce. It was one of the rare occasions Rollie had witnessed a befuddled Drake to be silent.

It took a week for Millie to stop being mother hen to both men. At first she was horrified seeing all the wounds, bandages and bruises. She also got over Drake Fargo's sharp tongue. Drake knew all about Millie except for the fact she was Black and hated people saying she was African American. She had never set foot in Africa and neither had her parents or grandparents. When she hugged Drake, he literally melted into her caring hands. There was an instant bond, and Rollie was proud of his partner and his lack of being even slightly prejudice. It didn't take long to realize Millie's closest friend was

Frankie Bean. She called him Beanie. He was from Florida, or so he said. Rather than have a chauffeur drive them everywhere they went, Beanie drove the old Rolls Royce by himself. Beanie was a white guy who adored the ground Millie walked on. They were about the same age, and he held her hand as often as she allowed, which was quite a bit. He reminded Rollie of Clarence. His concern over Millie was genuine.

After three, weeks, Drake discovered he and Beanie had many acquaintances and knew people who ran in similar circles. They shared war stories, but avoided getting into intimate details. Beanie's only child, referred to as Bean, was also a private detective in Miami and had offered to help in any way they might need. When both Drake and Rollie were up and about without assistance, Beanie insisted they move into his condo. He would take Millie's spare bedroom until they were ready to return to California. The more they were around Beanie Rollie started thinking he was an old mob guy. He resembled Uncle Charlie in habits, tastes, sayings, and results. Beanie was a no-nonsense kind of guy, and Rollie was sure Beanie would give up his life if it meant saving Millie's. The guy was where the material comes from that creates illustrious characters.

Drake spent lots of time talking to Erinn in California. Erinn was rapidly becoming the love of his life, but he'd never admit it. He became a little boy when he talked to her, a boy with a huge crush. He was, on the other hand, macho-man, and he had to keep up his image so it wouldn't create a conflict between the man he wanted to be and the tough guy everyone thought and came to know he was. Whenever Drake walked into a room, his massive size and always present scowl alone put everyone on edge. Rollie was starting to know the real guy, and he liked that man a whole lot more than the one living up to the legend. There was no doubt in anyone's mind that Drake Fargo had become legendary and could become lethal in a split second. Few men standing six-feet eight, weighing over two hundred and seventy pounds move with the meticulousness of a cat on the prowl. Drake could scare the skin off a beast, albeit a shithead thief or a desperate killer. Erinn was the only person Rollie had met who could tame Drake Fargo.

Rollie didn't hear from his agent Mildred until they had been in South Carolina for almost four months. Most of his cuts and bruises had healed. All the stitches were gone, but from head to toe the body still ached. When the phone rang, Rollie was in the middle of telling a story. No one knew if the story was true or not, and it didn't matter.

"... and the special effects guy wheeled this long dolly of toilet stalls to the stage. He placed them behind a false wall, and they looked like the real deal. Six johns in a row with stalls, doors and everything. This young actor is dancing and turning in circles, so my stuntman buddy asked him what was wrong. The kid said he had to go and was afraid to leave the set. My buddy said he didn't have to leave, there were toilets set up just for the cast and crew right over there. He pointed to a large portable set that had been rolled out. The kid dashed into one of the stalls and relieved himself with all the normal human sound effects that accompany taking a dump. A crowd gathered. Cameras were ready, and when the kid came out everyone applauded and took his picture. The young actor wanted to die right there on the spot, and then the special effects' guy insisted the wannabe actor clean up the mess. You should have seen the look on the kids face." Drake joined Beanie and Millie in wild hysterical laughter. On the third ring, Rollie answered. "Who is this?"

"Who do you think it is big shot?" Mildred's voice couldn't be mistaken.

"Hi Mildred, what's up?" Rollie said it loud enough for everyone to hear.

"Can you be in Miami tomorrow morning?" Mildred asked in her usual impatient voice.

"Can I be in Miami tomorrow morning? What 's in Miami?"

"A commercial. I sent them your picture and reel." Mildred added.

"Hold on, Mildred," Rollie said.

"Make it quick," she snapped.

Rollie looked at all the faces in the room.

"What do you need, kid?" Beanie asked.

"My agent has a commercial for me, but I have to be in Miami tomorrow morning."

"No problem. I'll fly you down there in my plane." Beanie said.

"It's a nice one," Millie added.

"You've been on his plane?" Rollie asked. "You wouldn't fly out to California because you're afraid to fly, and you've been up in his plane?"

"You better answer your agent," Millie said with a glimmer in her eye.

"Do I have the job Mildred, or is this a cattle call for any actor in the vicinity?" Rollie barked into the phone in a tone even Mildred had not heard before.

"They faxed me back a signed contract. For an unknown like you, I got a huge payday, and it comes with great residuals if you make a good commercial. So are you going or what?"

"Where do I go?" Rollie asked.

31

"I'll send you a text, but I'm telling you right now, don't be late. It's a national spot for the new Ford Mustang." The line went dead.

"Wow," Rollie mumbled. "I got a national commercial."

"Great," Beanie announced, "we'll all go and be your cheering section.

"This is exciting," Millie added, "let's pack our bags."

"Wait a minute," Rollie protested, "let talk about your flying around."

"Don't spoil this, Rollie," Millie said and walked out of the room.

CHAPTER 3

The house was nestled on ten acres of ocean front property in Summerland Key, right smack in the middle of Key West. It faced the Gulf of Mexico where the ocean was crystal clear and displayed stunning shades of blue-green which were difficult to describe to anyone who hadn't witnessed it for themselves. Anthony Pataglia was surrounded by his family and the men who worked for him. They all had healed from the near massacre in New York and were ready to go back home and plan their revenge.

They took the fifty-foot boat out to fish and discuss the future. The crew fished while the men talked business in the vast cabin of the ship.

"It's time," Pataglia stated. Anthony was the God Father of a major crime family. His late sister was Rollie Kemp's mother. Rollie's deceased Uncle Charlie was Pataglia's half-brother that had disgraced the family. There was painful baggage a mile long in the family. Rollie's late father had also betrayed the family, killed two trusted soldiers and stupidly Uncle Charlie had tried to cover up the murders with more lies. They all paid for those misgivings. The family killed Rollie's father and made it look like an accident, and sent Uncle Charlie into stunning isolation to spend the rest of his miserable life in forced seclusion. As for Rollie's mother, her own brother cut her off and hinted if she stayed in New York something dark and devastating would happen to her son Rollie. The whole of the family pegged the kid as a father-like-son loser. Rollie's mom fled to Charleston and moved in with Uncle Charlie. When Uncle Charlie went home to die, they ignored him, and he died in some flea-bag hotel room. Enough time had gone by either they forgot about Rollie or decided to leave him alone.

Fabrio Tallagi stood up. He was Pataglia's most trusted soldier. Fabrio had been with the old man since he was a teenager and would do anything to protect and serve. A large man with no neck and little if any fat, he stood with the structure of a perfectly created linebacker. When he spoke, his voice became the first threat, his size the second. Fabrio started pacing, and the other men watched nervously. Only Gi Carlo, Pataglia's ever-present bodyguard ignored Fabrio.

"None of this makes sense," Fabrio said. "Louis Baxter is dead from stealing union money, but we didn't kill him. Mark Lipesky ordered the hit on your daughter, but it wasn't his decision."

"Than it had to be Moe Brayden," Pataglia said coldly.

"He knows better that hitting your daughter would start a war." Fabrio argued.

"Then who killed her?" Pataglia asked, looking around the room at the other men. No one spoke up. "I want the bastard who pulled the trigger."

"What about Drego Santino?" Billy Davis asked when no one else dared to bring up his name. Billy Davis ran a crew for Pataglia in Philadelphia and also participated in the legal shipping business they ran. Billy was smooth, sharp, and one of the few who thought things through before he acted. He had never been arrested and wasn't on law enforcement radar.

"What about Santino, Billy?" Pataglia asked. "He didn't kill Tawny."

"What's he doing with those two actors?" Billy blurted out.

"She was killed in his house and those two investments he calls actors were there at the time she was taken out." Pataglia ran his massive hand through his hair. He looked around the room, but no one had the answer to the only question that mattered. Who killed his baby daughter?

"The guy makes movies, Billy. Santino's invested a lot of dough in those two fools, and it's just starting to pay off." Fabrio shrugged his massive shoulders, "I don't see Santino slipping up when everything is on the line. He'd never cross us even though he put his New York connections to bed for the time being. The movie business is too much fun, and we're making ridiculous amounts of money from his films."

Frank Masseria stood up and poured a drink. Masseria was a tall skinny guy with dark hair, eyes and matching complexion. He was part of the Billy Davis crew from Philly, and considered an electronic genius by everyone who knew him. He could hide a tiny camera anywhere, and it would never be found. He could also use the latest technologies in sound, wire-tapping and electronic surveillance. "We've been watching Johnny Wade, Moe's garbage man, but he hasn't left Philly for months, and before Drew Lipesky went into hiding, we had him in our sights too."

"All the time?" Pataglia asked.

"No, he could've slipped out of town for a few hours, but never long enough to fly to California, kill the girl and fly back." Masseria shook his head. "His old man was behind the union money, but those boys have been eliminated."

"Well someone killed her!" Pataglia shouted.

"Maybe we have a new player trying to take over?" Billy Davis suggested.

"We have eyes on everyone, Mr. Pataglia. How do we go after a ghost?" Masseria asked.

"Who can be that elusive?" Fabrio quizzed.

"Gentleman, phantoms are something that appears only in our mind, but I guarantee you this is not one of them. This is a living, breathing physical reality, and he must be stopped." A decision was made. He nodded giving approval. "Fabrio, I want you to go back to California and start digging. Take another look at Rollie Kemp even though someone tried to take him out. I still don't trust him, and I'll never forget what his father did to us." He glanced at Fabrio. "Let's take a look at everyone he knows, including his partner, ex-wife, girlfriends and everyone else he does business with."

"Are you forgetting he shot me?" Fabrio clenched his teeth and involuntarily rubbed his shoulder where the bullet made its hole. "I'm not sure I can trust being around him without doing great bodily harm to a guy who thinks he's so tough."

"Get close enough to let him know we're watching, just stay away until I say otherwise. Remember he and his partner were in that house when Tawny died so they will remain in our sights until I know for sure who pulled the trigger. Pack a bag and get on the next flight out of Miami. I need to make some calls and arrange some meetings. If there is a new player, let's cut his legs off and get it done quickly."

"What do you want us to do?" Billy Davis asked.

"What do I want you to do? I want to know who killed my little girl, who pulled the trigger, and who told the killer where to find Tawny. Lipesky may have ordered the hit, but there were other players, and I won't rest until all of them are dead. That's what I want!"

Masseria exchanged a look between Billy Davis and Fabrio. "Do you want us to stay here in the Keys or go back to Philly?"

"Here, until we talk to everyone. No one knows where we are at this point. Let's keep it that way. Let's try to avoid another surprise until we know who's trying to take us out."

CHAPTER 4

Beanie's small jet was even nicer than a similar one Drake and Rollie flew down on. Beanie's aircraft was a Gulfstream G550 and if there were any other options he didn't have on the plane it was because they didn't exist. He had the interior customized with flat screen TV's, satellite receivers, the softest leather on earth, and all the amenities one could dream of putting into the body of an airplane. It was equal to his Rolls Royce in every way.

They quickly reached altitude, leveled off, and in what seemed like minutes thereafter, were in approach to land in Miami. Beanie had permission to put his craft down with the big boys and that all by itself was as impressive as anything he did. Rollie couldn't stop wondering what Beanie's back story was.

Watching Millie having the time of her life brought a smile to Rollie's face. Whenever Beanie pointed out the window, Millie leaned over his lap and peered out into the wild blue wander in awe. It surprised him. She had never mentioned Beanie. He knew their relationship wasn't a new one. They were way too familiar with each other. Rollie was suspicious and happy for Millie. He didn't trust strangers, and since Millie never mentioned Beanie, he was a stranger. Rollie knew it was a defensive maneuver because Millie was the closest anyone had ever come to love him like a mother.

After listening to Beanie talk with Drake, Rollie came away believing the rough-on-the-edges guy was real. They talked about serving in Special Services, Navy Seals and the CIA, but carefully avoided suspicious details, which might peel away some of the facade they both wore close to the vest. Whatever mystery Beanie had, he and Drake shared some of the same common ground both had traveled over. Rollie's distrust melted away, and he was happy Millie had found someone to share time with.

As they were leaving the airport terminal, Rollie walked by Fabrio, who just happened to pass them a hundred or so feet to his left. He didn't recognize Fabrio, but took a second look trying to remember where he'd seen him before. It didn't come to him, and before he could give it further thought, Beanie ushered him into a waiting limousine.

Fabrio continued walking and then abruptly stopped to look over his shoulder. He recognized a face that had passed by and immediately turned back, but Rollie was gone. He wasn't sure it was whom he thought it was, but Fabrio never forgot a face. The guy looked just like Rollie Kemp, but what would Rollie be doing in Miami? He hurried into the main corridor, searching over the crowd but whoever he saw had vanished. He heard the announcer make last call for boarding his flight to Los Angeles and had to hurry before he missed it. Perhaps it was just a coincidence and up close the guy didn't look anything like Rollie Kemp, but the knot in his gut told him otherwise.

It only took four takes for Rollie to complete the commercial much to the chagrin of his rooting section which watched his every move. The director was so impressed, he asked Rollie to stick around for a few more days. He was doing another commercial for some Chicken place and thought Rollie was perfect for. He took Rollie off to meet the producer's and sure enough he got the job. Beanie assured him the stay over was fine, and the delay would give them time to meet his son and share a few laughs.

The second night in Miami, Beanie took them out on the town. At a lavish restaurant, the one with the strange name, LaChey Von, they met Beanie's son. He resembled a hood right out of the movies, over-sized dark brown sports coat, lighter matching slacks and a snugly fit cream-colored crew-neck shirt. His feet were sockless in the undeniably soft Alligator loafers. His blond, wavy hair was cut short but not close enough to make his head appear larger than it was. Drake stood six eight, Rollie was six four and Bean was just a bit shorter than Rollie but twice as wide. He shook hands with an iron-vice grip and wore a tiny scar that slipped from his mouth and ran down his jaw. Rollie guessed someone cut him, and as he observed the scar without meaning to stare, Bean reached up and touched it. When he spoke, his voice came out a sinister hoarse loud whisper. Gangster films created characters like Bean, but none came to mind that visually described the man standing before Rollie.

"Got cut a few years ago," Bean said. He removed his hand and smiled. "I've heard a lot about you two, Rollie, Drake. It's good to meet up finally."

They all slid into a large booth. The waitress came, and Beanie ordered wine for everyone. He didn't ask what anyone wanted. He was in control and left little doubt that's how he did everything. This was his night, so Rollie and Drake sat back, exchanged a look and remained silent. Beanie tasted the wine, approved it, and gestured it was okay for the waitress to serve. Beanie ordered dinner for everyone, steaks and lamb, an interesting combination that no one argued about. Beanie beamed at his son.

"Why don't you tell 'em a little about you, son?" Beanie said.

"I do detective work," Bean answered.

"Been at it long? Drake asked.

"A while," Bean answered. A real conversationalist.

"I kind of fell into the detective stuff," Rollie volunteered.

"As opposed to doing what?" Bean asked as he sipped his wine.

Beanie and Millie drifted off to whisper sweet nothings and ignore everyone else.

"I went to California to become an attorney." Rollie started.

"That right?" Bean said.

"Yeah," Rollie sounded a bit on edge. "Didn't work out."

"How come?" Bean continued with his two or three word sentences.

"Got divorced." Drake chimed in.

"Don't we all?" Bean said.

"Tell him about the police academy," Drake said in amusement. He could tell Rollie was almost at the edge of his seat. Either punches were about to fly, or he'd get up and just walk away. The glare in his eye revealed excitement to see which way the wind would blow.

"So you're a cop?" Bean said and sat up.

"No," Rollie glanced at Drake, knowing macho-man was deliberately pushing him. "A drunk hit me a week before graduation. Legs took a toll, and I couldn't pass the physical."

"Oh," Bean was disappointed.

"After the accident, Rollie became a real actor," Millie said with a rich content smile.

"Really?" Bean said taking another sip of wine.

"That's how we met," Drake said. He knew Rollie was just about ready to get up. The fun wasn't over. Drake frowned at Rollie for being a spoiled sport.

"Tell me why I don't understand?" Bean said.

"He got fired working on a big film. Punched the director and then broke the stars' nose." Drake was amused telling the story. "Rollie has an anger management problem."

Rollie was furious, but before he could get up and storm out Bean spoke.

"Me too," Bean said quietly. "I have this habit of taking a swing first and then asking questions when the guy is on the ground. I hate surprises." He smiled at Rollie.

"Sounds like we have something in common," Rollie said as he relaxed.

From there, the conversation flowed easily for all three men. When the evening came to an end, Bean shook Rollie's hand vigorously and then turned to Drake with equal enthusiasm.

"I'm on a case and won't have time to enjoy your company, but if you guys ever need help, I'm a phone call away. We could work together, and I've never said that to anyone before." Bean smiled, kissed Millie's cheek and then gave Beanie a hug. He turned back to Rollie. "Your grandma is one of a kind. She talks about you all the time, just ducked telling me about the real you, the guy I identify with and like a lot. Take care of her dad I'll see you guys later."

Bean turned and was promptly joined by two other men, and together they all walked out of the restaurant. Both Rollie and Drake turned to Beanie. He shrugged.

"The kid's a lot like me," Beanie said gesturing with his hands, "Bean doesn't trust too many people. Those two guys work for him and stay in the shadows if you know what I mean?"

"We don't trust many either," Drake added.

"Okay, let's show you guys our little Miami getaway."

Beanie had a rather large six bedroom oceanfront condo in Miami right on the bay. The place took up half a floor with multiple balconies and views to die for. The furnishing was right out of Architectural Design. Lush fabrics, leathers, collectibles, antiques and expensive artwork lined the walls and took up space in all the appropriate places. As they settled in, Rollie knew there was much more to Beanie then met the eye. They shared an after dinner drink and settled into a variety of bedrooms on either side of the condo.

Rollie couldn't sleep. The evening conversation brought demons he had been fighting for years back. His family, or what little there was of it, had left holes in his person. The guy he looked at in the mirror was lost at times. There was a vacancy he couldn't fill or shake. He sat out on one of the balconies and the ocean breeze drifted in, making an attempt at creating a relaxing atmosphere. It wasn't working, and then his cellphone rang. He dug it out of his pocket and glanced at the caller ID. He didn't recognize it. He hesitated before answering on the second ring.

"Who is this?"

He heard tears and knew it was Kali, the ex-wife who wouldn't go away. His belly churned as it did every time the sound of her voice purred from her lips. He had never stopped loving her and had no reason on earth to understand those feelings. She had cheated on him, and only God knew how many men, ripped his heart out of his chest and stomped on it, and taken anything she could carry of his belongings and cash. In spite of all she had done, he still cared about her. A sicker explanation was he couldn't get her out of his head and continued to love her. He couldn't forgive her, but his heart forced him to do the opposite. He could never turn her away and when she begged for help he always gave in. He could still feel her body, the warmth and softness of her skin, the taste of her mouth, the bouquet in her hair and how she could blend into his space and become one fluid movement. No woman had done that before or after Kali.

"Rollie? Say something." She was whispering, like she always did.

"What do you need?" He heard what he mumbled and tried to retract it without success.

"I still love you," her quivering voice sounded off, threatened.

"What's wrong Kali?"

"They know you're alive, and they're coming to kill you." She broke down into gulps and sobs that sounded wet and hysterical.

"Who are they, Kali?" Rollie asked.

"I don't know. I just overheard them talking."

"Where are you?" He asked.

"I'm sorry," she was whispering.

"About what? What are you sorry for?"

"Everything."

She hung up on him. He held the phone in his lap for the longest time, unable to comprehend what had just taken place. She didn't know he was in Florida. Or did she? When she used drugs, she hung out with scum. If she guzzled booze, she usually ended up in bed with a total stranger. Sadly Kali often went go on binges and didn't understand how she turned up miles out of town and in need of a ride. She was the most beautiful woman he had ever known. Model material. Everyone thought she was a ten, from head to toe. When she slithered into hell, her looks became secondary to what drove her.

Rollie felt a warm hand on his shoulder and turned to see Millie standing behind him holding a box.

"May I join you?" She asked.

Rollie pulled up the other chair and made room for her to sit. She set the box on top of a small table between the two chairs and then sat down. Silently, she studied his face. Her eyes had a way, a tender love filled with joy and surprises.

"Why aren't you sleeping?" Rollie asked.

"I knew you were out here. I heard you answer the phone."

"I'm sorry. I hope it didn't bother..."

"Shhh, no it didn't bother anyone. Was that Kali?" Rollie nodded.

"Sometimes I feel so alone, grandma. I see family gatherings, moms or dads holding their children in their arms, and I long for that." The tears felt warm as they slid down his cheeks. "I wanted to be hugged when I was a little boy. I want those memories, and they're not there."

Rollie covered his eyes, embarrassed to be weeping in front of anyone, especially Millie.

She opened the carton and removed a few envelopes.

"When your mother died, that awful man you called Uncle Charlie brought this box over to the house and asked me to keep it for him. He went to New York and never came back, and I forgot all about the box until Beanie was cleaning out the garage to make room for his Rolls. When I moved down here, I had the movers put everything from my old garage into my new one and forgot all about it. Beanie found the box while you and Drake were healing."

He watched her open the envelope and produce photographs. She handed them to Rollie, one at a time.

"These were taken before your father fell from grace. Apparently you were a very happy little boy back then." Millie offered him a smile of understanding. "Your mother loved you Rollie, look at the pictures."

Rollie thumbed through the stack one by one. There were fifteen or twenty altogether, each one showing a baby at different ages, from birth to about six or seven. In some photos, his acutely ill mother was hugging or kissing him while, in others, his father was lifting a young child into the air, or swinging him around in circles. Both parents were laughing and having the time of their lives. Rollie studied each picture carefully, not remembering one minute from the images he was looking at.

"Why don't I remember any of this?" He asked Millie.

"You were young, too young perhaps. When things changed, when your father got desperate, their relationship became strained." Millie filed through the box and found another large envelope she opened and removed the contents. She handed newspaper clippings to Rollie.

"What are these?" Rollie asked as he took them from her.

"Stories about your father, his arrests, his drunken behavior, about the two men he killed, and one small paragraph about how his life ended."

Rollie studied each article and then set them aside. He glanced over at Millie as she stood up, and he joined her. They hugged and then she touched his cheek with the love of a mother.

"You were so broken when you came to our home. You wanted attention and begged for knowledge. Clarence gave what he had, and I tried to fill your void."

"You did more than that, grandma." He smiled. "Do you remember when I wanted to call you mom?"

"You had a mother and I couldn't replace her. Grandma worked better."

"I love you so much." Rollie said quietly.

"I love you too," Millie whispered back, fighting off the tears.

"What would I do without you?"

"You don't have to worry about that right now. I'm here. I just passed my physical and stress test the week before you came down and the doctors said I had the insides of a woman thirty and the exterior of an old woman. They will catch up with one another in the near future, but until then you'll have to put up with me a little while longer." She stood on her tiptoes and kissed him. "I love you Rollie Kemp, just the way you are. I couldn't be more proud of you if you were my flesh and blood."

"We might as well be related in blood, you cleaned enough of it off me when I got hurt." He laughed and then hugged and kissed her back. "Ditto, I love you too, and I like the new boyfriend."

"You giving me your approval?"

"I am," Rollie answered. "Beanie's a genuine kick in the butt."

"You can say that again," Millie said as she folder her tiny body up against his and held him with all her mite.

CHAPTER 5

THE WATCHER stepped out of the shower, removed the shower cap and fluffed out her kinky red hair. She sat at the makeup table and applied meticulous makeup to coincide with the raven wig. A new look she hadn't used before was curiously captivating. There was unexpected desperation for an existence, a beginning of something untried. She was determined to begin life over when the job was completed if a way to shake the two men who were on constant surveillance could be found. If she killed them, more would come. Since she failed to complete her last mission goons followed her everywhere. They wanted to kill her as badly as she wanted to do them, but they needed her service and people who lived a life like hers was hard to replace. At the same time, there was no doubt. They would finish her off sooner or later. The only chance she had was finding a way to evade their presence when she was ready to make a run for it.

Her computer chirped announcing a new email had just arrived. She moved in the direction of her desk, but stopped to look at her reflection in the doorway full-length mirror. Her body was firm and shapely. The legs were that of dancers, evenly proportioned from hip to toe. She sat down in front of her computer and typed in her password. Her email opened, and there was only one new message. She opened it. The message was short. CALL ME!

She opened the desk drawer, retrieved a key and then opened her hall closet. She lifted out a small brown case and unlocked it with the key. Inside she removed a disposable phone and plugged it into the wall. It lit up and chirped. Under the phone was a little red book. She kept phone numbers in the book, all written in code only she understood. She found his number and made the call. It was answered on the second ring. His voice was muffled.

"I've been trying to figure out what to do with you."

"I made a mistake," the Watcher said in a tentative voice.

"You fucked up like a dog pissing on my shoe. So the question is do I give you another chance or cut you up into little pieces for fish food? What do you think I should do?"

"Does it matter what I think?" She asked.

"Maybe," he answered.

"You're going to kill me either way, right?" The Watcher crossed her legs, trying to determine how many she could take out before they got her.

"You've done good work in the past, and I'd like to think you could do that again in the future. So here's the deal. You fulfill the job. You live. You flub it, you die. How does that sound?"

"How do I know I can trust you?" The Watcher stood up and walked back to the mirror where she ran her free hand over her body. She couldn't trust anyone, but this might buy some time.

"You won't trust me any more than I trust you," he answered flatly.

"What is it, you want me to do?" She struck a pose for the mirror. Her body wasn't all that unpleasant. Men still liked what they saw. What did that asshole call her? Eye candy. Yeah, that's what she was eye candy.

"We have a location on Pataglia. He's with a small army and some important people we'd like to see disappear. You go in and take 'em out. If you make it out of his compound, and off the island, I'll wire you a new payment, and we're back in business."

"Is this a setup?" She asked softly.

"Hardly."

"You said island and compound. The two don't usually go together."

"He's in the Florida Keys, smack in the middle. If you get all of them, you won't have a problem. If you miss, chances are pretty good they'll come after you. If they chase, your fate will be yours, not mine. Fast and evasive, maybe you can outrun them. Get caught and the odds are they do what they do best."

"When?" The Watcher moved back to her desk and sat down. She closed the drawer with her toes and smiled. She loved a challenge, and this was one she might live to enjoy.

"There's a flight leaving for Miami at six-thirty tonight. Have time to catch it?"

She glanced at her watch. She had plenty of time.

"Yes," she answered.

"There will be a chauffeur with a sign Cindy Porter waiting for you. In the trunk will be all the firepower you'll need. When you're done, he'll bring you back to the Tampa airport so don't hurt him."

"Will he kill me?" The Watcher asked.

"You always spoil things by asking too many questions." Abruptly he ended the call.

Cindy Porter, she liked the name. Florida was lovely this time of the year, and no limo driver was going to mess it up for her. Now she had to know if she could trust him again.

CHAPTER 6

Detective John Rader sat behind the steering wheel sipping cold coffee while his partner Frank Mustio stuffed his face with a thick hamburger. Rader was tall, athletically thin and intense about everything in life. Frank was a complete opposite, short, stubby, a few pounds north of being utterly gross and seemingly too relaxed to be a good cop. They had been waiting on surveillance for hours, and the silence hung over both as if they'd talked themselves out of words.

"I'm starting to question your hot tip," Frank said over a mouthful of burger.

"He'll be here," Rader answered sharply. He didn't glance over at Frank because he was hungry and didn't want to admit it. They had a bet going that Rader would not eat junk food and essentially stay away from red meat. Rader wanted to throw in the towel and eat like a pig. He missed the taste of meat, the scent from a barbecue and the rest of all the temptations that came from eating badly. He went healthy six weeks ago and was starting to regret it every day Frank ordered something nasty to eat. He lost twenty pounds and promised his wife, Ashley, he'd stay that way. She had suddenly taken on a renewed interest in how his body looked and what she could do with it. Sadly that hamburger smelled beyond good.

What's he supposed to be wearing?" Frank asked as he finished off the last bite of the greasy stuffed chunk of disgustingly scrumptious smelling Mammoth healthy burger sandwich. That's what the little restaurant called their calorie ridden creation.

"Brown bombers jacket and black jeans."

"Want a fry?" Frank held out a slippery open container with large French fries sticking out in all directions.

Rader reluctantly shook his head. Than he thought, maybe just one? He turned away. No. He refused to give in and then have to deal with the guilt and possibly being forced to tell a lie. No, sex with his wife was never better, and the conversations before and after were great. He and Frank had been partners since joining the force and with all his rotten habits, Frank was his partner, and both would lay their lives on the line to protect the other.

"Is that him?' Frank asked just before he stuffed the last fry into his mouth.

"Yeah," Rader peered out the window watching Bennie Muñoz lumber down the street looking guilty and acting as if he just robbed a liquor store. He kept looking over his shoulder, half expecting a boogeyman to jump out and make him. "Let's wait until he's climbing the stairs to his apartment. The door's locked. When he reaches into a pocket for his keys, we'll take him."

"The minute he sees us, you know he'll run." Frank said wiping his face with a napkin.

"That's why I wore my running shoes." Rader said not taking his eyes off Bennie.

Bennie climbed the stairs, reached into a pocket, and the two cops jumped out of their car and ran across the street. Bennie saw them coming and took off. Rader followed while Frank slowly cut through the alley to go around the building.

On the next block, Bennie was a missile entering a marathon, streaking as he circled the corner and ducked into a stairwell. Rader wasn't far behind him, but as he passed where Bennie was hiding, the little thug jumped out and hit Rader in the side of the head with his fist. Rader dropped to the ground, and Bennie raced on crossing the street.

He ran down the block, right by the back of his apartment and the moment he came to the alley, Frank stepped out with a trash can lid and smacked Bennie in the face. Bennie went airborne, and then landed hard on the sidewalk. Frank's over-sized shoe was awkwardly placed in the middle of Bennie's chest. A large package of white power wrapped in a clear plastic bag fell out from Bennie's jacket. Bennie's eyes frantically looked from the package up to Frank.

"Hi Bennie," Frank said with a smile. "You didn't hurt my partner, did you?"

Bennie spit out blood, desperately looking for a way out. There wasn't one. Then Rader reappeared, wiping blood from his nose. He wanted to kick Bennie in the head, but refrained. Instead, he picked up the package of white powder, opened the top and inserted his little finger into the middle of the powder. He put his finger in his mouth and tasted the powder.

"Well I'll be damned. Stuff tastes just like coke." Rader closed the bag.

"It's not mine," Bennie blurted.

"Maybe you found it?" Frank quizzed, raising an eyebrow into a perfect arch.

"Yeah, how'd you know?" Bennie said with a smile.

"A bag this size," Rader held it up, "what do you think, Frank? Five to ten years?"

"You gotta be shittin' me?" Bennie said. "I'm delivering. It's not my stuff."

"Possession is nine tenths of the law, and you my friend are in possession." Frank leaned down on his foot, pinning Bennie to the sidewalk with suffocating force.

"Look, I didn't mean to hurt you guys," Bennie stammered. "What about a deal?"

Rader gestured Frank to step back. Frank removed his foot. Rader helped Bennie to his feet. "What deal? What could you possibly offer us?"

Bennie looked up and down the street nervously.

"Cuff me and put me in the back seat of your car," Bennie said.

"What?" Frank said.

"They'll kill me." Bennie mumbled.

Rader spun Bennie around and clicked the cuffs over his wrists, and then he half dragged him over to the squad car. He opened the back door and pulled Bennie right up against his face.

"If you're screwing with me, I'll kill you." Rader's voice dropped into a threatening whisper. He pushed Bennie into the backseat and slammed the door.

"You gonna trust him?" Frank asked as he rounded the car and opened the passenger door.

"Don't have to, Frank," Rader said as he got in behind the wheel.

They drove out of the neighborhood and after a short ride pulled in beneath a freeway overpass and stopped.

Rader turned to glare at Bennie. The little man cowered.

"Can you get me out of town?" Bennie finally asked.

"Are you kidding me?" Frank snickered.

"No. After I tell you what I know, they'll know where it came from. I'm screwed either way, so if you can't get me out of town safely, I have nothing to say."

"Let's say we can do that, Bennie. I need some crumbs here to work with?" He glanced at Frank and found an incredulous stare coming back.

Bennie squirmed for a moment and then his eyes filled with tears.

"There's some bad shit about to go down," Bennie stammered.

"Who's your dealer?" Frank asked.

"He's nothing," Bennie spat out. He looked around expecting someone to appear at the window and take him out. "I need protection."

"I need a million dollars, but it's not gonna happen. Is that all you got?" Rader asked.

"While I was waitin' for, you know my package? I heard these two guys talking down the hall. They said it was gonna start a war." He glanced up at the two detectives. "Look, my lady is big, ya know? Baby's comin' soon."

"Should have thought about that before you picked up the package," Frank added like he didn't care about the story or where it was going.

"Yeah, hind sight is great, and all that crap, but this is now, and that I would'a-should'a crap isn't on the table. I'm a lover."

"Yeah, I noticed," Rader said feeling the side of his head where Bennie hit him.

"Sorry about that, but there're two of you. Listen, these two guys weren't part of the crew. They were members of the west coast family and..."

"Wait," Rader said. "What family?"

"You know, the guys making big movies, the union guys?" He turned from Rader to Frank and then back to Rader. "You don't know?"

"Know what, Bennie?" Rader asked.

"Crime families, the Pataglia's from New York and these guys who are part of the Brayden family are from Philly. But then they got interrupted by this guy..." His voice trailed off into deafening silence.

"What guy?" Frank studied Bennie's face.

"He was one of those, you know, dudes with black eyes? He said someone named Lou Baxter screwed up, and nobody who screws with Harold Fine lives to talk about."

"That's it?" Frank turned away from Bennie, shutting him off. "Let's get out of here."

"Yeah," Rader turned to the steering wheel and grabbed the keys.

"Wait," there's more." Bennie was suddenly sweating, with every pore in his body opening up to release the floor gates. "This guy with the darkness in his soul said Baxter nor Ronnie Mauten were a problem anymore." Bennie waited. "Are they dead?" His voice was a murmur of fear. The two detectives turned around at the same time.

Louis Baxter was run off the road in Malibu after being shot, and Ronnie Mauten had been shot in the forehead and stuffed in the trunk of a Rolls Royce at LAX. Both men were involved in union negotiations and studio motion picture productions, and both had been obvious contract murders. Harold Fine was a significant Las Vegas player law enforcement had been after for years.

"Are they dead?" Bennie repeated angrily.

"Yeah, they are." Rader answered.

"I knew it," Bennie blurted out. "He saw me in the hallway. Asked me if I heard anything? I said no, but I could tell by the look in his eyes he didn't believe me. He just nodded."

"Where did the drugs come from?" Frank wanted to know.

"I'm not sure. It was either a guy named Arnie or Drew. I was supposed to meet at the beach, in the parking lot next to the pier."

"So who were you meeting?" Rader asked.

"That's the whole point. The man gave me a package and said either Arnie or Drew would meet me. I should've known." Bennie started crying. "You guys saved my life. Had I gone to the beach at midnight, the dude with the darkness would've been waiting for me." He looked terrified, tears streaming down flushed cheeks, "I'm a dead man, aren't I?"

"Is that all you heard, Bennie?" Rader wanted to know.

"All they said was when Anthony shows his face, the whole thing will be settled. I don't know who Anthony is I swear." The life-long criminal looked like a pathetic loser as he withdrew into a fetal position on the back seat.

Rader shared a long silent look with Frank. He knew a con when he saw one, and this wasn't one of those moments. Bennie was all but giving up.

"How do you want to play this?" Frank asked.

"Let's call the Captain first. McBride has to make the call." Rader wasn't about to step on his own feet again. The guys down in organized crime had to be informed, and that meant the Fed's would charge in like Knights and white horses.

Frank glanced into the back seat. Bennie was whimpering, rocking back and forth.

"What do we do with him?" Frank asked.

"I wish I didn't believe him, but I do. Let's get a unit over to his house and get his wife out of there. We'll figure out what to do with them when we sort it out with the important people who need to make the tough decisions. That won't be us Frank." Rader offered half a smile.

"Thank God for small favors," Frank added.

"Bennie?" Rader spoke quietly.

The tough guy attitude was gone, leaving behind a shell of what he once believed was essential. Bennie glanced up at Rader, wiping his eyes with the sleeve of his shirt.

"You don't believe me, do you?" Bennie whispered.

"We're taking you in. I need to know where your wife is." Rader asked

"She's at work. We have no family here in America, but she's legal I swear."

"Where does she work?" Rader wanted to go home and forget today.

CHAPTER 7

Rollie shot one more commercial for a new martial arts chain and their clothing line Smacko. The line included jackets, tight fitting pants, ankle protection shields, and a stylish wrist and forearm shield to protect a sudden attack. The commercial turned out to be a complicated production, and a costly one. Rollie had never worked on a sixty-second commercial costing several million dollars to shoot. It was created and directed by a big time movie director, with stunt coordinators, special effect people, gun shots, explosions and a car chase. They applied and received permits to shoot in downtown Miami, right through the streets of some of the most expensive homes in the country, and concluded with a wild chase into the Everglades. Rollie was dressed in their latest gadgets and had a stunt double to handle the craziest of the stunts. Otherwise, Rollie volunteered to do most of his own stunts. Millie was delighted watching all the action while Beanie and his son Bean did business in various cars and motor homes and still managed to keep a vigil eye on the entire production.

Drake reluctantly became Rollie's assistant, even though he seemed to enjoy every moment.

Rollie's dialog and lines were another story. The lines were crisp and snappy and the dialog bordered on ludicrous. Right before, they shot the first few lines of dialog, the director took Rollie off to the side.

"You won't go ballistic on me, will you?" The director asked.

"That's the old Rollie, not to mention my grandmother is sitting over there watching."

The director glanced over at Millie and nodded.

"She looks tough."

"Don't cross her," Rollie said with a smile.

"She taught you everything you know, right?" The director said softly.

"Let's just say if you piss her off, expect your ears to ring for a week. Her slap can be vicious, and don't cuss in front of her. You've heard the term bible totting?"

"It's the south, Rollie. Here, everybody carries a bible to church."

"But if you use the Lord's name in vain, you will feel that strength of that bible when she smacks you in the head with it."

"She wouldn't...?" The director glanced over at Millie. She waved back with a smile.

"Don't say you haven't been warned," Rollie said. "She doesn't care who you are or what you do for a living. You slander the Lord, you're gonna pay."

"She carries it with her?" The director asked while getting nervous.

"Right there in her purse. She never goes anywhere without it." Rollie enjoyed making him nervous. "Your salty tongue could bring the wrath of God up close and personal."

"Let's talk about your lines," the director changed the subject. "Our client is right over there sitting next to your grandma. He thinks they were written by an academy award winner, but in truth they were created by his twenty year old son. They're stupid, no more like infantile, and make no sense, but the old man loves them."

"So you want me to say them exactly as written?" Rollie quizzed.

"Exactly."

"Okay," Rollie added flippantly.

"This entire production is to create a smooth sixty-second spot, understand?"

"Sure," Rollie said.

It took two days to shoot long chases that would be cut up into tiny little pieces and then reduced further into micro seconds. The chase sequences went smoothly. They did several takes and used multiple cameras and the director and client were ecstatic. They moved on to the action sequences and then the dialog. The thug crashed the first car and jumped out to fight Rollie, who was supposed to be in the second car. The moment the stunt driver slid sideways to trap the evil man's car against the bridge, the director cut the action. From another camera angle, Rollie replaced the stunt driver and was charged by the bad guy. They fought, moving around the highway which had been closed, and it all went as planned until the dialog started.

"That's far enough," Rollie shouted.

"You think wearing Smacko can stop me?" The evil guy said with a grin.

"That's why it's called Smacko," Rollie answered sarcastically as he moved in a circle.

"Well Smacko won't stop me." Soundiing tough, the bad guy tried to run by Rollie.

"Smacko."

"What?" The bad guy froze.

Rollie grabbed his collar and spun him around. The bad guy took a swing, but Rollie blocked it by holding up the Smacko arm guards. When the guy smacked the Smacko guard, he screamed and pulled his hand back in pain. Rollie smiled.

"Smacko, for your personal protection." Rollie held up his sleeve and kissed the Smacko guard. He looks like a muscle man kissing his biceps, and then he grabbed the bad guy.

"Cut!" The director screamed and jumped to his feet. Millie was sitting right next to him and was surprised by his sudden movement. She was enjoying the whole scene. "God."

Millie reacted so quickly it stunned the director into silence. She slapped her bible against the back of the director's chair. The entire crowd got quiet.

"Were you about to say a prayer?" She asked the director.

"Ah," the director stammered, searching his mind for a quick answer. He quickly looked around and found Rollie, smiling and gesturing "I told you so," back at him. The director, thinking fast, answered … "Yes, yes I was about to say God bless the spoken words, but we should be able to say them better." He smiled at Millie and she sat down holding the bible in her lap. Her frown melted away when Beanie hugged her and kissed her cheek.

"Does that mean you want to do it again?" Rollie asked with a wide grin. He glanced at Drake, who was also smiling and found Beanie and Bean behind him wearing stupid smiles that traveled from ear to ear.

"Yes," the director said quickly, "that's what I was about to say. Let's do that again."

On the fifteenth take, the director seemed satisfied.

"Cut," the director called out, "that's a wrap."

All the crew members joined the two cast members in light applause and then started tearing down the set so they could go home.

Beanie took them all out to dinner again to celebrate. During another sensational meal at one of Bean's favorite Cuban restaurants, Drake received a phone call on his cellphone.

"Hello," he said quietly so as not to interrupt a story Beanie was telling them.

"Drakey?" The voice was immediately recognized. Erinn, his one and only true love, although he had a hard time telling her how he felt.

Drake got to his feet. "Excuse me, I have to take this."

They all watched Drake walk off into another part of the restaurant and go out the front door. When he was gone, Beanie returned to his story.

"Now this is the good part," Beanie said.

Outside, Drake paced into the parking lot with his cellphone held against his ear.

"Is everything okay?" Drake asked.

"Yes, and stop with the worrying," Erinn answered.

"Where are you?" Drake asked.

"I'm at home silly. Where do you think I am?"

"I'm sorry. I didn't mean to..."

"I'm starting to think you want an exclusive on me?" Erinn said lightly.

"That could be a good thing, don't you think?" Drake said.

"Maybe," Erinn teased. "Will you stick around if I do?"

"I could do that," Drake answered slowly, "if you do."

"Mmmm," Erinn mumbled. "I miss you. I really do."

"I'll be coming home soon. We'll talk about this. You know your lifestyle is a little different than mine and..."

"And?" Erinn asked.

"Is it possible to put the two together?"

"Is it worth trying?" Erinn quizzed. She had that giggle that drove him nuts. They had lots of history. More baggage than most couples, and yet they kept coming back to each other.

"Are you out by the pool?" Drake asked. "I hear water or waves."

"No, I'm in the middle of my bathtub, quite naked and think about you."

Drake could imagine her in the tub. It was a good image, but he'd much rather be at her side than thinking thoughts of joining her in a large bathtub.

"I'd say I'll be right over if I was on the West coast. Since I'm not out there, I can whisper sweet nothings and get away with it."

"Whisper," she teased.

"You know how I feel." He said angrily, hating the gushy feelings he couldn't do anything about. He didn't want to admit it, but inside, he knew how much he loved her. She was, however, like having an untouchable dream, there one minute and gone the next.

"Tell me how you feel Drakey," she whispered.

They were three thousand miles apart. He could say anything and knew there was enough time to for her to forget it.

"I love you, Erinn," he said it quickly and got it out in the open, again. "I've always loved you, and you know it."

"I do, and you know what?"

"Don't say something cruel," he said quickly.

She ignored him.

"I love you too. I can't get enough of you and can't wait to have those huge arms of yours around my body."

Silence filled the phone line.

"Drakey?" Erinn spoke softly, "Are you still there?"

"I am. I need time to digest what you just said, you know, have it translated into several languages, and then printed out so I can read it. Perhaps after all is said and done I can comprehend how screwed up things are between us."

"Well, while your digestive system is doing its job, and I'm sure it will be fair when all is said and done, I have some news for you."

"News?" Drake shook out of the bummer he was riding. "What news?"

"I heard there was activity on Santino's little boat, so I sent a friend down to the marina to see if it was true."

"Was it?" Drake asked. His pulse quickened as his jaw muscle expanded.

"It was, and he has two visitors staying with him."

"Actors?" Drake said, knowing what she meant.

"Yes, the boys are back in town. I also heard a troubling rumor."

"What kind of rumor?" This wasn't right. She was sticking her nose where it didn't belong.

"Union rumblings that changes are coming, and our town may have some unwelcome visitors. This last part, Drakey, rings of bad things in the air and I don't know what to do about it." She cleared her throat, but the voice had panic intertwined within the words. "I think someone has been watching me," she finally got it out.

"What makes you think stuff like that?" Drake asked.

"I don't know for sure. It's just a feeling. I keep feeling like eyes are out there watching my every move, but when I look, they're gone. Do you think I'm being paranoid?"

"Yes, so stop looking or asking questions. Make it simple, stay close to your house. I'll be home as soon as we can get out of here. Will you call me every morning and evening?"

"Drakey," she protested. "Are you trying to scare me?"

"No, I want you do be careful. People talk, even friends. You don't know what people are saying behind your back, and they could be saying things to the wrong people. Just pull back on the reins and put everything on hold. Can you do that for me?"

"Since you asked so nicely, yes of course I can. Did you mean what you said?"

"We've talked about a lot of stuff here, Erinn, which part are you referring to?"

"Don't do that, Drakey," she said with a serious undertone touching anger.

"Then you must be talking about me loving you, and the answer is yes I meant it. Hell, I've been in love with you for years, too many to count. I'm sorry we keep screwing things up. I hate it when I run away, or when you disappear at the wrong time. Most of all, I loathe the fact we're not stronger when we are together." Three thousand miles or not, it was out in the open, and he didn't care.

"I love you too. Hurry home. I'll call you in the morning."

She hung up. Drake snapped the phone shut and hit the first thing his fist could contact. Unfortunately, it was someone's car, and his sudden physical expression left an unmistakable dent that would require significant body repair.

CHAPTER 8

THE WATCHER slid over the wall dressed in all black. She lowered a black bag down from the stucco covered brick fence that surrounded Pataglia's compound, unzipped it and removed night vision goggles, several handguns and an AKA machine gun. She brought enough ammo to take out a small army.

The need to get closer became imperative. On the other side of the shrubbery, she had a much better chance of silently neutralizing six guards, move inside, and kill everyone in sight. It was an incredible gamble; she wouldn't get all of them. That created a bigger problem for her as the opportunity to scoot over the grounds and make it back over the wall breathing was a near impossible task. On the other hand, she thrived on doing what others said couldn't be done. One haunting question ate at her. Could she get in and back to her car alive? If she missed anyone along the way or there were more men she didn't see, she was toast.

The first two guards were easy. The third caught her from behind and put up a good fight. He was a burly guy, slow on his feet but the power in his hands almost got the best of her until she slid a knife into his armpit and severed his artery. She was thankful it was dark, and the look in his eyes was missed.

She put a silencer on one of her handguns and put one bullet into the back of the fourth guards head. The fifth and sixth guards were napping and felt nothing.

She circled the house and didn't see anyone else. On the waterfront side, there was a swimming pool, and a boat dock with one large fishing vessel and two smaller speedboats along with three beached ski crafts. She crossed over a massive brick patio, ducking out of sight as a traveling cloud cover raced across the moonlit sky exposing humongous portions of the patio to bright light every few seconds. She glanced up at the sky and watched the clouds begin to gather and assemble into one monster storm laced threat. A storm would help.

Inside she watched a group of men eating and talking. There was laughter, and conversation. She couldn't see how many were inside, but Pataglia was sitting in the middle, surrounded by Gi Carlo, Billy Davis, Frank Masseria, and others she had never seen before. A maid served more food and drinks while, behind them, a cook prepared another portion of their meal. All the men were dressed casually in beachwear, shorts, golf and Hawaiian shirts and sandals.

THE WATCHER loaded the AKA and removed an extra clip from the bag she carried. She took a deep breath, planted her feet in a weight balance separation and took aim.

She opened fire. The bullets shattered the windows, tore the furniture and chewed everything in sight to pieces. Bodies dropped, but a few men managed to avoid the onslaught of machine gun fire and ducked out of sight. Instantly return fire from several locations in the house lit up the yard. The Watcher raced across the patio and kept firing her weapon toward the mansion. She reached a brick built-in barbecue where she reloaded the AKA. Her peripheral vision saw movement, the shadow of a man. His image disappeared, and then opened fire at her. Bullets ripped the bricks, and cement dust flew into her eyes. She pulled out the handgun and fired twice into the room the shadow had ducked. A few feet to the right came muzzle flashes, and the bullets just missed the Watcher.

With the AKA and revolver in tow, she took off across the patio. Gunfire followed her from various places inside and out of the house. One hit her shoulder, taking with it a serious chunk of skin. The cloud cover expanded, and the grounds fell into a blackened situation where nothing could be seen. She was convinced her job had been accomplished and raced at the six foot high wall surrounding the house. Forced to abandon the AKA, she scrambled over the wall as a hail of bullets riddled the concrete and followed after her.

THE WATCHER tucked the pistol into her waist and ran. She ran for her life, zigzagging over the grounds and to the street where she jumped into her car and sped off without turning on the lights.

Inside the Pataglia mansion, the wounded helped others get up. Billy Davis had by instinct, grabbed Pataglia and pulled him to the floor where he covered Anthony with his body. When he helped Pataglia up he realized the head of the crime family had actually been shot again. His shoulder and forearm were bleeding badly, and Billy grabbed a cloth napkin and wrapped it around the wounds.

"Gi Carlo?" Pataglia mumbled, "Where is Gi Carlo?"

Billy David started pulling chairs and the table upright, and there was Gi Carlo lying face down on the floor. Billy turned the thickset man over. He had three wounds. A new hairline was bleeding just above his left ear. His stomach was soaked in blood, and down the leg his ankle on the other leg was bleeding.

"I'm okay," Gi Carlo said trying to get up.

"Sit down," Pataglia ordered. He turned to Billy Davis, "Call Doc Brown and get him over here. Where's Frank?"

Two men were dead. The maid was taking her last breath, and the cook lie mortally wounded on the kitchen floor. Frank Masseria was hit several times in his arms, legs and shoulder but was breathing when Billy found him.

Pataglia glanced down at his arm, and then his eyes traveled sadly around the room. He turned to Gi Carlo with tears in his eyes.

"Who?" Pataglia asked in a voice lost in emotion.

"Whoever it was. We'll get him and those responsible." Gi Carlo answered.

Billy Davis ran outside and disappeared. A few of the unwounded cleared off the couches and helped Pataglia and Gi Carlo sit.

When Billy Davis returned, he was helping another man who had been shot in the upper chest and was breathing with considerable difficulty.

"They got all our guys outside. Hell, there had to be more than one person. How could...?" His voice faded into sobs. He helped the wounded man to the couch. "Doc Brown will be here shortly."

"What are you thinking Billy?" Pataglia asked.

"This is a stunt Arnie could pull off. It's like a movie stunt gone bad."

"You think Arnie Aronjelovich was involved in this?" Pataglia asked.

"I remember that movie he made, you know the one we financed about the serial killer gone crazy?" Billy made a gesture with his good arm. "Wasn't there a scene in that movie at the end, where he went nuts and tried to kill everyone from his past?"

"After he took out some guards, yeah I remember that movie. Enough to create this idea that's for sure," Gi Carlo said.

"If Arnie is part of this, then he's involved in my daughter's death." Pataglia said.

"Didn't you send Tawny over to be interviewed by Arnie?" Gi Carlo asked.

"Yeah, I did," Pataglia answered. He envisioned all the posters of movies they had financed for Arnie Aronjelovich. They knew Arnie was a weasel, and one of the best liars ever. What Pataglia didn't understand was if a rotten egg like Arnie would put his life in danger to get a movie made? Yes, and it was a sad but true answer. The guy would sell his mother out to raise financing for a movie. Would he cross the Pataglia family? Would he? Sure. Pataglia knew right from the beginning Arnie couldn't be trusted, but the lure of Hollywood and box office cash-flow spit out a romantic notion. How stupid they had been.

"So doesn't that put us right in the middle of William Drone's lap?" Billy Davis asked.

Pataglia nodded.

"We're going out to California as soon as possible because that's where we'll get to the bottom of this." His eyes drifted around the room. "If they want me out in the open, so be it. Let's get this up on top of the table where it belongs. You guys need this crap like you need a hole in your head. If we can settle our differences, we'll put this behind us, if not; we'll make their lives far more miserable than they ever dreamt."

"We'll all go," Billy Davis said.

"No, I need you and Frank back in Philly. Let's resolve the Drew Lipesky situation at the same time, or we'll end up having an all-out war anyway."

When Pataglia was a young man, he had to make decisions. The man, whom everyone in the neighborhood was afraid of, Antonio LaFatta was just a fat old man who used muscle to terrify anyone who got out of line. It wasn't his muscle, and he didn't care if the force he sent died. All he had to do was send another. There were plenty of empty-headed young men who looked up to him. It amazed him how eager most young men were to impress him. There seemed to be a line of idiots ready to replace dead guy just for the opportunity to die on another senseless mission. The baker, a loveable person who helped everyone took a severe beating when he didn't pay a debt he didn't owe to LaFatta. Anthony Pataglia decided that was enough. LaFatta sent another to give a second beating to the baker, and he never made it back to LaFatta. After LaFatta had four more men see the baker in an attempt to collect money, and they also came up empty-handed, LaFatta decided it was time he handled things himself. What he didn't expect was Pataglia to be waiting for him. Pataglia made him a one-time offer, move out of the neighborhood or die. LaFatta laughed and reached for a gun. It was the last move he ever made. The whole neighborhood helped Pataglia get rid of the body and any evidence that Antonio LaFatta had existed vanished. From that day forward, Pataglia found a way to create peace and prosperity all at the same time. If Arnie Aronjelovich, William Drone or the Brayden family were making a threat, it was time to stop it and get everything out in the open. A peaceful solution was better, but if a few were eliminated along the way, that worked too.

THE WATCHER drove the long way out of the Keyes and up along the gulf. She avoided Miami and instead drove to Tampa where she intended to catch a flight to Los Angeles. She stopped in Naples, rented a room and made repairs to her body. She was horrified when she peeled off the black clothing and discovered part of her upper arm was missing. A deep cut where the bullet impact would leave a scar and probably needed stitches. She would tape it using a crisscross maneuver she learned from her teacher, and wrap it multiple times to avoid blood seeping through on her flight back to Los Angeles. She stood naked before the mirror and was disgusted by the change this would bring to her beautiful body. Men would find the scar revulsive. She was damaged goods. She lifted her chin proudly but couldn't shake the feeling she might've missed Pataglia. In her haste, she missed one of the guards, and that oversight led to her getting hit. She didn't have time to go inside and finish the job. Some of the men took several bullets and were still alive. If, in her haste, one happened to be Pataglia, she had bigger problems to deal with. Her life would carry a wanted target on it. HE would be after her. She loved the cat and mouse game, but this was different. Mercy wasn't a word they used. They would kill her, and it wouldn't be quick or painless. They would make her suffer. She knew she could run, but they would find her. She couldn't stay buried forever. She might be able to take out a few of those sent after her, but eventually they would catch her. Damn! How stupid if Pataglia survived. They gave her a second chance, and she blew it.

She dressed quickly, removed any indication she had been there, and drove to Tampa. Along the way, she watched the context of her attack unfold in slow motion. The guy sitting next to Pataglia had pulled her target to the floor. If the images she envisioned were accurate, she missed Pataglia, and the man who pulled him down.

In Los Angeles, she had more work to do. Perhaps there was still a chance to redeem her clumsy attempt to fulfill her mission. The Florida job was only part of what had been commissioned. She would perform the west coast job efficiently and hope her visions were nothing more than a bad dream. In Los Angeles, she vowed, there would be no more mistakes. She would make sure the end was just that – the end.

CHAPTER 9

Fabrio wasn't happy with news of the shooting. He was angry he wasn't there to protect Pataglia and the wounds the old man suffered should be his. He'd take a bullet anytime for any of the Pataglia family members. His life meant nothing without Pataglia's help. He drove around Los Angeles in his rental car and checked on everyone he could find that either knew people who were at the party, were at the party themselves, and all who had bumped shoulders with Rollie Kemp.

He heard Santino's yacht was back at it's birth in San Pedro. The two actors were still on board and were being watched. Something wasn't right there.

One of Rollie's stunt friends spilled the story after a few drinks that his buddy was coming back to Los Angeles soon. Fabrio didn't know where the little creep was, but intended to visit as soon as he knew the two detectives had returned. They were first reported being killed, but he read right through that bull. For all, he knew Rollie and his partner Drake Fargo were still in town and keeping a low profile. He'd deal with them later.

He was hungry. Food was the last thing on his mind, but his last meal was hours ago. He started looking for a place where he could grab a bite. His cellphone rang.

"Yeah?" Fabrio said when he flipped the phone open. He didn't' have time to see who was calling.

"Fabrio, this is Joann." Joann was Pataglia's secretary and right hand. He did nothing without having her at his side. She was beautiful to the eyes and smart as anyone he'd ever met.

"Hi Joann, what's happening?" She never called, unless it was necessary.

"Anthony is insisting on making a trip out there. I've done everyone I can, but it's no use. He's going regardless of what I say."

"How is he?" Fabrio asked not hiding his concern.

"Wounded, angry, hurt and disappointed. What can I say? There is no way to stop him. You know how he gets."

"Yeah I know. When is he planning to come?"

"I don't know yet. I just wanted you to know he's coming. He determined. He knows they are trying to draw him out in the open, Fabrio. You must stop them from killing him."

He spotted a restaurant that looked intriguing and out of the area where he'd be safe from searching eyes. He got into the turn lane leading into a shopping center and waited for the light.

"They'll have to kill me first," Fabrio said lowly. "Call me when you know he's making the trip and where he's planning on setting down. He can't fly into LAX, there are too many eyes watching. Tell him to pick a private airport and stay off the radar. Let's keep things quiet. I'll do what I can out here."

"Okay," JoAnn answered and then hung up.

He parked in a shopping mall parking lot and ordered lunch from a little Indian fast-food restaurant. He loved lamb, and the aroma churned his empty stomach. It had been nearly fifteen hours since his last meal, and that was stupid. The little girl behind the counter wore one of those endless smiles that appeared to be phony until the spoke.

"Is the lamb meal tender?" Fabrio asked her.

She nodded, her eyes growing into large dark pools of joy.

"Oh yes, very tender and delicious." She continued to beam up at him.

Her skin was dark and smooth. She reminded Fabrio of the last woman he had dated, Muriel, one of the few humans that trusted him, and died because of it. Her face an image he'd never rinse from memory, nor could he erase her eyes as she died in his arms. The two young Russian kids sent to kill him missed and shot her instead. It was their first and last mistake.

"I haven't eaten all day and am hungry. Is it a large plate?" He watched her face, the smile grew and the eyes sparkled.

"For two dollars more I can give you a double order if you like?" She said.

"Yeah, I'd like that."

She turned and mumbled something in a language he didn't recognize to a man in the kitchen. He looked out at Fabrio and nodded. He turned away to prepare the order.

"Would you like something to drink?" The smile stayed put.

"I try to avoid soft drinks," Fabrio answered. She made him nervous. If only it was another time and place, but that was wishful thinking. He was here to do a job and nothing would stop him.

"Do you drink tea?" Her eyebrows curled into perfect arches.

Dang she was a pretty one. He knew his face scared most women, but she was so sincere in the way she looked up at him.

"Tea? Yes, green or white. Do you have either?"

"Oh yes," she answered with a joyful nod. "We offer both, or I could mix them for you and give you a taste of both if you like."

"Let's do that," Fabrio smiled. It felt good to smile. He hadn't returned a smile in a long time, except in following through with delivering pain. He wasn't supposed to enjoy hurting people, but when they threatened Pataglia or any member of the family, they were hurting him as well, and the peace it brought dishing out some kind of violence was phenomenal.

The girl made the tea in an extra-large cup and secured a lid over the top. She placed the large container along with a straw on the counter.

"Your accent is from New York?"

Fabrio was surprised.

"Yes, I'm out here on business."

"Oh," she sounded disappointed. "Then you will be leaving soon?"

"Yeah, soon." He watched her fuss behind the counter. Nothing was dirty, but she cleaned anyway. When she located a few crumbs, they were gently dumped into the trash. She glanced up at him.

"If I have time, I'll come back and try one of your specials."

"That would be nice. Do you like New York more than here?" She asked.

"That's where I work, so it doesn't matter. Have you been to New York?"

"Oh no," she answered and blushed. "My parents died eight years ago, and I must stay here until my sister graduates from school." She lowered her eyes to the counter where she aimlessly wiped a pristine space even cleaner. "There is no time for travel or fun. I work two jobs and must fulfill my promise."

Fabrio understood commitments and a promise. He had made both to Pataglia.

The man behind the counter spoke, and the girl nodded and then took a container over-flowing with lamb and rice down and closed the lid. She returned to the counter and carefully placed the food into a plastic bag. She added utensils and napkins in the bag and secured it before ringing up the sale.

"That will be seven fifty," she said.

Fabrio pulled out his wallet and caught her name on the small tag pinned to her chest. Olivia was printed over a white strip with a black marker. He handed her a twenty.

"Keep the change, Olivia."

"Oh no, I couldn't do that."

"But you must. I insist." He gathered up the bag and tea and turned to leave. He hesitated and turned back. He set things back on the counter, took a napkin and wrote his cellphone number on it. He handed it to her, and she took it. "If you would like to see me again, call me, even if I am back in New York, okay?"

She nodded, folded the napkin and carefully placed it in her pocket.

"My name is Fabrio," he held out his hand, and she shook it.

"I'm Olivia, but I guess you already knew that." She studied his face and saw there were an multitude of pain and story hidden within. "So if I don't see you tomorrow I can call you?"

"Yes. If I don't answer, leave a message, and I will call you back."

He turned and walked from the restaurant. She watched him leave, and he could feel her eyes on every step he took.

He got in the rental car, drove to the end of the lot and parked beneath a tree where he hungrily stuffed the lamb-over-rice meal into his mouth. Then it was back to business. He opened a map book of Los Angeles, and soon found a shortcut to San Pedro from where he was. It was a short drive to the 405 Freeway, a trip south to the 110 heading west, which would take him down to the harbor.

The two actors were either on Santino's yacht or somewhere between Seaside Avenue and Ocean Boulevard. They had been seen shopping in that neighborhood. He pulled out his cell phone and dialed a number given to him by Gi Carlo. He could use a little help. "Sammy?"

A raspy voice responded, "Fabby?"

"Yeah, it's me. Strap on a three-fifty-seven, and meet me in San Pedro."

"You want me to come alone?"

Fabrio thought for a moment. He could use all the help he could get. He'd like to have this thing out of the way before a wounded Anthony Pataglia got here. He would require more support now that Gi Carlo wouldn't be able to help him. Sammy was a good man. Whoever he asked to join him, they'd be known and trusted soldiers.

"No, I want you to bring some help." Fabrio answered.

"What's goin' on, Fab? You don't sound so hot."

"Tell whoever you bring, he might have to shoot someone."

CHAPTER 10

Rollie was up early and out on the balcony watching sailboats' maneuver through a planned series of motions in a near windless environment. It was easy to identify the beginners and the pros near the mouth of the bay. Several jet skis roared in circles, coming ever so close to the panicked sail-boaters, and Rollie envisioned their smiles. Cocky young men who live to ridicule those unsure of what they were doing. He brought out a cup of freshly brewed coffee and no sooner had he taken a sip, he was joined by Millie. She brought out a serving tray with breakfast covered with silver lids. When she lifted the lid, hidden plates of breakfast goodies were exposed that included eggs-over-easy beacon, toast, and mixed fruit that included blueberries, cantaloupe, melon and strawberries. Obviously, Millie had spent some time preparing the feast..

"You can't leave on an empty stomach," Millie said as she kissed his cheek.

"I hate to leave and yet I know we have to get back."

"Drake and Beanie are eating in bed." Millie sat next to him and started dishing out food.

"Don't you dare spoil Drake."

"Too late, he thinks he's tough and all, but he's a big teddy bear."

"Oh, great, now he's a teddy bear."

"Not as much fun to hug as you, Rollie. He gets all fidgety and stiff. When we hug I think I embarrass him. Don't you ever hug that poor man?"

"No," Rollie answered and started eating breakfast.

"Thank you for allowing us to watch you work on the commercial." Millie was still excited about all the action. The whole thing was fun for her.

"I think it should be me thanking you for all you've done. You're the nicest person I know."

Millie glanced out at the view.

"Why is someone trying to kill you?" Her voice sounded small and terrified.

Rollie couldn't face her, so his eyes joined hers. Silently, they watched boats move in and out of the harbor. As an enormous multi-storied passenger ship slowly moved out into the open waters, Rollie sipped his coffee while he formulated his answer. When he first met Millie, he was fourteen and carrying her husband Clarence home after he suffered a severe beating. Rollie had saved his life. Still a teenager, Rollie beat the hell out of Clarence's assailants, but his deeds hadn't altered the look Millie had in her eyes. She had that same look when she studied his face, waiting for an answer. Millie became his friend. She took care of his mother as she was rapidly dying from the cancer eating her insides. When she finally passed, Millie and Clarence insisted he move in with them. Uncle Charlie had gone back to New York to die and Rollie was left alone. Millie became the grandmother he never had. She insisted he called her grandma and not mom or mother out of respect for his late mother. She laughed a genuine gut buster laugh when she thought of being a grandmother. Millie couldn't have children. All her life she wanted to know how it felt, the joy it created to raise her own kids. There was no doubt in Rollie's mind Millie would have been a fabulous mother. When Rollie got hurt, she held him and sometimes that was for hours. When she found him in the backyard, up against the house crying, she cuddled him and said he needed to get it off his chest and to go ahead and cry his eyes out. She said once he got it out of his system, he could move on. They helped with homework, and when they didn't have the answers, they found them, regardless of how hard it was. They spent hours with him at the library, and when they took short trips, they wouldn't go without him. When he graduated from High School with honors, they were there shouting and clapping as regular birth parents did for their children. When Clarence died, Rollie lost the only father he ever had. His old man, the one that was called his birth father was a wise-guy bum. He was the epitome of a loser. Rollie's mother's older brother Anthony was a Godfather and head of the Pataglia Brothers crime family. Rollie's dad wanted to be a part of their family, but every time they gave him an invitation to join he screwed it up or embarrassed them. While out for the first time, on a money run, he killed two of the family's men, and that was the last straw. His dad was dead within a few weeks, and Rollie and his mother were run out of New York. Rollie wanted nothing to do with the family, not that they wanted anything to do with him, and so it was mutual until now. He wasn't sure the family was trying to kill him, but someone was, and he had to go back and find out whom it was.

"It's complicated," he finally broke the silence.

"Uncomplicate it for me," Millie said quietly. "You've never lied to me before Rollie Kemp, don't start now."

He turned his chair to face her and smiled.

"You know I wouldn't do that," he said softly.

Tears flushed Millie's eyes, and Rollie leaned forward to take her face in the palms of his hands. He rubbed her cheeks and then kissed her.

"I love you," he whispered blinking back his own tears.

"I love you too," she answered, not taking her eyes away from his. They weren't blood relatives, but they might as well have been at moments like this. "Is it something you did?"

"No, well, not exactly."

"What does that mean?" She reached up and held his hand against her cheek.

"We were working a case, protecting two actors from doing harm to their careers or making a huge mistake in public. The job required us to attend one of them big Hollywood parties you read about, but someone spoiled everything and murdered a young actress. We rushed the actors out of the house and into what we hoped was a protected atmosphere, but they broke out and ran off."

"You knew the girl, didn't you?" Millie interrupted.

Rollie had to smile. Was he that easy to read?

"Yes, she was my cousin from New York. I hadn't seen her since I was twelve, but I recognized her when I saw her at the party and later found out she was the one who died."

"Why would anyone think you had something to do with her death?"

Rollie shook his head. "We don't think that's it. None of it makes sense."

"There's more to that girl isn't there?"

"She was the only daughter of my uncle Anthony's."

Millie pulled back, sitting straight up.

"Anthony Pataglia? Your mother's brother?" Millie's face tightened. "Someone murdered the Godfathers daughter while you were in the house?"

"Yeah, but..."

"No buts Rollie. You can't think of an excuse that will make sense so don't try. They must think you had something to do with her death." She shook her head. "Didn't they promised your mother to leave you alone?"

"Grandma."

"Don't grandma me! Why else would someone try to kill you?"

"Because we helped the two actors, or we saw something we shouldn't have. There could be other reasons, but I can't believe my uncle would just decide to eliminate me for the hell of it."

"Do you need help?" Millie got up and started pacing. "Beanie knows a lot of people, but his son knows more. Maybe I should call Bean?"

"No, that won't be necessary."

"He's good, and he liked both of you."

"Millie, listen. We work alone as I think he likes to do."

"So you're going to take the mob on by yourselves?" She quizzed angrily.

"We're not taking on the mob. Dang, I knew you'd go off like this if I told you."

"It's too late, mister hot shot. You're not that tough."

"Wait a minute," Rollie spoke up, "I'm pretty tough, broken a few noses, and I'm perfectly strong enough to avoid being pushed around."

"What if you're out-numbered?" She walked back and stood inches from his face.

"I'm good," Rollie said and took her into his arms. He held her against his chest and could feel her heart pounding against him.

"I know you are. That's what scares me the most. You really believe you're infallible."

"Only at times." He held her out and lifted her chin so he could see her eyes. "I'll be extra careful. I don't trust anyone, and that's a good thing, right?"

"It's a start," she whispered.

He pulled her back into his arms and held her.

"This is nice," Rollie whispered.

"Yes it is, and I want you back here in six months to do it again."

"Okay," he answered and continued to hold her as tight as possible without breaking her.

The red-eye flight back to Los Angeles seemed longer than it should have. The plane was half empty. Drake had called Erinn before boarding and said they would see her first thing in the morning, figuring they could crash later in the day. The flight was scheduled to land at six-ten in the morning, and Drake insisted they rent a car instead of Erinn picking them up. Erinn begged to come, but he finally talked her out of staying up all night. He told her to get her beauty sleep, so she'd be as pretty as ever when he saw her for breakfast. Drake Fargo could use his silver tongue to sweet talk anyone when he put his mind to it. The moment they lifted off, Drake fell asleep. Rollie tried, but even to save his life he could not fall sleep on an airplane. He flew, but he hadn't discovered a way to relax and sleep wasn't even in his thoughts. If he wasn't the pilot and in total control of the plane, he felt the damned plane would fall out of the sky at any moment. He tried, but there was nothing he could do about his emotions. He hated to fly. It just happened to be quicker than any alternative he could think of.

Rollie closed his eyes for a second only to have a hand shake his shoulder. He opened his eyes and found a stewardess peering down at him.

"We'll be landing soon, sir. Would you please buckle your safety belt?" She smiled.

Rollie hated to fly. He never slept on planes. He shook his head and sat up. He peered out the window and sure enough, the vast expanse of Los Angeles and all its suburbs lay beneath the plane like a gigantic puzzle. A light laze hung over the area, reminding Rollie that the clean air of Florida and South Carolina was just a memory. California meant they would be thrust right back into the middle of a nightmare. Whoever tried to kill them was still down there, waiting. They would try again. Erinn said the two actors were back with Santino on his boat, but they didn't run him and Drake off the road. They had missed something in the investigation, and until, and unless they discovered what it was, they would be in constant danger.

The plane dropped down to the runway in one smooth motion. The morning sun was just starting to rise and burn off the morning haze. The hub of Los Angeles was alive with activity.

They drove out of LAX in a rental car. Once on the 405 Freeway, traffic was already jammed until they reached the 10 Freeway where everyone was going in the opposite direction, and it was smooth sailing to Pacific Coast Highway. As they got closer to the ocean, the fog was still hanging over them like a suspended wet cloth. In spite of the fog, they both rolled down their windows to enjoy the cool breeze coming in off the ocean. It felt good. They were home and ready to resolve their case. They were owed money for babysitting the two actors, and those two clowns owed them big time. Rollie planned to collect, one way or the other.

CHAPTER 11

A blazing sun devoured the persistent morning fog that hung over Malibu. Rollie and Drake pulled into Erinn's driveway, and both frowned. The gate was open, her car parked in the circular driveway. Rollie pulled in behind it. The front door was open. Drake pulled his gun. A silent gesture at Rollie for him to do the same. Cautiously, they moved into the house.

Inside, furniture was upended. A few drops of blood left a trail through the entryway, and into the expansive great room that overlooked the ocean. The glass slider leading to the patio was open. Drake waved Rollie toward the kitchen while he went outside. Rollie nodded, and with the gun held out in front of him, inched through the formal dining room, moved up against the wall, and took a quick look into the kitchen. He didn't see her at first, but as he stepped around a broken dish, there she was. Erinn was face up, with blood pooling beneath her head. She wore a powder-blue bathrobe with matching silk pajamas. She had on one dark-blue slipper. Her other foot was bare and bloody.

Instinctively Rollie dropped to his knees, brushed her hair back, and checked for a pulse.

Rollie shook off the image. It didn't work. Instead of Erinn, Rollie saw Kali lying face down in the bathroom. Blood, or what looked like blood, was all over the place.

When he pressed on her neck for a pulse, she looked up and laughed. When he spotted the ketchup bottle, she laughed even louder.

"You thought I was dead, didn't you?"

"Half expected it."

"What's a matter, Rollie? Can't you stand to look at me?"

"Let's get you cleaned up."

"No. I like the way I am."

"You're drunk, Kali, and high."

"So?"

"Is this what you really want?" Rollie demanded.

"I need to feel important, Rollie, and you don't make me feel that way."

"I'm trying to help you, Kali."

"No, you're manipulating me. I don't love you, Rollie."

"Okay."

"It's not okay. Why won't you fight back?"

"I'll fight when we get you help. I'll be there for you, and we'll do it together."

"I don't want you there." Kali was yelling. "I don't want you at all!"

Rollie's fingers caught Erinn's pulse. The back of Erinn's neck was in his hand. Rollie called out, "In here, Drake." Erinn's heartbeat was imperceptible. He holstered his gun. "Erinn? Can you hear me?"

Erinn opened her eyes. "Am I dying?"

Rollie didn't know. "No. Lie still."

"It hurts," she murmured through clenched teeth. She tried to get up.

"Don't move!" Rollie said.

Rollie heard Drake and glanced up at him with worried eyes.

"Hold her, Rollie, hold her hand." He flipped open his cell phone, and dialed 9-1-1. "I need an ambulance, and the police at 207 Ocean Front Road in Malibu."

Drake walked off into the adjoining room.

Rollie leaned closer to Erinn. "Help is on the way, Erinn. If you can hear me just squeeze my hand?" He waited. She finally squeezed. She opened her tear-filled eyes, and the corner of her mouth quivered. She flinched, remembering something. "Shhh, it's all right." She tried to pull away from him, her eyes blinking rapidly, gushing-tears. Rollie held her hand tighter, trying to calm her. "They're gone, Erinn, they're gone." Rollie watched her eyes wander off, trying to see into other parts of the house, and when she tried to lift her head, Rollie placed his hand beneath it. Blood trickled over his hand.

Drake returned and knelt down beside Erinn as his skin became pallid from anxiety. Drake's facial features filled with worry lines, and tears splashed out of nervous eyes.

Rollie could see his pain. Drake had deeper feelings for this woman than he realized. Drake replaced Rollie, holding her hand, whispering in her ear.

"I'm right here, love."

Erinn's terrified eyes found him. She tried to speak, her mouth moved, but nothing came out. She licked her bloody lips.

Drake kissed her hand, "Don't try to talk."

Siren's sounded, getting closer, louder.

Rollie watched Erinn's hand squeeze Drake's massive paw. Erinn wanted to tell him something and struggled to communicate. She was too weak. Rollie felt helpless. The siren got extremely close and stopped. Rollie got up but couldn't take his eyes off Erinn.

Somehow guilt raised its ugly head, and he felt responsible.

Drake whispered to Erinn. "Erinn, stay with me. We have a date, remember?"

Erinn's breathing became erratic, then she took a deep breath, and passed out.

CHAPTER 12

Fabrio got the call early. Joann wasn't happy when she told him Anthony Pataglia would be landing at the Long Beach Airport within the hour. There hadn't been enough time to get everything in motion. Fabrio still didn't know exactly where the actors were hiding. Sammy brought two men he knew from the east coast. They both had Texas ID's on them, and a permit to carry. He and Sammy caught up with Drego Santino, and they spread out. They spotted a few cops working their way around the docks, and had taken considerable care not to be seen. One of the vehicles concerned Fabrio. Either FBI, or someone from LAPD's organized crime had been brought in. He needed to wrap this up and get out of town. The last thing he wanted was a wounded Anthony Pataglia to worry about.

Fabrio grimaced as he watched Anthony Pataglia, dressed in jeans and cowboy boots, climb from the chartered jet. They had landed on a seldom-used runway at Long Beach Municipal Airport. Pataglia had one arm in a sling, and Gi Carlo wore a nasty looking wound along the side of his head. A bullet had obviously grazed him. Gi Carlo had other wounds but showed no signs of discomfort. Pataglia couldn't hide the irritation his wounds caused. The morning sun was warm, an indication the day would be a hot one. California was like that, one day hot, the next bone-chilling cold -- another reason Fabrio hated the place. Fabrio watched the fog systematically burn off. Through the murk, the sun appeared as an offensive, brownish, orange ball, surrounded by chaotic star crystals. New York never had an unsightly landscape. The Long Beach airport was off the beaten path and activity of a major airport. They were under the radar from law enforcement. Fabrio stood in front of the hangar and waited. Once everyone was inside, he closed the hangar door.

"You shouldn't have made this trip." Fabrio argued.

"They tried to kill me. If they want me out here, so be it." Pataglia said

Fabrio watched Pataglia for a moment and then shifted his attention to Gi Carlo.

"How the hell could you let him do this?" Fabrio asked.

Gi Carlo shrugged. "He won't allow you to fight his battles, Fabrio."

"Who the hell was the shooter?" Fabrio snapped.

"A pro. He vanished into thin air. I had guys all over the place. He slipped through." Gi Carlo hung his head down. "No one caught a glimpse of him."

"Both of you have been shot. How can you help me? You need to get back on that plane and go home." Fabrio was furious, and wasn't afraid to show it.

Pataglia's eyes were empty, his face colorless. "That's not going to happen. So tell me?"

Fabrio, hands in his jacket pockets shrugged. "A whole bunch of people were at the party where Tawny died. She was, ah, with several guys…"

Pataglia knew his daughter wanted to hurt him. "I need to know, Fabrio."

Fabrio knew he would find out sooner or later. "She was a drug user, and she slept with four or five guys that night. She wanted to get even with you."

Pataglia spun away, smacking the wall. He didn't turn back. "Who are they?"

"The last to see her were Ben Parker, Andre Garrison, Arnie Aronjelovich, Dylan Taylor and, ah, Rollie Kemp."

Pataglia turned around, his lips curling in anger. "You sayin' my nephew was one of the last to see her alive?"

"Yeah, it looks that way." Fabrio answered.

"Damn him to hell! How could Richie and Rollie be so different? Richie died for me, and it appears Rollie wants to bring me down." Pataglia paced. "I want all of them to pay."

Fabrio furrowed his brow, "Dylan Taylor didn't touch her."

"You know that for sure?" Pataglia asked.

"Yeah," Fabrio answered, "he's gay."

"All right," Pataglia was formulating a plan, "where are these guys?"

"Arnie and Rollie are in town. The two actors, Ben Parker, and Andre Garrison are hiding in San Pedro. Drego Santino is down there looking for them."

"Who else we got available?" Pataglia asked.

Fabrio couldn't stand to see the old man wince from the pain. Gi Carlo just stood there, with help from a wall that supported him. Neither man was strong enough to help in any way. They were a liability that could get them all killed.

"Sammy Tass brought two guys with him. Gino Marino, and Manny Castellano. They've worked for us before. They're at the marina right now, hoping' to spot the actors or hook up with Santino. We know they're hiding in a deserted warehouse, but there are lots of 'em down there."

Pataglia winced. "Any sign of Moe Brayden?"

Fabrio shook his head, "No, and we haven't heard Drew Lipesky's here either."

Pataglia limped off by himself. The others waited, saying nothing. Pataglia walked the length of the hangar. On his way back, he asked. "Doc Wardar says you took a bullet in the shoulder. How is it?"

"I'm okay." Fabrio answered. He'd never admit it hurt, and the damage still hurt like hell — like nothing he had ever encountered. His whole shoulder was on fire, but it hadn't open and wasn't bleeding.

"We're all in great shape." Pataglia looked at Fabrio and frowned. After a moment, he asked. "Who shot you?"

"A couple of private dicks moved two of the actors from Santino's place, and had 'em all tucked away in a rehabilitation center until the actors ran away. I stopped to visit Rollie, find out where the actors went, and we exchanged pleasantries."

Pataglia got annoyed. "So who shot you?"

"Your nephew."

Pataglia exploded, veins popped out along his temples, his face turned purple. "Rollie shot you? Rollie's a PI?"

"Yeah, and a part-time actor and writer."

"The little shit!" Pataglia hobbled over and got in Fabrio's face. "Did you shoot back?"

"Pumped one right into his chest, but he was wearing a vest."

"What about the other detective?" Pataglia fumed.

"Rollie was the only one there when I went to visit." Fabrio waited. He could see Pataglia was in deep thought, and didn't want to interrupt him.

"You talk to Santino?" Pataglia finally asked.

"Yeah. He's scared, but has no idea why anyone would hurt Tawny."

"You believe him?" Pataglia steadied himself.

Fabrio looked off. "I didn't trust anyone when I got here. I slapped Santino, and he peed himself. I had a gun in his mouth. It always works. He cried, pledging his loyalty. He told me all he knew, and offered to help find the actors." Fabrio shrugged, "He was telling me the truth. Everything he told me, so far, has checked out."

Pataglia stepped back. "Anyone follow you from Philly?"

"No."

Pataglia dropped his shoulders, "With Lipesky taken care of, we both know Moe Brayden will send Drew Lipesky out here to clean things up. You remember Drew, yes?"

Fabrio nodded. "He's crazier now than when we were kids. Nothing stopped him then, and nothing will stop him now.

Pataglia agreed. "We're splitting up. I want you to stay in San Pedro until you find the two actors." He glanced at Gi Carlo, "Gi Carlo and I will go visit Arnie, and Rollie. I'll invite two of William's friends to assist us. Call me on the cell when you find the actors."

Fabrio waited. The old man was in trouble. He could barely walk, and Gi Carlo wasn't any better. "We need information. Who knows all about Moe Brayden's organization, Gi Carlo?"

"Arnie Aronjelovich," Gi Carlo answered. "We know he's working both sides."

Pataglia's jaw bulged, "It's getting' so you can't trust anyone. Get that worried look off your face, Fabby."

"I can't let you do this alone." Fabrio said.

"I want those actors." Pataglia seethed.

"I think we need to know who tried to kill you first." Fabrio turned to Gi Carlo. "Let's go see if Arnie Aronjelovich pees in his pants, Gi Carlo."

CHAPTER 13

Rollie waited outside for the ambulance. It arrived five minutes after Drake made the call. Two EMT's swarmed into Erinn's kitchen behind Rollie. The man was tall, thin, in his late twenties. His nametag read, Barber. His face was scarred, serious dark brown eyes, and gentle movements of a professional. The co-worker, a woman in her forties was every bit an equal to him. Phillips was printed on her nametag. Short, stubby, she moved like a racehorse, in and out of the house until they had Erinn stable enough to move. While Barber worked on her wounds, Phillips used her two-way radio to communicate with the hospital. As they were bundling her to load up into the wagon, a Sheriffs car arrived. Right behind the patrol car came the unmistakable detective's car.

Drake held Erinn's hand as they rushed her through the house to the front door. Rollie went out to meet with the Sheriff Deputy, and the two plainclothes detectives. The tall, massively built deputy stood eye to eye with Rollie. His body would be an even match to any decent body builders.

The two detectives, one almost as wide as he was tall got out and strolled over to Rollie. Rollie was amazed the mighty one could still pass a physical, or for that matter get into or out of a car without a serious struggle. His partner, typical guy-next-door type was average height, weight and build. His hair was thinning, face bony, and attitude flat. All in all, the guy could disappear in a crowd, and no one would notice him.

The deputy asked Rollie, "Who are you?"

"Rollie Kemp."

"And?" The deputy had a notebook out, ready to take notes.

"And what?" Rollie asked.

"Let's start with what you're doing here?" The deputy lost the friendliness.

"Visiting a friend."

The thinner detective stepped forward and cut the Deputy off. He directed his question to Rollie. "Was the place like this when you got here?"

"Yeah," Rollie answered.

"You know the lady?" The lanky detective asked.

"I do." Rollie answered flatly. He was getting pissed, trying not to lose his temper.

"A real conversationalist, aren't you?" The detective said.

"I try to be." Rollie nodded.

"Let's start over," the slender detective said. "I'm Detective Peter Decker."

Rollie shook his hand. "Rollie Kemp."

"So you said. What do you do, Rollie Kemp?"

"I'm a private detective." It felt good just saying it.

The beefy detective stepped forward. "Name's Johansson and no, you're not a PI! You're an actor!"

Rollie almost laughed in his face. No one in Hollywood knew he was alive, and here this cop knew all about him. "I do that once in a while, when business is slow."

Rollie watched the deputy close his notebook. He stepped back. "You guys have this?"

Johansson nodded. "Yeah, you can take off."

Awkwardly the deputy kind of bowed, and walked backward to his patrol car. He got in, rolled the windows up, and made a radio call. Then he waved, and drove off.

Johansson mumbled. "Everyone wants to be a detective."

Rollie caught his gaze but didn't respond. He couldn't wait to see how good this guy was. Johansson eyed the shattered door jam and chuckled to himself. Rollie assumed it was an inside joke.

Drake climbed out of the ambulance and came over to Rollie.

Decker recognized him right off. "How ya doing, Drake?"

"Been better." He looked at Rollie. "Handle this for me. I'm going to ride in with Erinn. We'll be at the Santa Monica Hospital." He turned back to Decker. "Treat him good, Decker, he's my new partner." He turned back toward the ambulance, and then glanced over his shoulder as he was climbing aboard. "Pick me up when you're done, Rollie."

Rollie nodded. Partner? He watched the ambulance pull out. It raced up the hill, its siren blaring. When Rollie turned his attention to the detectives, both were carefully scrutinizing him. He started into the house. They followed.

"Let go inside, and I'll show you how we found things." Rollie said over his shoulder.

"It's a start," Johansson said with a touch of sarcasm.

When Rollie stopped walking both detectives stumbled into him. Rollie turned around, his eyes glaring at Johansson.

"We can do this together, or you two geniuses can find out what happened all by yourselves. What's it gonna be?"

"Damn!" Decker muttered. "Drake taught you well."

"We should take this smartass in," Johansson said.

Rollie nodded, "Good idea. Then I can explain to your captain how swell things went here at the crime scene." He headed toward their car. "Let's go."

Decker stopped Rollie. "He gets pissy when he goes without sleep. We've been at it all night."

"That goes for both of us," Rollie wasn't smiling. He didn't go into the facts that he'd been shot at, nearly killed, and fundamentally didn't have a clue what he was doing.

Decker walked into the house. "C'mon, Rollie, show us what you found."

Rollie glared at Johansson, who finally gestured he was sorry.

"We found her in the kitchen," Rollie said as he turned around.

The detectives followed, wandered about the house, and looked over the damage.

"So how long have you worked for my old friend Drake?" Decker asked

"Not long." Rollie said. He was waiting to see some impressive detective work. Instead, all he saw was two guys looking at broken treasures. Both were in awe of the view out the patio slider.

Decker glanced at Johansson. "I'll call the crime unit. Let's see if the geniuses who did this left us some prints or a little DNA?"

Decker pulled out his cell phone and punched in a number. He wandered off while Johansson sized Rollie up.

"So," Rollie asked, "in your professional opinion, what happened here?"

Johansson's eyes scanned the room. "Sloppy burglary. The perps didn't expect anyone would be home, got surprised, and your friend got in the way. We see crap like this all the time down here at the beach."

Rollie nodded. "I bet you do." And they probably all get away, he thought.

"You wait," Johansson, said, "Drake Fargo has a habit of drawing out the real weirdoes, and they all end up shooting at people."

Rollie shrugged, "That should give me something to look forward too."

Decker came back in the room. "Once in a while he runs into a good shot, so don't forget to duck when they start shooting."

CHAPTER 14

Fabrio took the Washington Boulevard exit off the 405 Freeway and drove east. The orange, poisonous haze hung over the city 24/7. They passed Sepulveda Boulevard where a few drunks still lingered from the night before. A lonely hooker waved at them. Fabrio felt the bile rise in his throat, and promptly swallowed. Los Angeles was a cesspool. New York was class, even with its dark side. Coming to L.A. was taking a vacation in hell. He passed the Columbia/Tri Star Studios, where modern structures met older soundstages. Steel gates and guards stopped visitors from access without passes or appointments. A line of cars waited to gain entry. Just east of the studio entrance stood a wall of modern glass and elegance. The newest addition to the studio complex, was a ten-story building that housed many production offices, producers, directors and other industry oriented businesses. Fabrio pulled their car into the circular driveway and parked. During the ride, neither, Pataglia, or Gi Carlo, said a word.

Fabrio helped the two wounded men from the car and ushered them into the elevator. With a hushed, swishing sound, they rose, doors slid opened, and they were on the sixth floor. The building had all the right touches, exquisite carpeting, ultra-modern light fixtures, and archways leading to each office. Fabrio found the office they were looking for. The door had fancy lettering, Arnold Aronjelovich Productions. Fabrio opened the door, and they entered. The secretary's desk, with twin dolphins cut in crystal, held a translucent glass top. A single telephone was the only item on the desktop. It was void of a human. Fabrio spotted Arnie in his expansive office, hanging a poster from his latest production. The poster was a typical horror-film advertisement entitled When the Fog Lifted. A half-naked woman was silently screaming as a robotic hand was about to crush her.

Fabrio, unnoticed, stood in the doorway and watched Arnie. The film director looked tired, and older than he did the last time Fabrio had seen him. The office was beautifully furnished with stylish leather sofas cut with thin-layered cushions of soft pink, and matching cream-colored lounge chairs. Pataglia had paid for all of it. Arnie's writing desk was a glass pedestal, with a naked woman holding up a speckled brown marble top with off-white dots. The custom-made desk rested over a thick area rug, which had square pictures of murdered or nude girls, and death scenes from Arnie's films. The pictures were sewn into the carpet. The marble floor matched the top of the desk and blended with everything. Arnie was more than surprised to see them when he turned around. The color in Arnie's face perished. He wore black jeans, a black turtleneck, and a pale gray sport coat. The diamond earring in his left ear was at least a half-carat. Fabrio stepped back and waited with Gi Carlo.

"How ya doin,' Arnie?" Pataglia asked.

Arnie stammered. "Anthony. My God, I heard. How are you feeling?"

"Like anyone who's been shot twice." Pataglia answered sharply.

Fabrio closed the door, and stood by it with his muscular arms crossed. Pataglia, hands in his pockets, limped around the room surveying the posters, and various stills of actors and actresses.

Arnie's frightened eyes danced. "Anthony! If I knew you were coming…"

"You would've run like a chicken, right Arnie?" Pataglia finished for him.

Arnie tried his best, to look surprised. He spread his hands out, eyes wider than they should have been. "Run? Why would I run from you?"

"Everyone seems to be on the run these days, Arnie. I'm not in the mood for a chase."

"I wouldn't run from you, Anthony. We're in business, we're friends."

Pataglia moved closer to Arnie without looking at him. "Let's talk about my daughter?"

Fabrio inched up to the desk, leaving Gi Carlo at the door.

Arnie sagged his shoulders. "I'm so sorry about your daughter. Please accept my condolences." He shook his head a little too much.

Pataglia spun so quickly Arnie's feet couldn't react fast enough to get out of the way. Pataglia grabbed Arnie and slammed him into the wall. "What did you tell Mark Lipesky?"

Arnie shook his head violently, "Nothin', I swear."

Pataglia raised his massive hand around Arnie's neck, "You only get one chance."

"They, ah," Arnie swallowed hard, "They're all blown out about the labor deal."

"They didn't shoot me over a labor deal." Pataglia whispered.

"I don't know anything about the shooting, on my mother's grave."

Pataglia squeezed Arnie's Adam's apple, choking off his air. "You were with Tawny on the night she died?"

Arnie nodded frantically, gasping for a breath.

"What did you promise her, you piece of shit?" Pataglia's face was glowing.

Fabrio stood behind Pataglia, ready to receive him. He couldn't remember the last time he saw him this angry, and out of control.

Pataglia released his hold for a moment. Arnie sucked air into his lungs. Tiny little sweat nodules popped up all over his forehead.

"I said I had a role for her in my next film." Arnie confessed.

Pataglia slapped him across the face. "You lied to get her in bed?"

"No, I swear, the offer was real." He jerked his head to the side, avoiding Pataglia's burning eyes. "She was perfect for the role."

"Is that the movie Mark Lipesky's financing?" Pataglia asked.

Arnie hung his head, his chin grinding into his chest, "I'm sorry."

"You're sorry?" Pataglia pulled him over to a chair, "Sit down Arnie." He gestured with a head movement.

Fabrio moved over, stepped forward and took hold of Arnie.

"I would never..." Arnie groped for words.

Pataglia slapped Arnie's head with an open hand. "Shut up."

Fabrio held the old man as he squirmed in his chair. Fabrio knew the little weasel would sell out his mother to make another film. He would lie, and thwart his own flesh and blood for the sake of the business. Pataglia now knew Arnie was double dipping, and heard through the grapevine that Lipesky had funded more than one picture for him. He had already crossed the line of loyalty. It was too late for apologies. The man was never a friend and whatever business dealings they had were now over. It was time to find out how far Arnie had gone.

Pataglia spoke slowly, "I want something from you."

"Anything," Arnie answered too quickly.

"Good." Pataglia said.

Fabrio picked up on the short response and nodded to Pataglia. Arnie was a rat. Obviously he helped the other side. It was written all over his face. The old man allowed greed to replace honor, and trust.

Panic seeped into Arnie's face when he saw the gesture. His upper lip twitched, and nervous-eyes started with the slow, but uncontrollable rapid-blink, "What do you need?"

"I want a list of everyone who works the west coast for Moe Brayden."

Arnie held up the palms of his hands, "Anthony, I ah…"

Pataglia smacked him on the side of the head, "I also need a list of the prominent people who attended Santino's party"

Arnie sat back in his chair and stared at Anthony. His eyes filled with tears, and they ran uncontrollably down his cheeks. He licked his lips and brought his shaking hands down to his side. "They'll kill me, Anthony."

Fabrio's voice growled. "I'll kill you if you don't!" He brought out his gun and gradually attached a silencer.

Arnie's eyes popped all over the room. There was no way out. "Some of their people were at the party, just to have fun." He eyed the gun, "There were only a couple of people there who know Moe personally. I'll give you their names."

"Depends on how good a liar you are, Arnie. Right now, I care about four things, and you seem to be involved in all of them. Who killed Tawny, who ordered it, who gave the order to come after me, and who the hell Brayden's connections are?"

"I don't know everyone who was at that party." Arnie protested.

Fabrio hit Arnie just below the ribcage. Air purged from his lungs.

Pataglia continued. "While you're at it, you might as well give me the names of those who spent time with Tawny -- other than you!"

"Anthony! I didn't..."

Fabrio slammed the gun barrel into Arnie's mouth.

"Save it" Pataglia whispered. "You were with her. People saw you. Who else spent time with her?"

Arnie gave a vigorous nod, his eyes bulging from his head. He tried to see what Fabrio was doing. "I'll write them down." He was choking over the barrel of the gun.

Pataglia gestured and Fabrio backed off. "Write."

Fabrio removed the gun from Arnie's mouth and pointed it to the back of his skull.

Arnie opened the desk drawer and took out a notebook. He started writing names. His hands shook so badly he had to stop every few seconds. Eventually, he tore the page from the notebook and passed it over to Anthony. Then he completed the roster of Moe Brayden's faithful and slid it to Anthony, as well.

"Leave anybody off?" Pataglia asked.

"No, that's everyone I know." Arnie whispered.

Anthony Pataglia studied the list and handed it to Fabrio.

"Who put the contract on me?' Pataglia asked.

"I don't know," Arnie answered weakly. He flinched, fully expecting a bullet to penetrate his neck. "I swear I knew nothing about that."

"Who killed my Tawny?" Pataglia whispered.

Arnie closed his eyes, shook his head, and quietly waited his fate.

Fabrio read over the list and recognized some thought of as personal friends. He knew all this was part of the business, but it still hurt to know someone they once trust were traitors. They had to move quickly to resolve the problem, and just as fast to repair the damage that would follow the resolution. Rebuilding would take time, and Pataglia would have to provide a peace pipe to those he needed. They couldn't take out everyone on the list, and if they tried -- it would start a war that had no end. There would be survivors, but they would be dealt with differently. Fabrio folded the list of names and put them in his pocket. He observed Pataglia and waited.

Pataglia viewed Arnie broadly, with disheartenment. "I appreciate the names."

"Any chance for me to get out of town until this blows over?" Arnie asked.

"Sure." Pataglia said.

Arnie wrinkled his face. "You're not going to...?"

Pataglia shook his head. "If I wanted you dead, Arnie, you'd already be gone."

Arnie tried to smile. "I didn't lay a hand on her, I swear."

"Why is that?" Fabrio asked.

Arnie shook his shoulders. "No matter what I try, I can't get it up. Haven't been able to in years."

"That mean if you still could, you would've?" Fabrio said.

"Never!" Arnie shouted.

Pataglia raised Arnie's chin with his hand. "Call JoAnn in New York, and tell her where you want to go. She'll make your travel arrangements."

"How do I thank you?" Arnie was near tears.

Pataglia turned away from Arnie and walked out of the office. Gi Carlo followed.

Fabrio waited. He wanted to pull Arnie's heart out with his bare hands. He wanted to hurt the man who hurt Anthony Pataglia, but wasn't given the approval to do so.

"You're scum." Fabrio said. The sound of his voice said it all. He put the gun back in his holster, took one more look at a pathetic, lying turncoat, and followed after Pataglia.

In the elevator, Fabrio glanced at the list again.

"You wanna know why, huh?" Pataglia asked.

"Yeah," Fabrio answered.

"We kill him now, we'll never know where the little creep is about to run to." Pataglia said.

Gi Carlo added, "We're gonna follow him. That's good."

Fabrio didn't like it. "We should'a silenced him."

"Before we do that, let's see where he goes?" Pataglia said.

Fabrio drove them around the corner. They waited. Pataglia kept looking at the list. Fabrio could see the puzzle when Pataglia read names thought of as loyal comrades. Tears formed. It wasn't the labor contract. One of the other families wanted to get rid of him.

Gi Carlo broke their silence. "You're right, he's running."

They all watched Arnie leave the building. Arnie, like a man possessed, ran across the street to the studio parking lot. He carried a large briefcase, and wasted little time jumping into a new Lexus. He closed the door, and the moment he started the engine, the car exploded into a massive fireball.

CHAPTER 15

Rollie completed his statement to the police, watched as the crime scene unit finished, and all law enforcement personnel left. He called the security company and asked them to send someone over to button up Erinn's house. He wandered through the spacious house, surprised that nothing was taken. This wasn't a burglary-gone-wrong. Obviously they came with a purpose, and got what they came for. Rollie walked around the back patio, and for a moment enjoyed watching the gentle waves. It had taken all day, and now day was closing. Moonlight, mixed with the setting sun, danced over a calm sea. Rollie struggled to clear his head. Something was seriously off the tracks. He wasn't a formidable detective yet, but smart enough to know danger was circling. He wore a sardonic smile, knowing he might've been a good cop, but never got the chance to prove it. To get away from Kali, he dropped out of law school and received approval to join the police academy. Rollie was facetious when he decided police work might help get drugs off the street. Was the decision honorable, or to run away from Kali and everything else? Maybe it was both. Or, maybe he was bored with life, unable to get a handle on a direction. Unlike everything else he tried, where boredom set in early, his enthusiasm didn't disappear when he applied for Cop land.

The more Kali tried to come back or apologized, the farther he tried to run, and he couldn't get far enough away. Then the damnedest thing happened -- he started enjoying the police academy. He was actually looking forward to graduation, to carrying a badge. Right after graduation he planned to apply for the detective exam and wouldn't have rested until he took and passed it. One of the best parts of being a cop was to investigate, to solve a crime, and be part of the conclusion. He tried not to forget what he learned, and that was what annoyed him now. He couldn't figure out what it was, not yet anyway, and Rollie liked to be meticulous in his findings. Labor deals cost studios millions, but why waste a whole bunch of people over a labor deal? If the labor contract was the reason, why hadn't they killed his uncle?

He went back into the house, and started turning off lights. If they wanted to take over, a turf war would've started in New York. This was something else. Since his uncle wasn't involved in the missing pension funds, that wasn't it either. He closed the patio door, and secured the deadbolt, but when he turned around a tiny blue light caught his eye. It didn't take long to find the listening device, and camera. He raced through the house and found several more. Angrily he ripped them all free, and tucked the whole lot into a garbage bag he found in the kitchen. What he found was top of the line surveillance equipment. What the hell kind of person used this stuff?

The headlights from the security truck lit up the house as the vehicle entered the driveway and parked alongside Rollie's car. Two kids, both in their early twenties, climbed out and started unloading four- by-eight sheets of plywood. Rollie came out to greet them. Both had clear nametags sewn onto their work shirts. One said Tank and fit the kid perfectly. He was overweight in every visible part of his body. The buttons on his shirt looked ready to explode at any moment. His head was shaved clean. His chubby face had a tiny goatee in the middle of his chin, and he wore a cross earring. His partner, Beau, also bald, had tattoos over both arms, his neck, and down into his chest. Rollie couldn't see what was on his chest, but it looked like the wing of a bird. Earrings in both ears appeared to be knives or daggers. Beau was skinny as a pole. Looked like he hadn't eaten in a week. The overweight kid came over to where Rollie waited.

"Hey, name's Tank."

"Rollie."

They shook hands. Tank turned off and pointed. "That's Beau."

Rollie nodded at the second kid.

"So," Tank started, "what do we need?"

"Front door is jammed. It won't close, and I don't think the alarm will reset." Rollie said.

"No problemo," Tank said as he looked at the front door. "Let's just cover the damn thing up until the owner decides what they want to do. That okay with you?"

"Whatever works." Rollie said. "We can get in from inside the garage."

"Cool. C'mon, Beau, drag that crap over here so we can wrap things up."

"You'll reset the alarm?" Rollie asked.

Beau stared blankly at him.

Tank pulled out a two-foot long flashlight and inspected the damage. Rollie was convinced the kid didn't have a clue what he was doing.

Tank nodded. "Yep."

"Yep?" Rollie asked.

"Did you lock all the other doors?" Tank asked as he continued to shine the hulking flashlight over the front door.

Beau just stood there holding the plywood.

"That I did." Rollie answered.

"Cool," Tank said. He moved into the entryway, opened the keypad, punched in a few numbers, and listened for a beep. It came. He nodded. He flipped open his cell phone, and with his thumb pressed one number. He waited and smiled at Rollie.

"Flower? Hi sweetie, this is Tank." He laughed. "Yeah, that was me, baby. Reset four-oh-one and I'll give this guy the new code. Then, sweet cheeks, we're gonna button the whole thing up so you can go ahead and dazzle the lines." He waited, he laughed, and the keypad buzzed. "Got it, love ya, later." He snapped shut the cell phone. With mocked professionalism, he slipped the phone into and oversized pocket and gestured to Beau. Beau was still holding the gigantic piece of plywood over his head and was grateful he could finally set it down. He placed the wood next to the broken door.

Rollie was amazed. "So it works?"

"Do fish swim?" Tank asked.

"Cool," Rollie said.

"Exactly, my man. That's how we do things at X Meets Y Security." Tank turned to the skinny Beau and handed him a nail-gun. "Secure it, dude." Then he stepped back to watch.

Beau took the electronic wonder, shot a few nails into various parts of the board, and then, like a madman finished with a flurry, opening fire on the unsuspecting plywood. Projectiles splintered the wood. It took only a couple of seconds. He stepped back to admire his sloppy work, and nodded proudly.

Rollie was impressed.

Tank lifted some transistorized device that hung from his belt, turned it on, pressed a few keys, and held it out in front of him toward the door. It beeped, a flourish of trumpets came from inside the house, and that was it. Tank turned off the gadget and dropped it back to its hanging position on his belt. He turned to Rollie.

"You're all set." He wrote down a series of numbers on a pad, tore off the page, and handed it to Rollie. "The new security-code numbers. They'll open the gate, the garage, and the inside door. Thirty seconds to turn it off should be enough, right?"

Rollie nodded. "Should be."

"That's it, dude. We're outta here." Tank said

Beau continued to admire the plywood nailing as Tank got in the security truck. Tank tooted the horn while Beau admired his handiwork one last time before he dashed to the truck. In a flash, they were gone. Rollie just shook his head. Modern technology still baffled him.

Rollie secured the gate and headed into town toward the hospital. He had travelled less than a mile up Coast Highway before he pulled over. There were times he wished he liked drinking alone. Sadly he hated going into bars without a date or a buddy. He needed time to think. Women called it intuition, men called it gut feelings, and suddenly his guts were ripping him inside out. The exasperating reality -- he had no idea what it meant. Someone had deviated from the path of virtue. He looked at the sack containing all the surveillance cameras and listening devices. His old man didn't know about listening stuff. Uncle Charlie wouldn't have had a clue. What the hell was he missing? Homeland Security, the FBI, maybe even some law enforcement agencies used this stuff, but not crime families – unless things had markedly changed since he was a kid. Maybe new blood, college educated types were pushing the old dinosaurs out? About to call Drake, Rollie thought better of it. If Rollie Kemp was going to be good at investigations, and digging, now was time to prove it. Obviously this was something any good private eye would instinctively do alone. He turned the car around and drove back to their office. Gripping the steering wheel with renewed confidence, he was compelled to work this out alone. If he could surprise Drake, by piecing things together on his own, then there was a chance he could do the same for the new Rollie Kemp.

The office was dark. He parked down the block and walked up the alley behind it. A dog barked, and then the whole neighborhood fell into a deafening silence. The rear gate to their office backyard opened with a creepy moan from the hinges. Trying to enter the premises quietly were a near impossibility. Right on the other side of the fence, the Herman's guard dog, Nick waited. Nick was part Doberman, part Pit Bull, and mean as hell during the day. At night, he got worse. Nick was also the only dog Rollie knew, that didn't bark. Rollie stood beside an old oak tree and listened. He heard Nick, wheezing through clenched teeth, on the other side of the fence. Rollie peered into the darkness, hearing the sounds of the night. Surrounded by crickets, a distant catfight, a motorcycle passing, and Nick waiting for anyone to enter his kingdom, Rollie glanced around, hoped no one was watching him make a fool out of himself, then he snuck into the shadows. One thing he couldn't escape though, was the feeling someone was watching, or listening to him. The premonition was overwhelming.

Rollie drew his gun and inched toward the back of the building. He had set the alarm but didn't see the red light on the keypad. Someone had been here and disabled the alarm.

He edged along the side of the house and ducked beneath the windows. He raised one eye over the sill and peeked through the glass. He saw nothing. Traffic on Lincoln was thinly scattered with long sequences between passing vehicles. A trickle of sweat ran down his spine. He gaze over the quiet neighborhood determined not to fall apart or let his mind to play tricks on him.. No one was out at this hour, except Nick. He returned to the backyard, and a tiny blue flash caught his eye. He ducked closer to the house. He stood up and took another look into the office through the window. It was right there -- a little blinking blue light below one of the desks. Damn. How much did they hear?

Somewhere close, leaves were crushed beneath heavy footsteps, and then a twig snapped. Intuitively, Rollie ducked just in the nick of time. Right above his head, wood splintered as a bullet penetrated with a thud. A shot fired at him from a gun with a silencer. He dropped to the ground as if he'd been hit, rolled over, and waited. What seemed like eternity, took only seconds. A car started, and roared off. Rollie jumped up and ran toward the front of the office. Down the block, taillights pierced the darkness. The brake lights were small round globes, and the car that turned the corner was a small coupe – like the one that almost ran him down at the beach. The car disappeared.

Inside the office, Rollie found the source of the blue light. More surveillance equipment was hidden around the office. The material was high tech, and expensive. Who wanted him dead? It didn't make any sense, unless uncle Pataglia was evoking his anger, or Kali had teamed up with someone with exceptional talents.

Straight and sober, she might be able to talk someone into believing Rollie had significant cash lying around. He'd bail her out, and she'd ask for more. She tried to rob him before, even told friends he was rich. She didn't know about investments, or that most people who had money – never had much liquid cash on hand.

Rollie glanced down at the floor. Crumbs formed a small pile beneath the area where the listening device had been planted -- crumbs from what? Damn if they didn't look like pizza crumbs. Rollie hadn't ordered pizza since the incident. He had just taken a shower when the doorbell rang. He donned a robe and got his wallet before the second ring. Rollie opened the door but found no pizza delivery. Kurt, whatever the hell his name was, hit Rollie in the face, and charged into his apartment like a raging bull. Kurt was Kali's drug supplier. He came with two buddies who held him while Kurt punched his lights out. Rollie faked the knockout, and allowed his body to collapse.

"He's a pussy," Kurt said.

"What should we do with him?" one of the buddies asked.

"Tie his ass up. Kali says he's got bucks hidden somewhere. Let's find it."

"He's seen us. What're we gonna do about that?" the second guy asked.

Kurt shrugged, "We'll kill him, but not until he tells us where the money is, so tie his ass up as I said."

While Kurt was looking through drawers, and kitchen cabinets, the two thugs picked Rollie up, and placed him on a dining room chair. They looked around for something to tie him up with, found some towels, and when they lifted his hands, Rollie snaked the towel around one of their necks, and smacked the other guy in the throat with a closed fist. He twisted the towel and slammed the other ones head over the chair. Both dropped to the floor and didn't get up.

"Hey, you guys don't have to hurt him yet," Kurt, said as he came back into the room. With two swift jabs, Rollie beat Kurt in the side of the head above his jaw. It cracked. Kurt dropped in intense pain. He grabbed at his head, screaming

Rollie stood over him. "How ya doin,' Kurt?"

Through clenched teeth, Kurt spat out, "What are you going to do?"

Rollie casually retrieved a gun from his dresser. "I was thinking about killing you."

"You wouldn't." Kurt blurted out.

"Sure I would. Robbery can get ugly, and shit happens when three guys break into a cop's apartment."

"You're, not a cop yet, Rollie. They won't believe you."

"You think?" Rollie asked as he checked the load in the gun.

Kurt begged. "Please don't? This was all Kali's idea."

"Okay." Rollie said.

"You'll never see us again." Kurt promised.

Rollie picked up the phone. "I'm sure of that." He smiled and dialed 911.

Kurt was stunned. "You're not gonna turn us in, are you?"

"I am."

After the cops came and took Kurt and his buddies away, the phone rang.

"Yeah?" Rollie was half asleep.

"You bastard!" Kali screamed.

"It was one against three," Rollie answered.

"Now what am I supposed to do? I need something, Rollie, and you spoiled everything. He was my connection. How could you turn him in? They arrested him."

"I think he came to kill me, Kali. Is that what you wanted?"

"Yes, and he would've succeeded had he been more careful." Kali was shouting. "Maybe next time?"

"Next time? Rollie sobered up.

Kali was close to hyperventilating. "You'll see, tough guy."

"Why can't we just end this, and go our separate ways?"

"You owe me!" Kali shouted.

"What do I owe you?" Rollie asked.

"My life. You ruined my life, and everything."

"Kali."

"I need money, Rollie. You have money, and I need some."

" Hell of a way to ask for it."

"Fuck you, Rollie, fuck you!" She hung up.

Rollie drove to the hospital while his mind raced over bits and pieces of his past. Anger was a control device he had under wraps– until now. He balled his fists, and hoped for someone to get in his way. He thought his sudden bursts of rage were under control, but out came their ugly heads. If they wanted a fight, whoever they were, he'd give them a good one. One thing Rollie knew was how to dismantle the enemy, and defend himself. Rollie stopped at a red light. The car next to him spewed muffled musical sounds from a movie sound track – tires screeching, people screaming, gunshots, and a loud horn. The light changed, and the car behind him tooted his horn a second time. Rollie waved, let up on the brake, and drove through the intersection. He felt his fingers tighten on the steering wheel as the hospital came into view. Why couldn't he put Kali behind him? She did call the other night. And, she came after him once a long time ago. Back then, Kali was so juiced all the time, she didn't know what she was doing. He turned into the hospital parking lot and found a space. He sat behind the wheel for a long time. It made no sense regardless of how he tried to rationalize it. Why would his uncle care if he was alive or dead? To his knowledge he had never done anything to the crime boss. Everybody liked Rollie. He was a clown. Even drunk he made more friends than enemies. He never slept with another man's wife, at least not one he knew about. He racked his brains, and then it dawned on him. If they saw him on the stairs with Tawny, someone with a sick mind might think he killed her!

CHAPTER 16

Fabrio drove Pataglia, and Gi Carlo, to the Bel Air Hotel. He checked them in and delivered both men to a two-bedroom executive cottage. The place was a small house with all the amenities of a five-star hotel. The wound in Pataglia's shoulder was seeping. Gi Carlo looked as if he was on his deathbed. Fabrio helped Pataglia change the dressings and assured the old man he would call, and check in often. Fabrio never heard Pataglia acknowledge possible defeat, yet he mentioned it might be time to step down. The death of his daughter set the stage for depression, but there was more this time. The attempt on his life reminded Pataglia that all his efforts to shift the families from lowly criminal ranks into legitimacy had failed.

Fabrio was so worried he called Dr. Wardar, and asked him to visit Pataglia at the hotel. Fabrio had disillusioned Pataglia. He should have handled Tawny's killer, but Hollywood wasn't New York. He still had no idea who killed Tawny, shot Pataglia, or put contracts out on Louis Baxter and Ronnie Mauten. Fabrio felt as he did when he was a teenager. He was alone. The families were anxious, and all hell was about to unleash its fury on anyone in its path.

Fabrio called Sammy Tass and caught up with him in San Pedro. There wasn't much to see at night. Big ships, their nightlights ablaze cluttered the harbor on the left while city lights dotted the rolling hills on the right. They were cruising Ocean Boulevard when Fabrio's cell phone rang.

He flipped it open, "Yeah.

"It's Gino," came a raspy voice.

"Whatcha got?" Fabrio asked.

"Just caught up with Drego Santino." Gino said. "No sign of the actors yet."

"Where are you?" Fabrio asked.

"Sitting in front of Lucy's Tavern, ah, on the corner of Twenty First and Gaffey."

Fabrio knew where that was. "Where's Santino?"

"Inside Lucy's making some phone calls." Gino talked slowly. "His cell battery died."

"I'll be there in ten minutes." Fabrio closed the phone.

Sammy didn't say a word.

"Who did you send over to pick up Rollie?' Fabrio glanced at Sammy.

"Couple of union guys." Sammy smiled. "They'll hurt him but keep him alive until I call and tell 'em where to deliver him."

Fabrio nodded and smacked the steering wheel with his fist. "Damn actors! If they're not guilty, why the hell are the two of them runnin'?" He glanced at Sammy, "If you were a hot-shot actor, and came down here to hide, where would ya go?"

"A friend's boat, maybe. Get on one of those big freighters." He wrinkled his brow in deep concentration. "There's not a lot of stuff to do down here, Fabby."

Fabrio nodded. He glanced out over the shipyards. Tall ships, containers loaded with God only knew what, and lots of lights. The actors wouldn't be down there.

Lucy's Tavern was a local bar. Fabrio parked on Twenty First Street, told Sammy to stay put, and rounded the corner on foot. Gino and Manny were too easy to spot. They looked like two gangsters waiting for a Vic, in a stolen car. Gino recognized Fabrio and started to come out of his car, but Fabrio stopped him with a wave of his hand. He couldn't believe he had to babysit two more clowns. These two dumbells didn't realize their presence were threatening to everyone around them.

"Stay put." He walked to the side of their ride. "Santino still inside?"

Gino was early forties and looked like a movie star impersonating a wise guy -- black curly hair, dark eyes, olive complexion, leather jacket, and jeans. The driver, Manny, about the same age, wore all black. Fabrio wondered if the mother's of these two jerks ever taught them how to dress?

"Yeah, he's still in there. Said he was callin' some old friends. He knows the two actors must be wearin' the phone lines out tryin' to get some help." Gino grinned.

Fabrio looked through the window of Lucy's Tavern but couldn't see anyone. "I'll go see if he's had any luck." He glanced back at the two thugs. It was like looking at cartoon characters. They were bad news. Fabrio needed an excuse to get rid of them before they ruined everything.

"You want us to cum witcha?" Gino asked.

Fabrio shook his head, "Sit tight, and try to look normal. I'll be right back."

Lucy's Tavern looked like a thousand other bars. The place was packed – locals, dockworkers, and guys down on their luck. The linoleum floor hadn't been touched since the property was built. The floor was off-white at one time, but now was worn gray/brown, with lots of mileage. The bar, surrounded by stools, looked older. The cushions on the stools were torn, and the bar top, well scared with years of stories held within its cracks. Santino, was in the back, next to two old pool tables, using the public phone hanging from the wall. He spotted Fabrio, hung up, and apprehensively came to meet him.

Fabrio shook his hand, "Any luck?"

"They've been calling everyone they know, but won't say where they are. No one wants to help 'em, so they're runnin' scared." Santino looked off. "A young agent at CAA said the actor's mentioned Drummond's warehouse. I don't know the place, and he didn't either."

"You think they're still down here?" Fabrio was getting impatient. This was the first lead since he arrived in town. They were getting closer. Drego Santino was too old to keep up with the younger crowd. Fabrio regretted how he treated Santino, and now saw the apprehension in his eyes – like a puppy that had been hit and ducks every time a hand comes near. After he found out Baxter had no loyalty, he didn't trust anyone, even though he knew that was wrong. Fabrio trusted Santino but was disappointed with the old guy. A man in his position should have more information on the actor's whereabouts. What and where the hell was Drummond's warehouse? Was that a business, or another rich man hiding something?

"Oh yeah, they're still here. They got no place to go." Santino said.

"I owe you an apology, Drego." Fabrio said.

Santino responded. "No, you don't. You were protecting Anthony. No ill feelings, but thanks for the apology. I wish I could do more."

"Let's get outta this dump." Fabrio moved in the direction of the front door.

Fabrio opened the tavern door, and what he saw was like watching a scene from a movie. He put up his hand to stop Santino. Across the street, coming from a liquor store was Ben Parker, and Andre Garrison. The two actors moved toward a car parked in the lot next to the store. As they walked, Gino and Manny jumped out of their car – guns in hand. Unfortunately, a cop car was passing at that exact moment. The two cops spotted Gino, and Manny, chirped their siren, flipped on the spinning red lights, and were out of the squad car in seconds – armed and dangerous.

A roof rack of white lights lit up the area – and the two gangsters. The Policemen, with their weapons trained on the two wise guys, didn't see Ben Parker, and Andre Garrison. The two actors, however, witnessed the bizarre scene and immediately put two and two together. They calmly jumped into their vehicle, and drove off without looking. Their worried faces shadowed through the car windows as it disappeared from sight. Fabrio could do nothing but watch, and prevent Santino from getting involved.

"Put the guns down, and your hands up!" The cop was screaming! His voice had a nervous seriousness developing. One cop held a shotgun, the other a handgun. Both were frenzied, wide eyed, and on the verge of shooting the two men -- if they didn't obey.

Fabrio glanced back at Santino. The old guy wanted to bail. Fabrio shook his head. He turned to watch the arrest. Gino and Manny were utterly speechless. They had been so focused on catching the actors, they didn't hear the patrol car -- until it was too late. They dropped their guns, put their hands up, and then Gino saw Fabrio with Santino. Gino turned off and smiled at the cops. Fabrio caught his gaze and closed his eyes. Fabrio fully expected the young cops to blow them away. They didn't.

Gino took a cursory view of the cops, "Easy guys, we were just talking' about taking some target practice at the range tomorrow, and forgot," he crunched his shoulders together, "that the guns were still in our hands." He charmed "No harm done here."

"I bet," the first cop said. "Just keep your hands as high into the air as you can reach." The cop's voice cracked when he raised it to a shout, "Do it now!"

Gino glanced off in time to see the taillights of the actor's car disappear.

"Can we talk about this?" Gino asked, glaring at Manny.

The first cop nodded. "Sure, after I cuff your ass."

Fabrio wanted to run interference, go out and tell the cops they worked for him, but he wasn't ready to be hauled off to jail yet.

Manny said through his teeth, "This isn't working as we thought,"

The first cop smiled, "You think?" He holstered his gun while his partner trained a shotgun on the two men. Gino was cuffed first. "You boys have permits to carry these cannons?"

Gino looked at him. "You need a permit in California?"

Fabrio hoped he would shut up. A crowd gathering from the bar behind him and on the street.

People didn't understand the risk if all hell broke out. They wanted to watch.

"Where you guys from?" The first cop asked as he pushed Gino over the hood of the car, and put cuffs on Manny. Nervously he patted both men down. He pushed Manny face down, next to Gino.

"Texas." Manny offered enough seriousness to be believed.

The first cop laughed, "You two don't look like any cowboys I've ever seen." He glanced at his partner, "I'll call this in, get us some backup." He walked over to Gino, "We normally don't shoot tourists, but accidents happen. You do understand what I mean, right?"

Gino looked at Manny. "I don't think he has a sense of humor."

"You're right," the second cop added, "he don't."

"Is this how you treat all tourists?" Manny asked.

"Yeah," the second cop answered, "it's a California thing. We know how to greet armed folks from out of town."

The cops placed both Gino, and Manny into the back seat of the patrol car. The cops started looking through Gino's car as a second patrol car stopped. The crowd on the street and behind Fabrio grew, so he took the opportunity to get out. He turned to the crowd behind him.

"I don't know about you guys, but I don't wanna to be around when more cops arrive." He glanced at Santino, "Let's take a walk."

Santino agreed, "I'm right behind you."

Fabrio stepped out on the sidewalk, and half the patrons from the bar followed him. The group split up, half going one way, and the others walked behind Fabrio to the corner. As Fabrio turned to walk down the darkened street, one customer slugged him on the shoulder.

"Thanks dude. I got two outstanding warrants, and was worried about how I was gonna get outta there." He offered a toothless grim, "Not to mention tryin' to explain to the cops why I'm carryin' a piece." He opened his jacket, showing the gun stuck in his belt., " So now I owe you one."

"No Problem," Fabrio said.

"I'll buy ya a beer next time." The guy with the gun said.

Fabrio smiled. "I'll look forward to it."

The guy gave Fabrio a stupid salute and hurried off.

Fabrio surveyed Santino. "Does that guy represent everyone in California?"

Santino shrugged, "Out here, most young people carry guns, Fabrio."

"My God," Fabrio shook his head, "what's wrong with everybody?"

CHAPTER 17

Rollie found Drake sitting alone in the hospital cafeteria. He was nursing a cup of thick-gooey hospital coffee. Rollie set the bag of surveillance equipment on the floor and sat across from him. Drake had a haggard look, his face pale with concern. Rollie wanted to hug him, convince him things would be all right, but that wasn't a macho thing to do.

"How is she?" Rollie asked.

"Other than the broken rib, fractured jaw, nose, and eye socket, she's keen. Drake avoided looking at Rollie.

"I'm sorry, Drake. Is there anything I can do?"

"Find the bastard who did this to her would be a good start." Drake's voice cracked.

They fell into a deafening silence. Rollie watched, and saw the pain in his eyes, and knew he'd been crying. His face was swollen, puffed circles beneath the eyes, red-rims colored his tear-ducks, and his jaw kept sloping in and out.

"How'd you meet her?" Rollie wanted to change the mood.

Drake's face relaxed. "I went to the Polo Lounge in the Beverly Hills Hotel to have a drink with a new client. The client picked the place, asked me to meet him there, and then stood me up. Erinn was at the other end of the bar, waiting too. I moved closer, trying to think of a clever line, but damn if she didn't beat me to it."

Rollie encouraged him to continue. "What did she say?"

Drake closed his eyes, "She said, it's not nice to stare."

Rollie laughed, "You were staring at her?"

"Yeah. I couldn't keep my eyes off her."

"So?"

Drake ran his tongue over his teeth, "I told her my stare was incomparable. She said if I was unmarried, alone, and would buy her a drink, she might let me take her home."

"Just like that?" Rollie was genuinely surprised.

"I charmed her." His eyes drifted over the cafeteria. Drake cleared his throat. "We dated for a month or so, made love with such ease, like a married couple – and it scared me." He furrowed his brow. "So, I backed off. Now I know I hurt her deeper than I thought. Next thing you know, she ran off and married some guy named Lamont."

Rollie was sorry he brought the whole thing up, but ended more confused than when he started. "I thought she was married to Ted Wylan?"

"No, she married Ted after divorcing Lamont. Lamont beat her, put her in the hospital."

Rollie was burning with curiosity. "Do I want to know what you did to him?"

Drake lifted his chin. "I found him in their living room watching TV. He tried to hit me. I beat the hell out of him. He sued me and lost, and then the prick had the gall to say I didn't play fair."

Rollie decided he should shut up, but Drake wanted to talk about it.

"We got back together. No woman has ever held me like Erinn. No one has ever given me the pure pleasure we need to feel alive, except Erinn." Drake's voice drifted off.

"I understand that feeling," Rollie played with the napkin holder. Kali still had the string that had been wrapped so comfortably around his fingers. When he looked at Drake again, he saw a different man than the one he thought he knew. "What else is eating' you, Drake?"

Drake plodded on. "When my wife died, I thought I'd never have feelings again. Along comes Erinn, and scares me half to death. So I kept pushing her away, thinking she's out of my league."

"What league is that?" Rollie knew all about being in a league, with Kali, with a family that was now trying to kill him, and with Millie Jefferson. He watched Drake squirm, trying to escape, and wanting to talk at the same time.

"By the time, I woke up months had passed, and she was married to Ted. He couldn't keep body parts in his pants. I watched Erinn suffer through two miscarriages, and it all but destroyed her. The guy broke her heart, said he cheated on her, told her she was nothing, and after going through a deep-freeze depression, she finally got up enough courage to divorce him." Drake shook his head, "She got 'em though. He paid through the nose."

"So how is it now?"

Drake shrugged, "We've both had help from therapists, and discovered living is a good thing. She asked me to be her friend." He looked briefly at Rollie. "So now we're on-again, off-again, with a remarkable relationship. Our friendship, it's forever. She's my best friend."

"You gonna push her away again?" Rollie watched Drake. This was the first time Drake had opened up to him, and he didn't want to waste the opportunity.

"She told me, no more marriages – unless it's to me."

This was a good thing. "And you haven't run away yet?"

Drake raised his shoulders, then dropped them, "I'm tired of running."

"You want a juice or something?" Rollie was looking at the vending machines.

Drake shook his head, so Rollie got up to find something to eat. He came back a few minutes later with a full tray of junk. He handed Drake an apple juice and slid a plate with an open-faced turkey sandwich covered in gravy and mashed potatoes over to him. He got the same for himself. They ate in silence.

"You up to going over a few things with me?" Rollie asked.

"Sure."

Rollie took a bite of turkey, chewed it slowly. "We go to a party to watch over two certifiable actors who happen to be racing the wind, and have crime family backgrounds. An actress, who happens to be a mob boss's daughter, my cousin, and childhood friend is murdered. We don't know about the murder and whisk the two actors off realizing later one may have killed her." Rollie stopped. "The mob boss is my uncle, and someone's trying to kill me."

"Old news -- where you goin' with it?" Drake said.

Rollie took another bite of the tasteless food. An extremely attractive nurse came into the cafeteria. She took a deep breath and strutted like a cat-in-heat to the food counter. She smiled at Rollie. He returned the smile. Her white uniform pants fit snugly around an exceptionally firm shapely ass, and her breasts tugged against the blouse -- struggling for freedom. The two men watched the nurse select her food, pay her bill, and strut from the cafeteria.

Rollie continued. "So, later we're told the studio wants these two geniuses hidden. They pay us, and we hide 'em. The actors run away. People start looking for them. Then I get shot at, and someone breaks into Erinn's house and beats the hell out of her. The best part and my lack of understanding this is Erinn's house and our office are bugged with listening devices and cameras have been hidden throughout and whole..."

Drake cut him off. "What devices? What are you talking about?"

"Oh, I forgot, you don't know about this." Rollie brought the bag up from the floor and poured the contents over the table. Tiny cameras and listening microphones spread over the table. "High-tech stuff, Drake, and expensive. We can't even afford stuff this good."

Drake picked up the tiny little pieces and looked them over. "Does your family use crap like this?"

"No, they don't. My uncle wouldn't know which end to plug in." Rollie was sticking his neck out and knew it. He hadn't been around the family for years. They could be right in the middle of a high-tech existence, and he wouldn't know.

"Uh huh." Was all Drake could say?

"They don't plant listening devices, Drake. They just come after you like they did me tonight. You screw with them, and they end it. They don't listen first, debate about the ethics, and then take action. Hell, they just resolve it."

"They came after you tonight?"

"And missed, just missed I might add." Rollie studied the electronic equipment. He thought about it, about where the bullet hit. "We have a hole below one of our windows."

"Damn, Rollie, that's twice. You'd think they'd want it to look like an accident?"

"Shooting me in the chest was no accident."

"Unless we have two different groups." Drake paused. "Let's talk about you ex-wife?"

"She's a user, Drake. She's all fucked up."

Drake cut him off. "You sure? What does she know, Rollie?"

"I don't follow?" Rollie didn't want to go there. He knew Kali had done it before, but if it was his ex-wife, what the hell was she involved in this time?

"She knows you work for me, knows where the office is, and called you there. What else does she know about? Have you told her anything?"

A young doctor came into the cafeteria, looked around, and found Drake. He walked to their table. "Mr. Fargo?"

Drake shot to his feet. "Is she...?"

"She's resting comfortably, and asking for you."

"Will she, ah, be okay?" Drake waited.

The doctor nodded. "It will take time, but yes, she'll heal nicely."

Drake looked at Rollie. "Come with me?"

Rollie got up, "Sure."

Erinn had tubes running every which way. Her face was covered on one side, and her left arm was in a cast. Drake entered her room and immediately sat beside the bed. He picked up her hand and held it. Rollie came in behind him and stayed in the shadows. Rollie watched how gentle and affected the big man became.

She stirred, opened her one undamaged eye, and smiled. "Hi Drakey."

"Shhh. Don't talk." Drake sat at her side, and held her hand as he would a piece of art.

"The person who beat me," she whispered, struggling to get it out, "I'm sorry to say, I told where the boys are hiding."

"It's okay." Drake assured her.

"No. I'm sure they're going to be killed. Right now they're hiding in Wally Drummond's warehouse down in San Pedro."

"Wally Drummonds warehouse?' Drake repeated.

"Drego Santino is down there trying to find them. I didn't get a chance to call him back"

"Drego?" Drake sounded suspicious.

"Mr. Santino. You were at his party, remember?" Even with her pain Erinn smiled.

"I remember." He lifted her tiny hand into his massive paw and kissed it. She was his delicate heirloom. "I want you to rest, okay?"

"His warehouse is nicknamed big boy. It's one of the largest single-story warehouses on the south side of the marina. He keeps all his antique automobiles there because it's easy to move and ship them. Don't let whoever these people are hurt those boys, Drakey."

"I'll do my best." Drake kissed her fingers and gently placed her hand under the covers. He brushed her hair back and kissed her forehead.

"Go on, get out of here. I'll be fine." Erinn had tears in her eyes.

"I'll be back." Drake promised.

"I know," she whispered. "Be careful. Whoever came to see me -- they're not nice."

In the parking lot, Rollie walked to his SUV while Drake walked in tight circles. Waving a fist, he stared at Rollie.

Rollie watched him. "You're not doin' so good, are ya?"

"No," was all Drake could get out. "Why are they shooting at you, Rollie?" Drake's muscles were tightening every inch of his body. His face became colorful. "Why would they beat Erinn, and leave her to die?" He smacked the top of the vehicle with an open hand. "I understand wanting the two actors, but you, you're related."

"They saw me on the stairs with Tawny."

"Who saw you?"

"I don't know, Drake, but obviously they did and they're trying to kill me."

"Why would they..." Drake stopped talking.

Rollie cut in. "I left the family, remember? I changed my name. I insulted them. My uncle hates me 'cause I didn't go back while my cousin Richie stayed." Rollie frowned, "Now they think I might've killed, Tawny."

"What makes you think like that?"

"They shot at my uncle, killed cousin Richie, and I'm still alive." Rollie answered.

"That's not an answer," Drake said quietly. "Tell me why you're starting to believe all this negative crap?"

"I don't know." Rollie shot back. "Maybe it's cause they're shooting' at me."

Drake didn't buy it. "You really believe your flesh and blood uncle, would have you killed?"

Rollie nodded. "Yeah, that's what I'm sayin'."

CHAPTER 18

John Rader hadn't slept over two hours on any given night since the young actress was murdered. The call came right after his head hit the pillow. Two armed guys had been picked up in San Pedro. The suspects said they were from Texas, but had New York accents.

When Rader reached the station house, he met up with an African American detective built like a pro-football linebacker. They shook hands.

"Carl Macey."

"John Rader."

"C'mon into my office for a minute." Rader followed him. "The fax said if we picked up any loose ends from the east coast, to call you regardless of the hour,"

Rader sat down in an impeccably clean office. No pictures, files, plaques, or excessive furniture -- just the desk, and three chairs, one behind and two in front of the desk." How'd you find these guys?"

Macey sat behind his desk and planted two massive, muscular, arms on top. "They jumped from a car parked on Gaffey Street with guns in their hands. Unfortunately for them, they stepped right in front of a patrol car. The arrest was easy."

"Where do you have 'em?" Rader was amused the rugged detective had a nervous twitch. His left eye kept blinking while the right remained focused.

"Put 'em in a room together hoping they would start talking. So far they haven't said anything. They just sit there staring at the walls. C'mon, I'll introduce you."

They walked down the hall to the interrogation room. Standing behind a wall of one-way glass, they watched the two wise guys. Rader could tell they knew the drill. They'd keep quiet, and let the cops prove they had something. If the smart-asses were lucky, the cops wouldn't find anything, and they'd get released. The smaller arrogant one looked at the other guy and smiled. The big guy, dressed in all black, ignored him.

Rader knew. "You'll get nothing outta these guys, they're pros. Did you consider separating them?"

"Yeah, when they first came in."

"I D's?" Rader was in a hurry. This was another waste of time.

"Texas driver's license. Apparently they're legit." He put his hands behind his back and turned toward the glass. "Ran prints, and names through the system and got goose eggs."

Rader was surprised. "No background at all?"

"None. That's why I called you. They're too clean, nonexistent, until the arrest."

"Witness protection, or maybe big-time snitches? How could smart mouth guys like that not be in the system?"

"Must know some pretty important people." Macey said.

Rader nodded. "Care if I talk to them?"

Macey turned his palms up, "Knock yourself out."

Rader entered the interrogation room with a broad smile. His eyes sparkled, and you'd think he just won the lottery. He sat across from the two gangsters. "How you guys doin'? Want something to drink?" He looked from one to the other, "Okay. Name's John Rader." He waited for a response, knowing he wouldn't get one. He opened a file and read. "So," he glanced at Gino, "You're Gino Marino?"

Gino offered a sardonic grin, "Is that what it says on the license?"

Rader glanced at the file, "Looks like it, yeah, that's what it says." He lifted his eyes back to Gino, "So that must be you, right?"

Gino tossed Manny a smirk, "No wonder he made detective."

Manny nodded, "Yeah, a real genius."

"Ah, and you, you must be Manny Castellano?" No response. "You related to Paul Castellano?"

"Never heard of 'im," Manny answered.

"Nah, of course not. Why would you know the boss from the Gambino family?" Rader laughed, "So I guess you called Anthony Pataglia?"

Gino looked at Manny, and both gave Rader a shrug.

Gino asked. "Who's that?"

"Oh, c'mon, Gino. You know Pataglia?"

Gino shrugged. "Haven't a clue who you're talkin' about."

Manny, still cuffed to the table, leaned back as far as possible. "We gonna need an attorney?"

"Maybe," Rader answered, opening the file again. "You guys know a good one?"

"How 'bout callin' Elliot Titlebaum for us?"

Rader whistled. "He's expensive, isn't he?"

"Is he?" Gino looked at Manny. "You think we can afford a high-priced attorney, Manny?"

Manny leaned back in his chair and smirked at Rader. "Ya get what ya pay for."

"I'll see what I can do." Rader stood up. "Can I ask you something?"

Gino crunched his shoulders, "You can ask anything your heart desires. The answer, if ya get one, depends on the question."

"Fair enough," Rader nodded, "How come you both sound more like New York than Texas?"

Manny chuckled and threw a glance at Gino.

Gino pontificated, "Grandparents kept their accents. People ask that all time. How come two guys from Texas sound like New Yorkers?" He sighed. "Amazing, isn't it?"

CHAPTER 19

No matter how many times they drove around together, Rollie hadn't seen the dark side of Drake. They were silent during the entire drive to Drake's beach house. Rollie scrutinized Drake, and realized he hardly knew the man. Drake's strong jaw muscles kept flexing. Drake was always so laid back. This side of him was strange – a powder keg ready to explode. They drove north on Pacific Coast Highway and entered Malibu. Die-hard surfers were out, and even in the cool weather, the bikini-clad multitude of on-lookers sunbathed on the sand. Without so much as a glance, Drake passed through it. When they reached Malibu Canyon Road, Drake turned left past the shopping mall. He made a few turns and pulled into the driveway of an old, in-need-of-repair, beach house. It didn't look like much on the outside, but when Rollie followed Drake into the expansive great room, he realized the entire interior had been extensively remodeled. The kitchen was state-of-the-art with marble countertops, and stainless steel appliances. The walls in every room were smooth plaster, with rounded corners and edges. The furniture was for a large man and obviously custom-made. The sofas and chairs sumptuous leather. Masculine touches engulfed the area with rich paintings of the old west, and nautical items splashed in all the right places. A sitting area, in front of giant bay windows, looked out at the Pacific Ocean. A hundred yards of sand dropped down to turbulent waters. Beyond, a glimpse of Catalina Island floated in a misty haze. Rollie glanced around, and found the rest of the house was furnished like a typical bachelor pad, skimpy on collectibles, and fat on comfort. Over the fireplace was an enormous picture of Erinn, smiling down at anyone who wished to observe what a beautiful woman she was. Drake stopped to stare up at the picture, and then marched into a hallway where he opened a closet door. He walked into the closet, and kept going. "You coming?" He shouted from inside the closet.

Rollie followed, pushed some clothes to the side, and found another doorway, which was open. Beyond the door was a bathroom-sized weapons room. Various guns, knives, clubs, bows and arrows, and other weapons of destruction hung everywhere. Rollie stopped to admire the arsenal, but Drake was on a mission. He removed several handguns, a tapered knife, belt clips, and a few other items. Rollie watched, and waited.

"Take your pick of two handguns, get extra ammo, and come on out to the kitchen table." Drake turned and walked off.

Rollie looked the goods over, picked up several guns chose two that felt good, took down one of the knives, tested its balance, and then trailed after Drake.

In a kitchen that overlooked the ocean, Drake studied a map. Rollie sat in silence. When Drake glanced over, Rollie had spread his weapons out on the table.

"What's going on here, Drake?" It was awkward, like talking to a stranger.

"Ask," Drake said.

"Let's start with, who the hell are you, Drake?"

"You know who I am."

Rollie shook his head. "No, I don't think so. I only know what you told me. I trusted that was all of it, but it doesn't come close, does it?"

Drake peered out the window. "Whaddya want to know?"

"How about everything you haven't already told me?" Rollie shut up. Drake obviously had a hidden agenda that surfaced when things got nasty. Rollie witnessed guys like that in college, and later at the police academy. Usually they were insecure men with the need to excel when facing failure, but Drake was different. They had plenty of conversations before, but it was peripheral dialog to satisfy the moment. Rollie knew that was borderline stuff, and not the real man. The silence Drake carried, was the heart of the engine that drove him. Obviously it took a slap in the face to wake the sleeping animal within.

Drake took a deep breath, hesitated, and acknowledged Rollie. "Okay. I started out joining the Marines. Captain thought I was resourceful, and moved me into Special Forces. A funny name for a group who'd go in first, settle things, and then call the others in to clean up the mess. I drifted into the Secret Service, did a short stay with the CIA, hung around, being promised a place in a new national security organization that was in the incubator, and waited until they needed me. Right before, my tour was up, this Indian kid who said he was pure Cherokee, went nuts. When he got drunk, he was stronger than any two men I had ever known, and schizophrenic as any other nut case. I walked into the mess hall for lunch, and he stabbed me in the shoulder. Then, he tried to slit my throat, but missed. He pulled his gun, and I took it away from him. Didn't expect him to have a second one. Crazy bastard unloaded five, maybe six shots at me. Life flashed by, the Indian killed a nurse, the Petty Officer, and wounded two other people, all the while trying his best to waste me. When I finally got a hold of him, he smiled, and tried to shove a second knife in my gut. I sidestepped his hand and planted his first knife into his chest. The damn fool died with a smile. They said I was a hero. I didn't share I was scared to death. They begged me to stay, offered a long-term contract, but I'd had enough. Came to California with my wife. We had plans. Settle down, start a family, buy a house with a white picket fence, and live happily ever after. She got an infection in her leg, turned out to be bone cancer. Six weeks later she was gone. In 1983, at the ripe age of twenty-three, I found a job with Harry Wilson, one hell of a good private investigator. Two years later he had a heart attack. Damned fool went and died on me too. He had no kids, no wife, and few if any relatives. His death was as though I had a dreadful dream. His attorney came by and read his will to me. That sweet old jerk gave me everything, his agency, house, car, dog, money and all his worldly belongings. It wasn't much in those days, but the house, this house was paid for, and so was the office. When the shock wore off, I discovered he didn't owe a penny to anyone. No debts. He had a few bucks in the bank, so I invested in Microsoft and a few other start-up companies and got lucky. From what you told me, you know all about that. Over time, I met a few women that didn't mean anything until Erinn fell outta the sky. Now we're friends in love. We can make love, and walk away. We fight, and walk away. If I run she goes and gets married, and divorced. I come back and pick up the pieces. That's it. That's all there is to Drake Fargo. Oh, and I went through a phase where I didn't give a shit about anything. I guess that's the period that made me good. When I woke up, and realized some of what I did was dangerous -- it was too late. The job, it's a rush, kid. When the adrenaline flows, it creates a rush I can't explain. When you look in the other guy's eyes, and it's either him or you, and he knows you don't give a damn -- the whole game changes. Fear becomes your strength, and there's no better weapon."

"Okay." Rollie felt like he'd just taken a tranquilizer. "What happened to the dog?"

"Died of old age. Been thinking about getting another one. I miss the greeting."

"What happened when you were in Special Forces?"

Drake thought about his answer. "There is a bunch of stuff I need to forget. I was a bad guy back then, Rollie -- bad with the blessing and protection of our government. It was a long time ago."

"That's everything?" Rollie hoped it was.

Drake watched the ocean." What else do you want to know?"

"I don't know." Rollie thought. "As complicated as you are, I'm sure there is more."

"I put my underwear on the same as you. I believe in God, and know he frowns on lots that I do. I pay taxes, and I still love that damn woman."

"Ah." Rollie nodded.

Drake expanded his chest. "What the hell does that mean? Ah?"

"Anger." Rollie almost laughed out loud. "You said I needed anger management. It appears you have a similar problem."

"You got bigger anger problems, kid. You got issues you don't deal with, and I don't go around asking you a million questions."

"No, you don't." Rollie said.

"See what I mean?" Drake was getting testy.

"No." Rollie wondered how far he could push.

Drake was furious. He slammed a closed fist into his palm. Rollie didn't flinch. Drake gathered the map, and weapons into a pile. "We're goin' to San Pedro when it gets dark."

"Can't we see more in the day?"

"Yeah, and we could watch each other bleed to death after they shoot us." Drake said.

Rollie had said enough. Finally, Drake had come clean. His cell phone rang. He flipped it open, without looking at caller ID. "Yeah, this is Rollie?"

"You staying out of trouble, hot shot?"

The gravelly voice caused him to pause with the sarcasm. "For a day to two, why do you ask?"

The voice got angry. "You don't even know who this is, do you?"

"How are you Mildred?" Rollie glanced at Drake. The big man took a beer from the fridge, snatched up his cell phone, and walked through the glass slider to the outside deck.

"Don't Mildred me, hot shot. You can call me Miss Wanamaker."

"I sort of like Mildred better, ah, Mildred."

"Why?"

"So we'll sound like friends, you know, two people that like each other."

"That's why you should stick with Miss Wanamaker."

"I don't think we should argue over aesthetics." Rollie said

"Now you're getting cute. You wanna know why I called?"

"Now you're scaring' me." Rollie half expected her to say she was dumping him

After a long hesitation, she said. "You think you can make an appointment?"

Rollie glanced over his shoulder at Drake. He was busy watching waves, and talking on his cell phone. "When?"

"Oh, I get it. I need to fit this appointment into your busy schedule, right?"

"Now that you put it like that, Mildred, no. I ah…"

She cut him off, "A week from tomorrow, 3:30, Universal Studios." She stopped talking.

Rollie quickly figured the mess they were in would be resolved by then, and if he were still alive he would go to the appointment. "Mildred?"

"Yes or no?" She demanded a response.

"Of course I can make it. Do I, ah should I, ah…"

"Just go as the big handsome hot shot you are, and don't be late."

"Who am I seeing?" Rollie felt like a little boy talking to his teacher.

"Casting director, Ron Talbert. He saw the film of you playing that dog, and now he wants to see if you can say a few words without the dog suit."

"I can do that." Rollie foolishly bobbed his head and then scanned the room to see if Drake was watching. Thankfully he wasn't.

"Call me after you see him." She hung up on him.

Rollie stared at the phone before closing it. Drake stepped back into the room.

Drake's voice was almost as ruthless as Mildred's. "Don't go back to the office until this gets settled." He waited for Rollie to acknowledge him.

"I thought we had a business to run?"

"I just talked to Rader. He says the cops at the harbor picked two guys up."

"Two guys?" Rollie didn't get it. "What two guys?"

Drake took a deep breath. "Their ID's said they were from Texas, but their accents were New York. Rader said they had a couple of cannons with lots of ammo, but had a license for the pieces --, so they weren't charged. Cops put 'em on a plane back to Texas."

"And we can't go back to our office because?" Rollie asked.

"Because probably there are others, and next time they won't miss!"

"So do we investigate or hide?"

"We need to know where our clients are." Drake picked up a revolver and checked the load. "I've never lost a client before, so we need to get them back, and avoid getting shot. The last part's important."

Rollie agreed. "Makes sense."

"Get your guns!" Drake snapped. He saw the knife Rollie picked out. "You gonna share with me how you know how to use that?"

"You're not the only one who had an Indian friend."

"I'm going to the hospital. I'll be back in a couple of hours. You gonna stay put?"

"I don't know. If I take off for a while, how do I lock up?"

"The house locks itself. Take the Audi in the garage. Key is in a holder above the light switch." Drake was snippy.

"No, wonder you don't have another dog."

Drake glared. "What's that supposed to mean?"

"If the poor thing got out, he'd never get back in." Rollie said.

Drake fumed for a moment, tossed angry eyes at Rollie and then abruptly walked to the front door. "Don't go near your house either. And if you do go out, get back here before dark." At the door, he turned back. "By now they probably know where you live."

"And you don't think they know about this place?" Rollie quizzed.

Drake laughed. "If they knew about this place, Rollie, you and I would be dead."

CHAPTER 20

Rollie took every short cut he knew to get back to his house. He wasn't the type to get paranoid, yet his eyes took in more of the scenery with each glance then he thought. No strange cars, vans or vehicles with tinted windows, and no one standing around pretending to be busy. Still, he made sure no one was following or waiting for him. He drove within a block of his house, walked to the sand, and stood admiring the ocean. Behind the sunglasses, however, he scanned everything in sight. He put his head down and took a stroll along the edge of the surf. Late day always brought a breeze in from the ocean, and most watercraft were on the way back to the marina.

Three blocks later, Rollie walked up a path, cut through a yard, and made his way to the street. He walked inland another block, and then zigzagged back toward his house. He saw no cars, or foot traffic on his block. He approached his neighbor's house first. After he had pushed the doorbell, he turned to watch the street. The door opened behind him. He turned and found a devilishly sexy young woman, clad in a tiny bikini, at the door.

"Oh, hi Rollie. Is everything alright?"

Rollie thought fast. "Hi, Sandy. Yeah, everything's great. I was expecting a package today, and hoped they might've dropped it over here. Has anyone come by the house?"

Sandy was one of those baby-doll girls. She was married to a hulk, as handsome as she was beautiful. The whole neighborhood referred to them as the Ken and Barbie couple. Sandy was early twenties, married to a handsome stockbroker named Tom something or other, and wherever they went – everyone noticed. Men loved to watch Sandy, and the women adored the muscular Tom. There were times Rollie saw Sandy out on the beach, and he too loved to watch. She had one of those oh-so-perfect bodies, and she knew it.

"No," Sandy was shaking her cute little head. "I haven't seen as much as a mail truck today, Rollie. I worked in the front yard most of the afternoon, so I would've seen a delivery guy, you know what I mean?" She blinked her sexy blue eyes.

Rollie showed disappointment. He could imagine every man living on the block sitting behind their curtains, looking at Sandy through binoculars. She loved to wear the tiniest of bikinis, like the one she was wearing. When she bent over, only God knew how she managed to keep everything from popping out. "Well," Rollie hesitated, "maybe tomorrow?"

"I'll keep my eye out for you." Sandy was still smiling.

"I appreciate that. Say hi to Tom for me." Rollie nodded, trying not to be too obvious with his wandering eyes. It was hard not to look.

"I will." She stood back. "What do you think of my new bikini?"

Rollie was caught. He knew, she knew, he wanted to take a longer look, so she accommodated him. She held her shapely arms up and gave him a sexy pose. Rollie felt warm and fuzzy. His eyes roamed over her, trying to look at the bikini, and then the price tag saved him from making a complete fool out of himself. The little neon-green label was still handing at the back of her top. He thanked God for small favors. "Your, ah, the price tag is still attached." Awkwardly he pointed beneath her breast.

She didn't move. "You're kidding, right?"

Rollie shook his head. "No, it's right there for everybody to see."

"Oh my God!" Sandy blurted. "How embarrassing." She spun around. "Could you?"

Rollie wasn't sure he could hold his hands still long enough to remove the tag. Sandy made him nervous. Even with her back to him, Rollie glanced down over her curves and felt mortified. What if Tom suddenly came home? What if a neighbor saw them? Not cool.

"Are you all right, Rollie?" She asked.

"Oh, yeah, sure. Hold still."

Sandy giggled. "I am holding still, silly. Can you break the string without tearing the top?" She glanced over her shoulder, looking up into his eyes. "It would most likely be easier if I took the top off, right?"

"No," Rollie almost blurted it out. "I can do it." His fingers twitched. "All I have to do is ah?" He examined the skimpy top. "I can, yeah that's what I can do. I'll just tear the little tag off."

"Wait." Sandy continued her smile. "I'll get the scissors." She dashed off into her house.

Rollie watched her go. Guilt. No, not really. If she didn't need to be looked at, she'd of covered up, right? So he looked, no, it was more of a gawk. Yeah, he was gawking.

Sandy ran on her tiptoes back to the front door and handed Rollie a tiny little pair of scissors. Thankfully, he still managed to cut the little plastic do-dad. Without thinking, he reached inside the tip of her top and retrieved both pieces of the plastic thing. His one lone finger brushed against her breast. She ignored the touch, but Rollie didn't. As quick as possible, he snatched both ends into his palm and removed his hands. He handed the pieces and tag to her, along with the scissors. Rollie stiffened from the heat passing through his skin. He fruitlessly tried to stop the blush from spreading.

"There you go." Rollie mumbled.

Sandy gave him the million-dollar reception. She moved too close. Lifted up on her toes, and kissed his cheek. "How can I ever thank you?"

Rollie lost his wit. "Ah, next time you and Tom toss a steak on the grill, put an extra one on for me. I'll bring the beer." He backed up.

Sandy stood still. The look on her face said she accomplished her goal. She loved to tease, and had mastered it. She was gregariously wonderful. "I'll do that," she purred, "and you have a wonderful evening."

Rollie nodded, collected his thoughts, and the rest of his body – and backed away from her. Sandy didn't budge. He waved, turned, and walked as fast as wobbly legs could carry him to his house. He didn't turn. He was afraid to. He could feel her eyes. She'd wait until he went inside, and closed the door behind him. Then, and only then, would her door close.

Rollie came home on a mission. Sandy's detraction didn't help. As fun as it was, there was something he needed to do. He stood behind his curtains and watched the street. Relieved, he turned to the business at hand. Rollie had hidden Louis Baxter's ledger inside his old nautical deep-sea diving helmet. Rollie bought it a few years ago and never found the right place for it, so it eventually occupied a space in the corner of his great room. There the caged glass window could overlook the sea, and hunger for an opportunity to be the recipient of one more plunge into the murky waters of the pacific.

Rollie closed the blinds, removed the ledger, and opened it. Inside, the pages were full of numbers, payments, schedules, locations, banks, and lastly – names.

Rollie scrolled down the list. The names were in alphabetical order. There, in the middle of the page, written in pencil, was one name he didn't expect to see. Before he jumped to conclusions, he needed to be certain. The muddy ordeal was taking shape.

He read over the pages, the entries, and understood, for the first time, why everyone was out to cut throats. The cops had a copy of the ledger, but obviously they didn't know what was written between the lines. Without Louis Baxter, they'd have no idea what the written word meant. Rollie couldn't explain it to them, without implicating himself. He couldn't disclosed anything written in the ledger.

He closed the book and replaced it inside the mask. Someone knew he had it but didn't know where it was hidden. That might be the only thing keeping him alive, and only God knew what they would do to him to get it back. The lives of everyone around him were in danger. They'd kill everyone Rollie knew to get the book back. Everyone!

Outside Rollie snuck around the garage and ran into two men. They were dressed in overalls like typical laborers.

"Whoa!" The bigger of the two caught Rollie, preventing him from tripping over.

"Sorry." Rollie said. "You guys lost?"

The stocky guy hit Rollie in the chest with a closed fist. The punch hurt like hell. It was right where he'd been shot, and still wore the lesion. The punch, however, didn't budge Rollie.

"I don't think so," the smaller man answered.

The beefy guy pulled out a piece. Rollie hit him so hard, the gun dropped from his hand. The smaller man had his hands buried in overalls, and before he could remove them – Rollie smacked him in the nose. His jab was getting better. The guy's nose burst and blood gushed out. Rollie whacked him again, and he dropped to his knees. The bigger guy, still shaking off the first punch, reached out to grab Rollie. Rollie was expecting it and popped him in the side of his head. The punch sent the stocky guy to the sand. Rollie grabbed his hair and yanked his head up.

"What did you have in mind?' Rollie asked.

"Nothin'" the beefy guy mumbled.

Rollie smacked his throat, just below the Adams apple. The guy gagged. The smaller man tried everything to stop his bleeding nose to no avail. Rollie picked up the fallen handgun and put it against the bigger man's head. "So I guess if I shoot you, no one will miss ya, right?"

"Wait!" The stocky guy yelped.

"You got two seconds." Rollie whispered.

"We were told to pick ya up."

"And?" Rollie persisted. He glanced at the smaller guy, hit him again, and his nose continued to bleed. Rollie pulled the beefy guys hair, and his eyes bulged.

"To hurt but not kill ya."

"Who told you to do this?"

The big guy hesitated. Rollie cocked the gun and placed it by the man's temple.

"I'll tell ya," the stocky guy blurted out, "but you ain't gonna like it."

"Why's that?' Rollie was seething.

The beefy guy glared at Rollie. "Because they're gonna kill ya, that's why."

CHAPTER 21

Fabrio's cell phone rang. He was no closer to finding the actors than before. Now he was missing a few men, and time was running out. Pataglia was calling to get answers. He reluctantly flipped open the phone. "Yes, mister Pataglia."

"I heard about Gino and Manny. You have anything?"

"No." Fabrio wanted his answers to be short. He and Sammy had zip. They couldn't find the warehouse, and everyone they talked to lied. What kind of town was this? How could you trust anyone who worked in Hollywood?

"I've arranged a meeting," Pataglia said. "Pick us up in an hour."

"I'm with Sammy," Fabrio said this to see if he should take Sammy with him.

"Is his car still down there?"

Fabrio glanced at Sammy. They didn't trust him enough to bring him. "Yeah, his wheels are down here."

"Give him enough money to keep him busy. He has your cell number?"

"He does." Fabrio felt uncomfortable. He brought Sammy in. He trusted him.

"Good." Pataglia said, "He can call you if he finds them, right?"

"Yes." Fabrio said.

"See you in an hour." Pataglia hung up.

Fabrio drove Sammy back to his car, gave him money, and told him to call when he found the warehouse. When Sammy argued that he could take the actors, Fabrio said find 'em and call me. He left it at that, and Sammy responded as Fabrio expected. Sammy was a soldier. He'd do what he was told. It was unusual for Pataglia not to trust someone Fabrio brought in. He tried not to think about it. The drive back to the Bel Air Hotel was creepy. There was a chance he'd have to finish this on his own. Pataglia was in no condition and would get in the way, and Gi Carlo couldn't raise his right arm. Gi Carlo came out to protect the old man, but Fabrio knew everything eventually fell on his shoulders. He picked the boss up on schedule. Pataglia looked pale and weak. Gi Carlo said nothing. Fabrio watched the proud bodyguard, knowing Gi Carlo would give up his life to save Pataglia's. Problem was Gi Carlo couldn't move without persevering anguish. Fabrio would have to guard them until they got back to New York.

The Drone mansion, set high on a knoll just north of Sunset Boulevard, had a spectacular view of Los Angeles. From the driveway, you could see tall, well-lit buildings, colorful rooftops, and distant oil wells that continually pumped day and night. Off to the west lay the rolling waters of the Pacific Ocean, and the islands beyond. While all the neighborhood homes towered over their yards, Drone's ranch home spread over the lot as if the designer couldn't make up his mind to stop, or extend the expansion. It was old Beverly Hills wealth at its best. A four-car garage, tennis court, swimming pool, and circular driveway large enough to park ten cars surrounded the house. They were met at the door by a butler. He quietly asked them to follow him.

Inside, antiques rested picturesquely in every nook and cranny. Exquisite paintings with tiny lights hung everywhere and the carpet were snow-white and so deep, and luxurious Fabrio wondered why Drone didn't require people lose their shoes in the vestibule, and start barefooted.

William Drone was waiting for them in his den, a room so colossal, it could consume several cracker-box houses within its monumental walls. Drone, one of the last true aristocrats was in his sixties, tall, thin, and well maintained. His white hair was meticulously trimmed. He wore black Italian loafers, gray slacks, a dark blue blazer, and a light gray shirt with an opened collar. He was sitting with four men dressed casually – like golfers. Among them was Elliot Titlebaum, a very special, high-priced attorney, retained by Pataglia for everything from straightforward arrests to murder charges. The other three were Tom Meyer, controller of the west coast trucking industry, Tony Don who enforced the waterfronts in Los Angeles and Long Beach harbors, and Paul Masseria, the financial genius behind the entertainment and garment unions. Clustered in a circle, they sat on deep-cushioned couches, and watched flames dance in the fireplace. No one was pleased to see Pataglia. Fabrio knew everyone in the room. Drone was the west coast boss for the Pataglia crime family. Titlebaum was an underboss. The others were Captains, ready to move up and take over. Together, they controlled labor, unions and the invisible workforce that ran the west coast. The Drone mansion, known by the Feds as The Hacienda, was majestic with its Mexican heritage. Fabrio heard the Feds had tried to penetrate the fortress for years without success. Most law enforcement agencies with organized crime units drooled for a chance to get Drone, but all their efforts had failed. Drone had the house swept daily for bugs and electronic surveillance equipment. To the casual observer, Drone's business was clean, and above board. The part that wasn't visible operated under the clandestine cloud of fear, and retaliation. So far removed, even the Feds couldn't connect the dots.

Fabrio knew Pataglia trusted Titlebaum. He was an old friend. Old was the dominant comment as he was the same age as Pataglia. They went to school together. Titlebaum served many purposes aside from being a brilliant lawyer. He knew all the right people and indiscreetly could arrange various services to his clients. Titlebaum's father, Allan was also a lawyer and represented some of the most notorious crime figures in U.S. history. At the turn of the century, during the 1920s and 30s, Alan Titlebaum kept many from being deported or sent to prison. As the mob-family business grew and expanded, the tentacles of crime families spread their holdings. Many chose a fifty-fifty approach, meaning at the very least, half of their entire holdings were legitimate businesses. Alan set things in motion and then passed his legacy over to Elliot when his son was fresh out of law school. Alan retired to Miami and died peacefully at the age of ninety-two. Elliot, in a subservient, hands-off manner, steered Pataglia into dominant legitimacy, and made him, and all the family leaders, multi-millionaires. Along the way, Elliot grew in both stature and size. He lost most of his hair by age forty, gained considerable weight, and swore when he reached three hundred pounds that he wouldn't add another ounce. It worked. He still weighed three hundred pounds. Elliot assisted the

Pataglia brothers in choosing family members, and surrounded Anthony Pataglia with the best. Now everything could fall apart. Fabrio no longer trusted any of the men in the room. Fear dotted their eyes, and trust that had brought them together and produced untold wealth – was gone.

Pataglia waited for William Drone to speak. "What are we to do now, Anthony?" Drone asked. He glanced at the other men. "Baxter's ledger is missing."

Pataglia stared at Drone. "And you think I had something to do with that?"

Drone sat back, contemplating his next move. "Fabrio, where were you when Louis lost his life?"

Fabrio stepped out of the shadows and stood behind Pataglia. "I was in New York."

Drone smiled. "What about when Mark Lipesky vanished into thin air?"

"I was at a Chris Botti concert. You know him?"

"Indeed I do." Drone said. "I can hear him playing a song that reminds me of watching freight trains as a child, heading south like a flock of geese. I'm afraid his trumpet lyrics fill my heart with memories of a family that is in deep trouble." Drone's eyes drifted into the fireplace. Flames reflected and danced off his black empty corneas. "Louis Baxter was stealing from the pension trust funds, but he also knew about the gardening tools."

Pataglia sat up, genuinely surprised. "You said we were out of that deal?"

Drone nodded. "We took your advice, Anthony and turned down the delivery. Louis Baxter, along with his partner, Ronnie Mauten, intercepted one transmission and, acting alone, without our participation, took delivery. We believe payment was made with pension money. It appears that quite a lot is missing."

"Mother of God!" Pataglia spat out. His red face glowed. "You can't be serious."

"Quite serious," Drone said. "The problem is if you didn't take Louis and Ronnie out, and no one in this room ordered the hit, then Moe Brayden did."

"It's time we stick together and resolve what's on the table." Pataglia spoke with quiet, non-threatening tones of conciliation.

Drone glanced at the others. They all remained stone-faced and silent. "What happened to Gino and Manny, Fabrio?"

"They made a mistake. They're clean. Cops released 'em. The bad news is they were escorted to the airport, and put on a plane back to Texas. We're shorthanded."

Drone nodded. "Then we have the unions, and they're not happy with anything that will rock their boat. I loathe the valley rep. He's slime, and we are being forced to work with the likes of him. Your new contract has to bite the dust, Anthony."

"I know," Pataglia answered. He glanced at the fireplace, watching tiny flames shoot up and dance over the firewood. "Selling mini nuke bombs in shoeboxes makes us a hands-on part of a terrorist organization. How could we be so stupid?" He looked around the room, taking in each man with contempt. "And you all thought I was involved?" He shook his head angrily. "I've protected all of you for years, made you rich, and turned your businesses into pots of gold. This is how you thank me? Killing my daughter, my cousin, and shooting me?"

"That wasn't our doing." Drone glared at Pataglia.

Fabrio didn't buy it. "You saying Moe Brayden ordered the hit?"

Drone shrugged his shoulders. "It doesn't make sense, does it?"

Pataglia closed his eyes. Fabrio could see the old man's pain and disbelief. If Moe Brayden started this, and he was responsible for making an arms deal – it was beyond stupid, and Moe Brayden was anything but stupid. Homeland Security would be all over this. Once discovered, the Feds would have a hay-day. Fabrio couldn't share what he overheard, or they'd know he was responsible for Mark Lipesky. From what he heard, Moe Brayden didn't start this.

Pataglia finally spoke up. "No. This wasn't Moe. One or more of the other families," he looked around the room, "want all of us, out of the way. This is a takeover."

Fabrio nodded. "Only one to benefit is the Lipesky's."

Drone's jowls tightened. "Then we'll have to do something about that." His smile was thin and uncomfortable. "You must understand, Anthony, from out viewpoint it looked incriminating until they shot at you. We," his eyes traveled the area, "thought, ah, well we wanted to talk to you before any decisions were made. Our hearts were broken. We're family."

Fabrio felt sorrow crushing his chest. It still didn't answer why they would kill Tawny.

He glanced around the room, wondering if they had a rat among them.

Pataglia whispered. "If Moe Brayden, or the Lipesky's, want me out in the open, so be it. I'll step out and let them take their best shot. What I want to know is where on earth are those shoeboxes, and how can we destroy them?"

"We don't know." Drone said. "We're as worried about that as you."

"They didn't do this alone." Fabrio spoke up. "They had to have help."

"What can we do for you?" Drone asked. "How do we make this go away?"

"I don't know." Anthony answered, shaking his head, "Whoever tried to take me down in New York opened old wounds. I hoped those feelings were sealed and buried."

Fabrio hesitated when his eyes locked with Drones. He saw a flash of guilt. "You've talked to Moe Brayden, haven't you?"

Drone stammered. "Before you arrived, I called Moe." Drone sounded embarrassed. "He has assured me, he didn't start this."

Fabrio knew that was true, but also knew Moe Brayden would jump on the bandwagon as soon as Pataglia was gone.

Pataglia frowned. "Moe has backed Lipesky for years."

"Let's not forget Mark disappeared." Drone chimed in.

Pataglia shook his head. "His son, Drew will follow in his footsteps."

Drone nodded. "We know he's insane. Won't walk away easily."

Fabrio glanced over to Pataglia. The whole thing made less sense now than when they first arrived. Someone was methodically killing family members. Who? Was it someone in the room with them?

"Whoever they are, they took my daughter knowing I would come out west." Pataglia was frowning, still having a hard time putting all the pieces together.

"Then why the shooting in New York?" Paul Masseria finally broke his silence.

171

"We need to find out," Pataglia answered. "Any one of us could be next."

Tom Meyer blurted out. "What about those actors you're looking for?"

"And the private dicks that are also looking for them?" Tony Don added.

"Where is Drego Santino?" Drone asked Fabrio.

Fabrio shrugged. "He's in San Pedro looking for actors. One of my friends is helping him. They'll call when their located.

"Why don't we surprise the whole lot?" Drone was thinking out loud.

"I don't know what you have in mind, William, but you do marvel in the unexpected. What surprise might do this?" Pataglia asked.

"A tricky business, Anthony, but not impossible. You need to talk to the actors and get their side of the story." Drone glanced at Fabrio. "You need to know why those private dicks chose to hide the actors, and what they know about all this. Then, my friend, we will call in the troops. The unforeseen is always a joy to watch from a distance. We know Santino is kosher, and once we question and clear the actors, we'll make dinner arrangements, and all of us will go out for a nice evening on the town."

Fabrio looked to Pataglia and got a nod.

"By the way, do we know who the private dicks are?" Paul Masseria asked.

Pataglia hesitated. "Drake Fargo owns the agency. My nephew, Rollie Kemp, my late sister's kid, is his partner."

Drone seemed surprised. "Rollie Kempanelli?"

Pataglia nodded bitterly. "Changed his name a few years ago to Kemp."

Drone nodded, "Ah, clever." He looked at the fire, "We know about Fargo. He's done lots of work for many of us in this room and for the studios, but most assuredly he's dangerous. If Drake Fargo lost clients, there's no way he's giving up until he gets them back." He chewed on his lower gum. "He'll have to be dealt with."

Fabrio added. "We think Rollie is involved in the murder somehow."

Drone turned to Pataglia, "How does that sit with you Anthony?

"His father was a punk, beat my sister, and made us look bad. Rollie refused to come back and deal with family problems, went and changed his name and thumbed his nose at us. I don't care what we have to do to the little shit. He's a disgrace to our family."

Drone was uncomfortable and adjusted his sitting position. "I see." His hand covered his chin. "We have a friend, actually he's a police detective involved in some matters of interest. I believe his services will be invaluable when the time comes. I'll get an update from him, and see where we are. If we know who killed Louis and Ronnie, we'll know who shot you, and we'll have a lead on where those nuke bastards went."

Fabrio wasn't happy. The glare of disappointment flooded his eyes. People were dying, nuclear bombs were missing or had already been sold, and one family was trying to take over another. His lips pursed tightly. Pataglia wanted to bury his daughter and move on, but it wasn't going to be that easy. They still didn't have all the players. The Lipeskys, along with Moe Brayden, and possibly other families, all wanted changes. They wanted to go backwards, and that meant his life was about to be altered. He wasn't quite ready to accommodate them. Pataglia was wounded, and his long-time girlfriend,

Victoria was pregnant and wanted to get married. Gi Carlo looked like death warmed over, and Fabrio didn't have a life. He lived for others. Where was the kick in doing that twenty-four seven? If they didn't find the bombs, they'd be considered terrorists. He needed a sexless relationship with a good woman. Now he needed the time it would take to get one. Time, apparently, wasn't on their side.

"Okay," Pataglia said, "let's find out who's on Lipesky's side, and who's on ours. We should be on a plane in the next few days, so we have lots to do in a short period of time."

Drone smiled. "The liberty of grasping zero hour can be an illusion, much like the use of an ornamental mirror that one sees foolishness and truth on one side and deception on the other. Either way, Anthony, it should be exhilarating." He got up. "Come, let's all have a drink, make some calls, and plan a game of elimination."

"What about the nuke shoeboxes?" Fabrio asked

"Let's hope we find them before one explodes." Drone answered.

CHAPTER 22

In the San Fernando Valley, Rollie found a parking space behind a fast-food Chinese restaurant off Ventura Boulevard. The two guys who assaulted him were bound together in the back seat. Rollie assisted in getting them out. Their hands were tied behind them, secured to their belts, and leashed together like dogs.

"Walk like good little boys. If either one of you open your mouth, it will be the last thing you ever say." Rollie looked them square in the eye. "You got it?"

They both nodded. The little guy's nose still seeped with red goo, and the side of the big guy's head was swollen and turning black.

Rollie walked behind the two men, a short block in the alley behind the Teamsters office. They entered through the back door. On the second floor, Rollie found Danny Bilotti's office. Danny was an old stuntman acquaintance turned rat. Danny became an enforcer and grew through the ranks of the union. He solved problems before they got out of hand. Danny knew details of all union involvement and off-the-book involvement. Obviously he arranged for the two men to visit Rollie. Danny Bilotti went from nice guy to slime ball in a couple of short years. Rollie braced himself, his knuckles rolled and ready.

He entered the office and found two men sitting in the waiting area. Rollie's spine tightened -- his fists closed. He stood in front of the two men he had tied up. The two union guys in the office stood up. They looked like ancient boxers. Both had scared faces, big bodies, thick arms and legs, heavy bellies, dark hollow eyes, and black, curly hair.

The first one offered a hand to Rollie, "Name's Tag."

Rollie shook his hand. "Rollie Kemp." They assumed he was a buddy of the two bruised men. Their punched faces didn't raise a flag – yet.

"You here to see Mister Bilotti?" Tag asked.

"Yeah, is he in?" Rollie tried to remain calm, not sure he could take all of them if things turned. Even with their hands tied, the two attackers were dangerous.

Tag looked at his friend, then back at Rollie. He shook his head, "You guys got an appointment?"

Rollie gestured with an open hand, "Nah, we're old friends. We were in the neighborhood, and thought we'd stop by."

Tag laughed. He looked at the other guy, "He's just in the neighborhood, Willie."

Willie moved closer to Rollie and got up in his face. "The man don't see anyone who ain't got an appointment." He stood inches from Rollie.

That did it. Rollie smiled. "Tell ya what, guys. Why don't you ask him?"

Willie poked a finger into Rollie's chest, a jab right on his breastbone. It hurt like hell. "Why don't you guys take a hike? The man is busy."

He went to poke Rollie again, but Rollie grabbed the finger, and snapped it. The others heard the knuckle pop and the bone crack. Willie cried out, grabbing the

176

broken finger. Tag came closer, so Rollie smacked him in the face -- one of Rollie's better punches. It dropped Tag to his knees. Blood trickled over his knuckles. Willie, meantime, holding his finger, shot toward Rollie and got punched just above the jawbone. He staggered, and dropped to a chair. His face turned purple.

"Get outta the way," Rollie said quietly.

Willie thought about it for a flash, and when Rollie raised his arm the big man stepped to the side. Rollie walked by the two goons, pushed his captives through the door with Private printed in large bold black letters on the glass.

Danny Bilotti was sitting behind the desk when Rollie and his two prisoners entered. Danny was in his fifties, short, muscular, shaved head and covered with tattoos. He had a real cute young girl sitting in his lap, sticking her tongue down his throat. Both Danny and the girl looked at Rollie.

Rollie smiled, "You busy?"

The girl frowned, drawing her pencil-thin eyebrows together, "Well, like yeah!"

Rollie nodded, "I need to ask him a few questions."

Danny was flabbergasted. He gestured with his head for the girl to get up.

The girl looked sixteen. She glared at Danny. "Like we're in the middle?"

"Let's take a break, kid." Danny smiled awkwardly at her, "Come back in twenty minutes."

The girl stood up, brushed her ultra short mini-skirt down, picked her panties up from the floor, and shot piercing gray eyes at Rollie. "You're a jerk!"

"I know," Rollie nodded.

"Fuck you." She spat it out between clenched teeth.

"Maybe later." Rollie said.

"Maybe never asshole." She glared back at Danny, "I'll be back in twenty. If you're not ready, then I gotta get back to school."

Danny grinned. "I'll be waitin'."

The girl gave Rollie one more look, a death wish and stormed from the office. After the door slammed, Danny rolled closer to his desk, stared at the two guys Rollie had tethered together, and smiled at Rollie.

"Sorry for the interruption," Rollie said as he pushed the two men down on a small loveseat. They groaned. Rollie sat down on top of Danny's desk.

"No problem. I needed a break anyway." He glanced over Rollie's shoulder, at the door. "You met Tag and Willie?"

"Yeah, they ah, they might need some medical attention like these two do."

Danny nodded. "This must be important?"

"Depends on what you intended to do to me." Rollie answered, never taking his eyes off the muscular man. With the speed of a snake, Danny opened his desk drawer. Rollie spun around and slammed a foot into his chest. Danny rolled backwards into the wall. Rollie followed him and straddled Danny's legs.

"Some people need to talk to you, Rollie. I was hoping' you wouldn't get hurt, that's all."

"Anthony Pataglia?" Rollie asked, watching Danny closely.

"Nice man." Danny answered.

"He asked you to come visit me?" Rollie asked while he checked the other guys. We wanted to make sure they hadn't moved. They hadn't.

"A friend suggested it." Danny said.

"Same friend that did Louis Baxter and Ronnie Mauten."

"You're in real trouble, Rollie. Way over your head."

Rollie jerked Danny forward, inches from his face. Rollie needed control. The loss of temperance was milliseconds away, and he couldn't afford to lose it. "You have five seconds."

"Or what, tough guy?"

Rollie lost the will to hold back. He popped Danny with a sharp jab to the breastbone. The wind collapsed from Danny's lungs. His faced flushed while his lungs searched to restore the loss of oxygen.

When Danny regained the ability to breathe. "Are you crazy?"

"I don't know, am I, Danny?" Rollie held on to Danny's shirt.

Danny Bilotti relented. "They didn't ask me to help, Rollie, they told me. They know you and I go back a long time. C'mon, Rollie. You're a standup guy. I wasn't gonna hurt ya. They said to keep you, that's all"

Rollie released him. Danny fell back against the wall. "So you turn me over to them, and then what did you think would happen?"

"I don't know man." He glanced out the window. "You got people lookin' for ya. I don't know what you've done, but it might be good to stay here, you know, outta the way for a while?"

"Specifically who's looking?" Rollie asked.

Danny rubbed a hand over his bald scalp. "You know I can't tell you." He closed his eyes, raising his shoulders, and dropping them, heavily. "The troops are gathering. You must've crossed 'em, dude. They're talkin' like you're a dead man."

Rollie leaned over, "Tell me, dude, just between you and I, what are they looking for?"

Danny shrugged, "Word on the street is it was either you or one of those actors who killed the wrong girl. Accident or otherwise, man, it was a bad move. Payback is a bitch."

"What came in on the freighter?" Rollie had to test him. The ledger listed this office address as the delivery point. Danny's whole face changed expressions. Eyes danced nervously, upper lip twitched.

"Stay out of it, Rollie." Danny said

"Stay out of what, Danny?"

"I'll say you got away. Get outta here. Go to Vegas and stay there." Danny said it too fast. He avoided Rollie's glare.

Rollie reached out and pulled Danny half way over the desk. He slammed his elbow over Danny's throat and leaned heavily to cut off his air. "I'm out of patience."

Danny held out his hands, and Rollie let up. Danny gulped air. "You were in the wrong place, and witnessed something you shouldn't' have. I don't know anything else."

Rollie's mind was ahead of him. "How many guys they have?"

"Enough." Danny couldn't resist. "They got guys all over the place. You heard someone blew Arnie Aronjelovich up, right?"

Rollie hadn't heard and shook his head. "When?"

"Yesterday, right in the studio parking lot." Danny's face was bright red.

Rollie released him and stood up. "What was on the freighter, Danny?"

"Shoe boxes. I don't know what was in 'em. Must've been important shoes."

"Where are these shoe boxes?" Rollie was back in his face.

Danny frowned. "You gotta get out of town, dude."

"I can't do that." Rollie's voice was soft, controlled. Danny recognized it spelled danger, and looked for a weapon. "Let's try the question once more. What was in the shoe boxes?"

Danny reached under the desk for a gun, and Rollie kicked it out of his hand, dragged him over the desk, and popped him with several rib punches. Danny dropped to the floor, his hand raised. "Okay! They had bombs, nuclear stuff."

"Where are they?" Rollie knew they weren't here.

Danny shook his head. "Guys picked 'em up couple days ago."

"What guys?" Rollie pulled Danny up and tossed him on top of the other two men.

Danny shook his head. "I don't know, man. Look, word on the street is there's a contract out on you. Just get out of town for a while. Let it blow over."

"Who killed the girl at the Santino party?" Rollie asked.

Danny hung his head down. "I swear, I don't know. Go ahead and hit me, dude." Danny braced for a pounding.

Rollie tore the phone from the wall and crushed Danny's cell with his foot. He invited the two goons in the hallway to join them, and then tied all five into a circle. He bound their feet to the desk, tied their hands behind each man, and then wrapped them together with rolls of plastic runners he found in their closet. When he finished, the group resembled bobble-head dolls. One by one he taped their mouths shut. Danny was last and talked while Rollie worked.

"You're a dead man, Rollie. The only hope you have is to hide so they can't find you."

"They want me bad enough, they'll find me." Rollie said. Methodically he completed the job and got ready to tape Danny's mouth.

"You're not gonna to leave us like this, are you?" Danny asked.

"I am." Rollie answered.

"We could be here for days." Danny protested.

"Yeah, that's true. Oh, I have one more question. What are the bombs for?"

"All I know is it's a new scam to hold corporate America hostage. They weren't intended to be terrorist shit or nothin' like that. I don't know how it worked."

"Terrorists just the same." Rollie taped Danny's mouth. "The cops know about this?"

Danny violently shook his head no.

"They know about the child porn, you piece of shit?" Rollie glared at Danny. He had found over a hundred kiddy porn DVD's in the closet, and perhaps a thousand more VHS tapes all boxed up and ready to ship. Rollie was disgusted with all of them. Danny, his eyes bulging from his skull was pleading with his eyes. He knew Rollie had made up his mind. Rollie locked the office up and dropped the keys in the trash. On the way down the stairs, he ran into the young girl who was sitting in Danny's lap.

"I wouldn't go up there if I was you." Rollie said.

"Like I'm gonna listen to you." The girl snapped back.

"Suit yourself. Danny just called the cops because of that robbery, ya know?"

"What robbery?" The girl's eyes lit up.

"I thought I overheard him say you were involved that you'd be right back."

The girl didn't hesitate. She turned and ran down the stairs like a pro athlete.

Rollie sat in the car for several minutes. He called detective John Rader and told him about the porn and where he would find a group of men all tied up. Rader wanted to talk further, but Rollie got off the phone. Rader promised he'd call some of his buddies with LAPD and have Danny Bilotti arrested. Rollie didn't feel guilty making the call on his old acquaintance as Danny had slipped into the Hollywood rat hole and deserved whatever came down the pipe.

The day aged. Rollie headed back to Drake's house. His cell phone rang. He flipped it open. "Yeah, this is Rollie."

He heard her sobs, out of control hysteria. "Rollie, don't hang up."

It was Kali, the last person he wanted to talk to. "I can't talk right now."

"Please!" It was a scream, a demand, painful, and full of remorse.

"Kali listen..."

"No, you listen. They're coming to kill you."

The nape above his shoulders chilled. "Who's coming to kill me, Kali?"

She started crying, "I'm sorry." She sobbed uncontrollably, a watery nasal tone in her voice, "They beat me. I had to tell them. I thought he was my boyfriend, Rollie, but he works for them.   Nicky

Henderson is one of them. Oh my God. Oh my God, they're going to kill you."

Rollie pulled out of traffic and stopped. "Who Kali?"

"Five or six men are coming. They just left here."

Rollie heard the panic in her voice. "Where's here? Where are you, Kali?"

"In the Hollywood Hills somewhere. I don't know."

"I'll come and get you." Rollie insisted.

"No!" She screamed.

"How do you know they're coming after me?"

"I know, 'cause the man said he was going to kill you tonight. I gotta go, Rollie. You be careful, hear? I still love you." She hung up.

CHAPTER 23

Fabrio drove to the marina after picking up the two men William Drone arranged to accompany them. The two strangers sat in the rear with Gi Carlo. Pataglia sat in the passenger seat, clearly in utter agony. His eyes were closed, his head rested on the backrest, and one hand grasped the door handle. His knuckles were white. Fabrio glanced at him every few seconds, and wished he could do more. The black Chrysler 300 purred west on the 110 Freeway like a Panther on the prowl. As Fabrio approached San Pedro, traffic thinned. He exited the freeway and drove toward the marina. The two men in the back seat didn't say a word. Fabrio wanted to take Gi Carlo back to the hotel. He needed bed rest, and would be of little use if things turned sour.

Fabrio couldn't embrace all that had gone down over the past few days. Tawny was murdered, along with soldiers, Louis Baxter, and Ronnie Mauten. Were they set up, or had they actually turned against the Pataglia's? The missing pension funds amounted to millions, and yet both men were found with several hundred thousand dollars. Moe Brayden clearly hadn't started the mess, and the Lipeskys war had a short goal. If other families didn't join them, they were in adverse circumstances. Undoubtedly they would run out of a place to go. If neither the Brayden, or Pataglia families wanted to dirty

185

their hands on nuclear bombs, a third party was moving in. A set up like this took planning, and Fabrio wondered who was waiting for them at the marina?

Pataglia, without opening his eyes, asked, "Tell me your names again?" He slowly turned to look at the two guys sitting with Gi Carlo.

Fabrio didn't trust either one. Both were in their early twenties, one with short brown hair, the other with a kinky bright red mane, and a perfectly round head. The bushy red-hair made him look silly, innocent, and much younger than he was.

The redhead spoke up, "I'm Archie Damon, and this here is Roland Wynan."

Aside from the hair both had square jaws, and, like him, had no particular identifying looks that set them apart from anyone else on the planet. Their eyes, however, were intense and focused on the job ahead. They fiddled with their handguns, checking the load, making sure a cartridge filled the chamber, and the safety off.

"Good." Pataglia asked, "Have you worked for mister Drone long?"

Archie smiled, like the kid next door bragging about a home run he hit, "Me, I've been with him six years. Roland here, started two-years ago."

Fabrio studied them, squinting like his eyes were out of focus. "Does Roland know how to talk for himself?"

"Be nice, Fabby." Pataglia said.

Roland smirked "I do. It's just more fun to hear Archie talking about me."

Pataglia gave a slight nod, "That's good, thank you."

Fabrio noticed both men wore sneakers, black jeans, and black long-sleeve shirts. They wore no visible jewelry, watches or rings he could see. Pros. He turned to Pataglia with an approving nod. Fabrio's cell phone rang. He checked the caller and flipped open the phone. "Drego, where are you?"

"We're in the marina." Santino said.

"Alone?" Fabrio asked.

Santino cleared his throat. "No, Sammy's with me."

Fabrio turned to observe the enormous ships in the harbor. "We'll be there in a few minutes."

"Can I be heard?" Santino asked.

"No, why do you ask?" Fabrio answered.

"The boys you have, they came from William Drone?" Santino's voice drifted off in a whisper."

"Yes. " Fabrio frowned. He had no idea where this conversation was going. He adjusted his body in the seat. "Is there a problem?"

"Just being careful. Drone says the redhead could tear your heart out with his bare hands. Drone said he wasn't just a martial artist, but a complete and thorough psychopathic killer who enjoyed nothing more than to inflict more pain than his victim could endure."

Fabrio nodded casually, glancing into the backseat at the small man with bushy red hair. "I'll keep that in mind." Drone earlier had mentioned to Fabrio, that while Archie appeared to possess manic-depressive insanity, you could trust him with your life. Drone sent the redhead to protect Pataglia. So, in spite of Santino's warning, Fabrio was grateful to have this moping, smiling, entertaining character to watch over them. He needed all the help he could get. Archie was like watching someone with moonstruck madness-- you wanted him around, and couldn't wait to get away from him. "Where, exactly, are you right now?"

Santino coughed. "In the marina. You won't see us, but I'll be watching for you. We haven't seen anyone yet, but we're about to split up and spread out."

Fabrio looked out and realized they were adjacent to the marina. "We're here. Has anyone seen the actors?"

"Guy who runs the marina liquor store said they came in a couple of hours ago, so they're still here." Santino got quiet. "Did you find Rollie Kemp?"

"No," Fabrio snapped, "We'll deal with him later."

"As you circle the marina, you'll see my yacht." Santino said. "Park in the far lot at the other end, as close as you can to the building with a bright yellow stripe around it. Me and Sammy will work our way over to the building right behind that one and meet you up on the second floor."

"Is that the warehouse we're looking for?" Fabrio asked.

"Yeah," Santino answered. "It's the one with the yellow stripe, and hundreds of antique cars inside. We'll be in the empty building behind it."

Fabrio spotted the striped building as it started to rain. "When is that cop supposed to show?" The windshield wipers swished silently back and forth.

"He should be here any time." Santino answered.

"See you in a few minutes." Fabrio closed the phone. "That was Drego. He's with Sammy. Says the actors were spotted a couple of hours ago."

"So they're still here?" Pataglia said.

"Yeah, they're here." Fabrio answered. Maybe now they'd get some answers.

Archie looked through the mirror with a smile, "These guys well-armed?"

"Probably, and they're not going to give up easily." Fabrio answered.

"Park on the other side of the building." Archie said.

"Why?" Fabrio started to argue.

"Cause they might see us," Archie sat forward and looked at Pataglia. "I'm here to protect you. Tell him to listen to me."

Pataglia curled his upper lip. "Park on the other side, Fabby."

Fabrio threw Archie a look, but Archie ignored it.

"You wearing the vests I gave ya?" Archie said.

Pataglia's response was short, "Yes."

Archie straightened his jaw, "It won't help a shot to the head, so you to stay behind me. I go first, Fabrio second, and then you follow. Don't let me down. You understand? I need you right behind me, then Gi Carlo. Roland will trail." He looked at everyone, "Does that work for you?"

Fabrio saw Gi Carlo give a slight nod. Pataglia didn't like taking orders, and reluctantly agreed. They were about to put their lives on the line for a psychopath.

Archie beamed. "Good."

Fabrio circled the buildings and parked. Archie glanced out the window into the near empty parking lot. The drizzle was coming down heavier. "Stay here while I go check the building, and find a way in." Cautiously he inched the door open, and got out. He leaned back in, staring at Pataglia. "How sure are you one of these actors killed your daughter?"

Pataglia frowned. "Fabrio found out that they were the last ones to be with her, the last to see her alive. If they didn't kill her, they know who did, so we need to keep them alive long enough to get the truth."

"They'll talk to me, Mr. Pataglia," Archie spread a sadistic grin over his face. "Everyone, eventually, talks to me." He closed the door and disappeared into the rain.

CHAPTER 24

Rollie drove East on the 10 Freeway, South on the 405 and eventually West on the 110 Freeway toward San Pedro. Traffic was crowded but moving. Rollie realized he was going sixty-five, and it amazed him how quickly he had to slow down for an approaching traffic jam. He would creep on for a few yards, then jump back up to sixty-five. The sun slowly dropped into the ocean, on a fatal crash course to end the day. The sky vacillated from burnt orange to neon pink. Distant cloud puffs rumbled together like dirty cotton-balls, and threatened to launch a violent storm. They hadn't said a word since Rollie told Drake about the ledger, what he found scribbled on the pages, and what he discovered at the union office.

Drake finally said something. "You really can read that ledger?"

"Uncle Charlie was good." Rollie stared ahead even though he knew Drake was glaring at him. "Is that why you're pouting?"

"I'm not pouting." Drake snarled.

Rollie had a slight disparity. "Uncle Charlie said the Feds believed criminal bookkeepers were mentally deficient, so back in 1952, maybe a few years later, Meyer Lansky taught the families how to manage their holdings and investments. He created the theory of double dipping. Keep two sets of books. One that could be looked at by anyone, and one that only a handful would understand. Lansky was a financial genius. He taught everyone, from Lucky Luciano, Carlo Gambino and eventually the Pataglia's and Brayden's. The Feds put many away on racketeering, murder, restraint of trade, plotting robberies, but not accounting."

"What's your point?"

"You have to go back years to find any member of a crime family that was arrested for making money from legitimate investments. Money that is carefully managed stays that way. Haven't you ever wondered why crime families never run out of money?"

"Never thought about it." Drake responded. "What aren't you telling me?"

"What we need to know wasn't in the ledger. We have dates, amounts paid to various people, and companies. The list is long, and the dollar amounts reach into the millions." Rollie shook his head in frustration. "Both actors' names were on the list."

Drake smacked the dashboard with an open palm. "As if all the millions they make ain't enough, they need more?"

"No, that's not it. Their names were listed as donors. They're both payees, not recipients."

Drake fell into silence. Rollie could tell he didn't get it. It made him feel better because he didn't get it either. Drake fumbled with his unruly hair, brushed his clothes off, and stared out the windows. "What do we do with the ledger?"

"I don't know. Maybe Rader's hands?" He changed the subject. "What did Erinn's doc say?"

"She'll recover physically. Mental is another story."

"Did Erinn ever tell you who came to the house and messed her up?"

"No, but she did get a call." Drake crunched his molars, "Told her the actors are trying to get out of the country. They've tried hiring a boat, plane, and drivers, without luck. Their so-called buddies have slithered off. No one is coming to their rescue."

"What did Eddie Rosewell say?" Rollie wanted to keep the conversation going.

Drake glanced at Rollie. "He said you called?"

"Yeah. I called everyone I know, but Rosewell said studio information was between him and you."

"You're getting' good, kid. Eddie claims the studio won't lift a finger to help the actors until this gets settled and they're cleared of charges."

Rollie watched cars zip buy, recklessly weaving in and out of traffic. "You wanna talk about it, or pout all night?"

"I've been thinking." Drake said.

"Oh, is that what you call it. Neat." They drove a bit longer. "Okay, what are you thinking?"

"Bombs, murder missing pension funds, your uncle getting shot, your nephew killed, actors paying the mob for God knows what, and a lunatic trying to kill you and Erinn. All that."

"Makes for some righteous moments, doesn't it?" Rollie watched the sun disappear and caught a glimpse of the Green Flash – the mystical moment when the sun drops beyond the ocean floor, and the sky fills with a bright green flash. The sighting was a rare optical phenomenon, and Rollie was thrilled to witness his first. The day was over, but the nightmare was just beginning.

"What else are you hiding?"

Rollie shook his head. "Nothing. Oh, I did forget to tell you. Right after, I left the union office, Kali called on my cell. She was hysterical." He took a breath, watching a smaller ship make its way to the dock. He had a hard time discussing Kali, and awkwardly annoyed she was still in his life.

"Am I supposed to guess what she said?"

"She said five or six guys are coming to kill me."

"Five or six?"

"Yeah." Rollie nodded.

"And they know where we're going?"

Rollie shrugged. "I guess so, she didn't say."

"Our fees are going up by the minute."

Rollie glanced over at the big man. He was grinning. "You always have this much fun?"

"I try. How 'bout you?"

"Maybe." Rollie tightened his grip around the steering wheel.

"Think they'll find us?"

Rollie shrugged. "From what's happened so far, it should be easy."

"That a boy. Way I see it, if we know about the location, they do too."

"You knew, didn't you?" Rollie glanced over at the big man.

Drake shot a look back at Rollie. "That she was involved? Sure. She called you, knew where you were, even warned you." He stared Rollie down. "And what did you do?"

"I guess I didn't want to go there."

"You can say that again. Love is hard to understand."

Rollie's jaw tightened. "All we gotta do is figure out who's coming, beside my uncle's goons. Apparently we've been sucked in by whoever's after us."

"Us?"

Rollie braked as traffic came to a stop. He chose to ignore Drake's sarcasm. "Don't ya love traffic in L.A.?"

"It could get worse." Drake snapped.

"Yeah, we could be walking."

"That's a thought." Drake stared out. "I think we fucked up."

"I think two different people shot at me. I'm not sure who planted the cameras or listening crap, 'cause that's weird stuff. There must be three groups."

"Interesting." That's all Drake said.

They moved up another few feet and stopped.

"So, are they after me, you, or both of us?" Rollie quizzed.

"Now there's another interesting thought."

"Yeah. I do that sometimes." Traffic picked up, and soon they were going seventy. Rollie smiled at the speed of traffic and moved into the fast lane. "I don't get it."

"What caused the traffic jam?"

"Don't try to make sense of it. There is no accident, just traffic. I always look around, but there isn't one. Must be a reasonable excuse though, don't you think?"

Drake nodded "What's reasonable?"

Rollie braked, slowed down again. "The ghosts and phantoms that live in this town." Rollie watched the crowded freeway crawl along like a giant anthill. The drizzle moved inland, and droplet's starting hitting the windshield.

"Just like." Drake agreed.

Rollie got off the Freeway, took Seaside, and turned into the marina. The wind had picked up from the usual late-afternoon breeze off the ocean. The sea became choppy, and small boats moved with the constant motion of the sea, bobbing up and down in steady rhythmic flotation. The sky filled with dark, ominous clouds. Rollie slowed as he drove around the wide roadway, and stopped in a wide public parking lot. A steady drizzle was tumbling over the area. Only a few pickup trucks and a single SUV were on the lot, and all of them had boat trailers attached. He pulled in and parked. He looked out the window, and Drake followed his gaze to a seventy-foot yacht. It looked like an aircraft carrier compared to the other boats. On the top deck was a speedboat and two-passenger helicopter. Modern rescue conveniences, Rollie thought.

"Is that Santino's boat?" Rollie couldn't take his eyes off the huge craft.

"Yeah, that's it. He loves to throw parties on it."

"We should all have one like that." Rollie said, admiring the gigantic craft.

"Not my cup of tea." Drake said, "I don't like going out on the water."

"Fish seem to enjoy the water."

"True. Zip up your jacket."

"It's not cold." Rollie still didn't like the jacket, even though it saved his life.

"Bullets don't know cold, zip it up." Drake glared at him.

Rollie saluted, "Yes, sir."

"Let's go, and don't be a smartass."

"Don't take everything away from me, Dad."

Drake narrowed his eyes, his upper lip curled in an angry snarl. With his hands, Rollie gestured for Drake to lighten up. They got out of the car and walked the long way around the lot. Then Drake started walking toward the yacht. The sprinkle was steady, and the skies above were about to hemorrhage.

Rollie glanced around. "You think it might look obvious, us walking right at it?"

"Don't think anyone's home, so it won't matter." Drake crossed over to a retaining wall. Rollie followed, "Erinn said Santino was out looking for actors."

Rollie glanced over the marina, "So where's Wally Drummonds warehouse?"

Drake gestured with a twist of his head, "That huge building with the ugly stripe."

Rollie followed his gaze, seeing the massive structure with an enormous neon yellow stripe running around the entire building. "No wonder he calls it the big boy. Damn ugly thing must have twenty-thousand square feet."

They walked over to the edge of the water and sat down. Rollie wanted to look around, but Drake shook his head.

"Why are we sitting in the rain?" Rollie asked.

"Because." Drake answered dryly. "Your uncle still financing, Santino's pictures?"

"Probably." He watched the boats bounce. "Why?"

"Make sense that Santino would be down here helping your uncle, doesn't it?"

"Yep." He watched a seal glide through the water.

"Who gets to 'em first, and where are they?" Drakes voice was low, a near whisper. "Are they still in that building, or on the move again?"

"Still there." Rollie glanced out at a small sailboat coming into the marina. Two guys were wrestling with the sails, and Rollie knew they didn't have a clue what to do. One of the guys almost fell overboard. "Besides, actors are too dumb to risk movement."

"My money says they're armed and scared."

"How much money we talking about?" Rollie perked up.

"Five bucks."

"Make it ten, and we'll see who's the best shot." Rollie held out a closed fist.

Drake touched the fist with his, "You're on."

Both stood up. Drake looked at his watch. "It'll be dark in half an hour."

Rollie walked off in the opposite direction. Drake followed a few feet behind. Rollie put his hands in the jacket pockets, dropped his head into the wind, and kept walking toward a ramp that led down to a series of docks, and hundreds of boats. When they reached the bottom, they were out of sight from the parking lot, and all the surrounding buildings.

"When it gets dark, we need to separate." Drake said

"You think?"

"There you go again!" Drake snapped. "Can we be serious for a second?"

Rollie glanced at this wristwatch. "So, according to your calculations, in a half hour, we might be shot at, killed, or if we're lucky, get into one hell of a good footrace, right?"

"There are lots of possibilities."

Rollie knew he had balls, enough fear to make it work, and plenty of guts to handle anything, but he wasn't sure he could look a man in the eye with an "I don't give a shit look," and mean it.

"I'm heading over there." Drake gestured to the far end of the dock.

"Okay, and after that, what's our plan?"

Drake got a puzzled look on his face. "Plan?"

"Yeah, you know. We came down here for a reason. Do we know what the reason is, and how we're going to accomplish getting it done?"

"Oh, that." Drake said. "The way I see it, we need to grab the actors first, and then get the hell outta here, 'cause if one of them killed the girl, bad is gonna happen."

"I still don't think either one killed her."

Drake spun around, his eyes searching Rollie's face, "And what makes you say that?"

"Her neck was broken. She was posed. It was a professional mob hit."

"You know these things?" Drake asked.

"I heard about how they do things from the time I was old enough to listen. My old man's friends liked to brag about stuff. So did Uncle Charlie."

"Why put a hit on the girl? Why not just kill her old man?"

"I think they're confused, Drake. Obviously they can't just walk in and kill a guy like Anthony Pataglia without starting a war."

"They tried in New York." Drake said.

"Yeah, but they missed."

"Oh, I got it. They wounded him on purpose?"

"Whatever. Now they have to use their tiny little brains to figure out a way to draw him out here. They're stupid, Drake, and stupid people don't think things out. They just do them."

"Wow, this is good stuff. Go on."

Rollie sneered at him. "You knew, right?"

"Yeah, but it's nice to know we're on the same page."

"Pataglia's coming for the actors. He believes one of them killed his baby. The Brayden soldiers knows he's comin', and probably ordered the hit."

Drake nodded, "I got that far."

"So, back to the big question?" Rollie waited.

"Why they want you dead?" Drake quizzed.

"No, not that. The other thing."

"Reason? Our plan?"

"Yeah." Rollie rocked his head from side to side.

"The third group, the one that tried to kill you?"

"What about 'em?"

"You gotta stop 'em."

Rollie was apprehensive. "Why me, and not you? Let me guess. 'Cause I'm related, and it's my job to see it through?"

Drake smiled, "And there you have yet another option."

CHAPTER 25

The view through the binoculars wasn't crystal clear, and she couldn't sharpen the focus. She saw the Chrysler 300 enter, pull around the buildings and obviously park. Next the detectives showed up. Even without a clear vision she could tell, it was Rollie Kemp and Drake Fargo. They walked down the boat ramp and could no longer be seen. The Watcher hated the tremor. Her left arm responded with a twitch. She couldn't keep the hand from shaking. She allowed the message to get under her skin. The email arrived at noon: Last Chance! You have brought about a great deal of embarrassment. Redeem yourself. You now have an insurmountable debt and should you have one more lame and impotent conclusion with your endeavors, you may as well attempt to shuffle off, but rest assure there is little chance to throw off the scent. The game of hide-and-seek will precipitately be concluded. Proof of success is now required. We are waiting to hear from you. Bastards! They knew she always completed the job. They knew she would make good on her contract. What was with the threat? What would prevent her from going after them? Perhaps the time had come to retire?

There was little doubt how much she despised the ocean, the humid air and the God forsaken mist that constantly fell and kept everything sticky. The marina brought a flurry of memories back. Her first contract, after going out on her own, happened in the exact marina she now waited. The mark was a singer, part of a group that made headlines worldwide. He was an embarrassment to the other members of the band, and so they paid to have him removed. It had to look like an accident. No guns or knives. The guy was a heavy drinker, and they, whoever they were, wanted him to die of natural causes. It was fogy, cold, and wet. She watched him down a pint of Jack Daniels, and then he set out to walk his dog. The Watcher happened to be on his dock. She stopped to pet the dog and accidentally bumped into the singer. The guy slipped off the dock and fell into the icy water. The Watcher and the guy's dog waited until he stopped thrashing. She read in the morning paper, the dog was found running in circles and the singer's body was found floating between two boats. They assumed he got drunk and fell in. His death was ruled an accident. She vowed never to return to the area, and had the sniffles for a month. So much for making meaningless, solemn promises.

The failure in New York ate at her. Each of the three men received two hollow-point slugs. One was enough to gut a man. Two was meant to overkill. The problem was, she killed the wrong guy. Richie Pataglia looked like Anthony's twin. She didn't know about Richie, but that was another blunder. She hadn't done enough research -- a colossal mistake. There was no place for her to go. She had to finish the job. As long as The Watcher had done this, she had never made a miscue –, and now the errors had grown into a catastrophe. First came a witness who could identify her, the miss at running him over. The night scope that failed, and all that followed by the colossal error in New York. Damn! What would Sonny think?

The Watcher had been taught by the best hit man ever -- Sonny Harris. Sonny was the king of contract players. If you wanted the finest gem in the sea, the flower of the flock, you hired Sonny Harris. When he got cancer, he wanted his legacy to live on. He introduced her to everyone he knew. It didn't happen right away, but within the first year, she was the queen.

She wiped a tear, remembering the day they met. She lived alone, and it was a drag. Living in a new state where she knew a few of her co-workers at the market, she was beyond lonely. All the male employees were married, and she was extraordinarily vulnerable. Stuck in Houston, it wasn't a pleasant town to hook up with a new man. All the good ones were married or gay. She shopped in the grocery store daily, in search of something different to create a feast for one. Sonny was pushing a cart around, not quite shopping for food. His mission was to scope out his next victim. The manager of the grocery store, a fat slob named Danny Blue, also ran drugs. He got greedy, shorted a shipment of coke by cutting it in half -- half for him and half for the buyer. Danny Blue didn't think anyone would notice his diluted sale. The buyer did, and went over Danny's head to the source. No way to reconcile with a thief, so Sonny received the contract.

While watching Danny Blue, Sonny bashed his cart into The Watcher's. He was moving so fast he knocked her right on her ass. Her dress flew up around her waist. The moment he looked down at her, she froze. She was lying on the floor, spread-eagle, with her pink thong fully exposed. She loved frilly things you could see through. Obviously Sonny did, as well. He raced over to her side, never taking his eyes off her crotch, and apologized.

"I think you're apologizing to the wrong part of my body." She said, even though a bit titillated by his stare. The guy was one hot animal.

Sonny shook his head. "No, doll, that's the right part, and I hope it's not damaged."

When he finally did look into her eyes, her whole insides flipped around. Her heart rate tripled. Sonny had the bluest eyes she'd ever seen. His face was pure masculinity with high cheekbones and little dimples in his cheeks. He had the half shaven look a rock star, and boy did it look good on him. His hair was longer than most men wore it, wavy, and pitch black. He had a smile that increased blood pressure without effort, and teeth so perfect they looked phony. There weren't, however, and nothing else was phony about Sonny Harris. The bulge in his pants didn't go unnoticed either.

He helped her up, but only after he adjusted her skirt. His hand brushed against her thong as he lowered the material down to her knees, and then he examined her legs. He ran a hand over her skin, and his fingers gave out electric moments of pleasure that made her shiver. No man ever made her feel so alive as Sonny did.

"What are you doing?" She whispered breathlessly.

"Just making sure the goods aren't damaged." He was smiling. He had a smile.

"Are they?"

"I think they're good to go." With that, he helped her up.

His smile was contagious. She felt weakened just looking at him. "Where exactly would you like them to go?"

"These gorgeous limbs are going to follow me back to my motel room."

She brushed her skirt down further. "And why, precisely, would they follow you?"

She looked directly into his blues, and found them sparkling as he took her in with one exaggerated glance. "Well, doll, I think you're inquisitive, aren't you?"

"You sound like a bad boy. Are you bad?" And she was hoping he was.

Sonny nodded, slow, and deliberate. "I'm a very bad boy." Then he turned and walked away. "You comin'?"

Her crotch twinged. "Well yeah." She hoped to come in more ways than one.

She left her cart, he left his, and they walked out of the grocery store right over to the Travelodge Motel. They tore each other's clothes off. They made love four or five times that first night, and it continued into the next morning. They couldn't get enough of one another. Even when he went to work, he'd come back to the motel in the middle of the day just to undress her, and play the man thing. He played better than any man she'd ever met or hoped to meet.

When he told her his job was done, and he was moving on, she was surprised.

"Wanna come with me?"

"Where would we go?"

He had a twinkle in his eye. "Does it matter?"

The Watcher had no family, no ties, and no reason to stay in Houston. She moved from Columbia South Carolina just months before, and she certainly had nothing to go back to Columbia for. Her mother married some creep who couldn't keep his hands off her, so she stabbed him in the groin with a kitchen knife. He survived, but he wouldn't be hopping in the sack with anyone for a while.

"No, it doesn't matter a lick."

She helped him pack, noticed the guns, and not long after that she learned what he actually did for a living. "What's it called, this job of yours?"

"I'm a contractor."

"What do you build?"

"Not that kind of contractor."

"But people make a contract with you? Isn't that what you said?" She remembered teasing with him, but in her gut she knew what he did.

"That's what I said."

"So they contract you to do what?" She wanted to hear him say it.

"Would it make a difference what I did?"

"No,"

"Regardless?" He looked deep into her eyes.

She giggled. "Whatever it is, it must be exciting, or you wouldn't do it. If it's that exciting, I not only want to know what it is, but if I can do it too?"

"Well, doll, it's exciting, it's dangerous, and you can learn to do it."

She wanted to be a part of whatever it was. "Sounds wonderful."

"You ever hurt anyone?"

"I stabbed my step-father. That should count."

"Kill him?"

"No, but I wanted to."

"Disappointed when you found out he lived?"

She nodded. "Very."

"Then you will enjoy this."

She knew she was right. "You contract to kill people, right?"

"And if I do?" Sonny waited, hands on his hips.

She kissed his face. "Will you teach me everything you know?"

"It would be my pleasure, doll."

And teach he did. At first he took her with him, and allowed her to watch. He taught her how to shoot, use a knife, silence someone with her hands, break a neck, and shove a nose up into their skull. Along the way, he taught her a host of other tricks of the trade. She caught on fast and was soon doing jobs on her own. They moved to Los Angeles, and found a place that faced the ocean. They bought a sailboat. In less than a full year, she was receiving contracts that paid as much as his, and became as prolific. She returned home from San Francisco one day, and found Sonny drunk, his eyes red from crying.

"What is it?" She was so damn worried.

"Doc says I have cancer."

"So you'll get it fixed and get treatments."

"Sorry, doll. No operation. It's terminal."

"How long?"

"Six months, give or take."

She understood. "Will you have lots of pain?"

"Won't let it go that far."

"How you going to avoid that?" She asked.

"I know this person. I'll put a contract out, and when I least expect it, bingo bango."

"I think I know this person."

"Yeah, I'm sure you do."

"How you gonna pay for this service?" She was all business with him.

He looked at her. She was serious. "You think it'll be expensive?"

"Very."

"Then I'll leave everything I have to cover payment for the service. My bank accounts, property, cars, and contacts should cover the costs."

"All your belongings, and contacts?"

"You bet."

She agreed. "I think that will cover your debt."

"I'll make the call when things start getting rough."

"Until then?" She smiled when she said it.

"Life continues as it is. Screw around a little, do a few jobs and take a vacation or two."

"I suppose you want the same company you've been keeping?"

"Always." He smiled and curled into her lap. "I love ya doll."

"Ditto."

Eight months later, she received a notice in the usual way. A personal ad in the newspaper: "Wanted a strong-willed person who can recharge academic needs and assist in preparing for final exams." Boring business with little potential. Will pay minimum wage plus a bonus if assistance can be completed in time. Please send resume to P.O. Box 77B4C22, Los Angeles, CA. She accepted the contract, and one day when they took the sailboat out she noticed his pain first hand. Without giving thought, she shot him once behind the ear, another in the heart, and threw his body overboard. He wanted to go out just like any other hit, and he wanted to be surprised. She accomplished both and proudly fulfilled his last wish. Then she genuinely missed Sonny.

Rollie Kemp had twice eluded her, but there wouldn't be a third. Her grip tightened around the steering wheel of the old station wagon she had rented from Rent-A-Wreck. Rollie should be dead just like Tawny

Brock. She delivered on the girl and then fell apart in New York. Now it was messy, and she had Rollie to thank for getting in her way.

She drove through the marina, like any boat person. No one would notice the old car. There wasn't much to see. A few SUV's with boat trailers, a lone car parked by a strangely painted building. She looked at the car, a Chrysler 300 and kept going. She circled the marina twice, seeing several more cars that might or might not mean anything. No one was walking around, and it was intensely dark. Lightning lit the distant sky. She drove further into the marina area and parked out of sight. She was wearing black sneakers, sweats and hooded jacket. She had black gloves that were paper-thin, and she carried several guns and knives. She'd take out Rollie first, and then the actor. If Pataglia happened to raise his bushy head, she'd take him to satisfy her debt. She wore a Kevlar vest with a throat protector, had two Glock 9mm pistols, a pocket full of loaded magazines and a Beretta snuggly strapped on her ankle.

The marina was a whopping shadow, poorly lit where there were lights, and dangerous to cross regardless of where you started. The constant drizzle would help. A few boats bobbed in the water with their running lights on, but otherwise it was pitch black. It was eerily quiet as she slipped from the car, and ran back toward Santino's yacht. She knew Santino was down here looking for actors. Maybe he got lucky and found them? Laughably, everyone thought one of them killed the girl. They'd never know the truth once she killed them.

CHAPTER 26

Rollie casually strolled over to the marina junction box, looked around, unscrewed the panel with his knife, and cut the wires. The dock area became extremely dark. A few boats bobbed through the channel slowly heading for their slips. Otherwise, he stood in the black-of-night.

"Now we can't be seen," Rollie whispered to Drake.

Drake blinked in the surrounding darkness, "How the hell are we supposed to see?"

"Adjust," Rollie whispered back. Stay here. I'll be right back."

Rollie hiked over the railing and moved like a cat up the steep embankment. Every step meant a calculated risk of falling. He trudged up the rocks, alongside the marina, and peered over the top. He was even with the parking lot. He watched several people walk into a darkened structure on the other side of the lot. Rollie tensed. He glanced down into the marina where he left Drake, but couldn't see him. Damn! It unquestionably was dark. He moved over the rocks, careful not to slide down, and froze when an old station wagon made a methodical trip through the area. It passed through a second time, and then disappeared around the other side of the marina buildings. He strained to see if anyone came from the direction where the station wagon vanished. No one did.

Headlights flashed over Rollie's face. He ducked and cautiously peered over the edge. A dark, four-door sedan passed -- an unmarked cop car slowed, doused its lights, and disappeared behind the buildings across the lot.

Moving to his left, along the ridge, Rollie felt the guns he carried -- how cumbersome the muzzles were. The 9mm Glock was tucked in the curve of his back and dug into his skin. The 38 snub-nosed Smith & Wesson rubbed awkwardly on his ankle. He wondered if undercover cops and wise guys had similar complaints. Stupid things hurt. The knife fit uncomfortably down his left leg and was way too long. It wasn't a good choice, and now he regretted picking it. He hadn't given the weapons much thought until the discomfort hit him. He wondered if his love life, or lack thereof, would get another chance. Funny how much there was he had yet to try. Now wasn't the time to analyze it, but it would be addressed when this was over. Take some time for Rollie. Not just the goofy stuff, but things most relevant to him like grandma.

A seagull screeched. Rollie turned, and nearly tumbled down the slippery rocks. At the end of the dock, a man and a woman were climbing out of a relatively large fishing boat. It had to be at least thirty-six feet, sleek, and possessed a long bow. Rollie guessed it probably cost several hundred grand or more. He melted into the rocks and waited. The couple staggered along the dock, took a few steps to the side of the boat, and then started up the ramp where Rollie was flattened against the rocks. He pulled himself deeper into the sharp edges of the stone and held his breath.

"This is a great night so far," the man said.

"What part was best?" Her voice was throaty, sexy.

"Great sex before a guy eats is not a bad way to start the evening."

"The dinner was good afterwards."

They stopped walking, just inches away from where Rollie clung to the rocks. The edges were slippery from the drizzle, and Rollie hoped the couple would hurry up before he slithered down the rocks in a body avalanche.

"Know what was best?" The man asked.

"What?" She giggled.

"Desert."

"Which one?" She rubbed against the guy.

"The last one, baby. It was the best sex I've had in years."

"I bet you say that to all the girls?"

"What girls? I've never said it to anyone until now."

Even Rollie could tell a lie when he heard one, but the woman was too drunk to notice. They stood toe-to-toe, running their hands over each other, and Rollie started to perspire.

"Really?"

"You're something. I love the way you get into it, get all sweaty."

She whispered, "I'm blushing. Wanna go back to the boat?"

Rollie wanted to shout yes.

"Let's go get a few drinks first. I need to replenish my strength for the next round."

Rollie started a downward cascade over razor sharp rocks. He scrambled over the rocks trying to stop his descent and slipped another four or five inches before his shoes caught a break.

With Rollie just inches away, she purred, "You sure?" She was all over the guy.

The man took her hand and led her up the ramp toward the parking lot. "C'mon. I need time to repair the damage."

Rollie adhered firmly to the rocks, grateful for their movement.

"Isn't that what those little blue pills are for?"

"Even they need time to work again." The guy said.

They both laughed and disappeared into the night. Rollie inched his way over the angular shore boulders. There had to be another way to get back down to the ramp. He heard a sudden noise, spun around, and heard another loud crack, a car backfiring, maybe a gun being fired. Rollie grappled, slipped, lost his grip, and slid down over the slimy knife-edges of the protruding stones.

CHAPTER 27

Rader spent hours looking for the ledger. Someone had taken it. About to call it a night, the phone rang. He didn't need to answer but relented on the fifth ring.

"Rader," he sounded rushed on purpose.

"Is this John Rader in robbery homicide?"

"Yeah, who's this?"

"Bill Mullwood over in the Van Nuys division. Wanted to thank you for that tip today. What we found on their hard drive would make ya sick. Porn kings. I don't know how they got all tied up, but it was a nice package. They were using eight and nine year old kids, sick bastards. Anyway, we got a woman here claims she's the ex-wife of a guy named Rollie Kemp, a PI in West L.A. or Santa Monica. You know him?"

Rader set his briefcase on the desktop and sat down. Already he was sorry he answered the phone. "Yeah, I know Rollie well. We went through the academy together."

"He's a cop?" Mullwood asked.

"No, he was the vic in a TA right before graduation. Didn't mend fast enough to complete. Went into acting. You'd know his kisser if ya saw him."

"You gotta be me kidding me, right?" Mullwood chuckled. "The guy was almost a cop who turned to acting, and then became a PI? His acting ability must suck, right?"

"You askin' me for my opinion?" Rader said.

"Not particularly. This broad is a real nut case. Says there are five or six guys going out to kill her ex. If you caught the look you'd know what I mean about taking her seriously, but I thought I'd make the call anyway. Any of this make sense to you?"

"Not sure." Rader said as he thought about all the possibilities.

"The broad could be a real looker, ya know?"

"Did she say anything else?" Rader thought about Rollie's mysterious phone call, and the visit Rader now wished he'd paid closer attention to.

"Can't take what she said too seriously, Rader. Looks as if she's been using for a long time. There's not much brain material left here, but she's an insistent little bitch."

Rader hated pointless ramblings. He'd heard all about Rollie's ex. Seen pictures of her before she fell into hell. She was pretty, but she also used drugs, and cheated on him. Why was he sitting here listening to this crap when he could be home with the wife and kids having a beer, or out shooting baskets with the boys while Angie fixed dinner and teased him about later? When she called asking about him coming home, she had that playful thing in her voice. He could tell when they were good, and she was ready, willing, and more than able. Her voice got raspy and reeked of sensuality. They got married right out of high school, and Angie was the only woman Rader had ever been with. They were virgins, and when he held her in his arms the very first time he felt his whole body explode inside. He never had that feeling before and no one had come close to repeating it. Several women in the office tried, as did some on the beat, but no one could replace Angie, and there was no way he'd ever cheat on her, no way. He loved her in ways you only read about. They were good together. Oh, they fought once in a while, but they never took anger to bed. If she didn't apologize, he did. They cried together and would sometimes hold each other just for the pleasure and comfort of it. He missed her and wanted to go home. It had been a long enough day.

Rader almost didn't want to ask, "Where is she now?"

"Downstairs with the EMT's. Somebody punched her around and left her a real mess."

"She say anything else?"

"Some other guy, whose name is, ah, hold on a sec," Rader heard a report fall, lose paper spreading over the desk or floor, "shit," the detective mumbled, then more shuffling through paper, flipping pages, getting stuck like in a notebook, "yeah, here it is. Some guy named Drew Lipesky left with her boyfriend; a guy she says kidnapped and held her prisoner. His name is Nicky Henderson. She claims Nicky sells drugs and this other guy --"

"Hold her until I get there. Take me fifteen, twenty minutes." Rader's heart jumped a beat when he heard the name Drew Lipesky.

"Rader, hold on, this could be a waste of -- "

"Just hold her!" Rader hung up, left his briefcase on the desk, and hustled towards the elevator. On his way down to the garage he called Angie on his cell phone.

"Ange, I got a lead on these gangsters we've been expecting, hon, so save my plate and wear something easy to remove until I get there, okay?"

"Thanks for calling. You're always so sweet." Angie said.

"You being sarcastic?" Rader asked as he walked to his car.

"No, I love it when you call. Take your time, and if you get in late and I'm sleeping, wake me. I can't go all night without you. I've been thinking about us all day."

"I'll wake you." Rader promised. "Regardless of the hour."

"I'll be waiting. You be careful, hear?"

"Yeah, I will." He closed the phone and took a deep breath. The night air felt good. Maybe Rollie's ex did have a connection. Rader needed to catch a break before a whole bunch of people died. He had a dirty cop in the house, and dangerous guys from back east in town. The kind of perverted malevolence he never wanted to see. They had enough evil in California. Simply put, the crime family guys had to go even if it had to be in a body bag.

CHAPTER 28

Fabrio didn't like to wait, and despised counting on a stranger to protect them. When Archie didn't come right back, Fabrio became angry and got out of Chrysler 300. The drizzle turned to rain. He leaned back in, looked at Pataglia, and then turned his attention to Roland and Gi Carlo. "Stay put until I get back."

"We're like sittin' ducks here." Roland protested.

Fabrio's eyes darkened. "When Archie returns, follow him inside. Otherwise, wait here until I come back. Understand?"

"Yeah, okay." Roland said.

Fabrio turned back to Pataglia. "You okay?"

"I'm fine. Go see what's up."

Fabrio saw the grimace and felt guilty. He quietly closed the door and moved off. The pace of the rain picked up. Over the ocean, the sky lit up from a spectacular spider web bolt of lightning, followed immediately by bellows of rolling thunder.

Fabrio, with the grace of a large cat, moved from a dark corner behind the striped building and ducked down a ramp. The rain was now a steady downpour. Everywhere he looked, shadows moved. People were running for cover all over the marina. Some belonged, and some didn't. He saw Sammy Tass move in the shadows ahead of him, but before he could signal Sammy, a man appeared behind his comrade. Sammy didn't see the guy, and Fabrio could do nothing to help him. The man hit Sammy in the back of the head. Sammy's head snapped back from the blunt force and collapsed in a heap. Fabrio sprung up, and ducked back when two other men joined the first. All three stared down at the fallen Sammy, and then one of the guys fired two shots into Sammy's body. The piece obviously had a silencer, but Fabrio saw the muzzle flash. He swallowed hard, to eliminate tossing his stomach. Sammy was his friend.

Fabrio waited in the shadows, gulping air. Damn, how he wished he could cry. The three men walked into the striped building, and Fabrio ran over to the dock entrance. Down dockside, Fabrio inched up the second ramp and stepped out on the sidewalk that outlined the entire marina. He wondered why all the lights were off. It was a strange night, blacker than the murky darkness of being locked in a cellar, like the one his old man used when he was a kid. A sudden noise, he turned to the left, and was met by Archie's hand pulling him to the ground.

"You can't walk around like that. They have a small army." Archie whispered.

"How many?" The sudden surprise by Archie pissed him off and probably saved his life. He still wasn't sure he could trust the redhead.

"Don't know. Maybe a dozen."

"Where's Santino?" Fabrio asked.

"Waiting for us in the deserted building. I told him to sit on his hands."

"Let's get Pataglia outta that car before they see him." Fabrio said

He started to get up, but Archie stopped him.

"Gi Carlo's not gonna be much help, and I don't know you Fabrio. You any good?"

"Yeah." Fabrio answered between his teeth. He hated to be questioned, and more so by a young punk kid like Archie.

"We're outnumbered by a bunch, so we need to depend on each other." Archie spoke softly, and yet his words were direct.

"We can take a dozen." Fabrio murmured.

They both heard it at the same time -- a small noiseless sound among the night air. Fabrio sucked up against the ground, as did Archie. They waited. Shadows moved, and the rain started pounding the ground. Five, maybe six men passed them. Fabrio tried to count, but from the ground it was impossible. Fifteen feet sprawled between them and the collection of armed thugs. Fabrio glanced over to Archie and shook his head no. When the goons had passed, Fabrio and Archie stood up. Both scanned over the grounds.

"They know we're here." Fabrio said under his breath.

Archie agreed. "Yeah, they do. We didn't exactly hide on our arrival."

They snuck back to the abandoned building where the car was parked.

"Looks like they want Pataglia out of the way. They'll need to kill all of us, won't they?"

"Let's upset their plans. You're not ready to die, are you?" Fabrio asked.

"No."

"Good, neither am I." Fabrio tapped his knuckles against Archie's.

CHAPTER 29

Rollie sat at the base of the rock formation, embarrassed from his fall, and grateful no one witnessed the clumsiness. Aside from a few minor cuts and bruises, the only thing hurt was his pride. He stood and brushed himself off. About to step up to the level of the parking lot, a hand covered his mouth and pulled him down the ramp to the boat level.

"That was pure artistry." Drake mumbled.

"You saw me fall?" Rollie whispered. Even though, no one could see it, he knew red blotches covered his face. Perhaps the rain would carry them off before Drake noticed?

"Yeah. Graceful."

"It wasn't as bad as it looked. And why are we whispering?"

"You didn't see them?" Drake gestured with his head.

"Only thing I saw was the drunk couple." Rollie answered defensively.

"They see you?"

"No." Rollie didn't think they did. Hopefully they were too drunk?

Rollie glanced off, boats bobbed up and down. Some had lights on, mainly to carry electric current flowing through the wires. Sporadically dispersed throughout the marina, were a few larger mini-yachts with live-aboard provisions. Through a boat window or two, the flicker of television sets flickered. Otherwise, the blackness of the surrounding sea brought a new meaning to the words pitch-black. In a moonless sky above, storm clouds were expanding, laying the groundwork for a tropical California assault. It seldom rained in California, but when it did, it usually came down in buckets. The rain that fell was steady.

Drake examined the sky. "Looks like the rain's gonna stick around."

"It never rains in California." Rollie said as he too scrutinized the sagging skyline.

"They came in three cars."

Rollie nodded, "I saw two of 'em."

"I thought you said you only saw the couple?"

"I lied," Rollie answered.

"Then you missed one."

"How many were in the cars?" It was Rollie's turn to banter.

Drake looked thoughtful. "Three, maybe six."

"What happened to four or five?"

Even in the dark, the whites in Drake's eyes glowed with anger. "They parked all over the place. One car looked like one Rader drives."

"Yeah, I saw that one too. They must have a dirty cop with them."

Drake nodded. "Maybe."

"Should we split up, Drake?"

"If some of them came down here to eliminate you, we should stick together. Six to eight guys spread out in too many directions." Drake was being charitable.

"Didn't you say three before?"

"I also said maybe six," Drake explained.

222

"Then where'd the eight come from?" Rollie demanded.

"Three cars hold lots of bodies, Rollie." Drake walked down the ramp in the direction of Santino's yacht. Rollie became his shadow, walking right with him. Without looking, Drake mumbled. "You're annoying me, Rollie."

"You said we should stick together."

"I'm gonna smack you."

"Drake?" Rollie stopped walking.

"What?" Drake was real pissy but still whispered.

"Think about it. Who sends ten to twelve men to get one? What kind of threat am I?"

"You're a pain in the ass."

"Besides that."

"As exasperating as you are, you're right." Drake said.

"If my uncle's here with his friends, we might not get to the actors."

"Not if that's who was in those cars." Drake agreed.

"Who else could it be?"

"Your ex-wife?" Drake answered with missing a beat.

"Don't be ridiculous."

"Depends on who shot at you?" Drake added.

"Well, we both know my uncle's goons shot at me once."

"So, it must be one of the other desperados your ex-wife mentioned?"

"Maybe Kali told 'em stuff?" Rollie didn't want to believe that, but if Kali got desperate enough, she might do anything. If she told one of her friends that he had lots of money, maybe that was who was after him? Damn. He looked at Drake. "Let's call for backup?"

"Yeah, for the first time, I think you're right. It's not worth getting in the middle of something we can't prevent. I'll give Rader a call, and we'll lay low until he gets here." Drake pulled his cell phone out and dialed. The call wouldn't go through. He snapped the phone shut. "No service. Try yours."

Rollie pulled his cell phone out and had the same problem. "What good are they if they never work when you need them?"

"Well, genius," Drake said, "what now?"

"We'll watch and see how things develop. You bring a deck of cards?"

Before Drake could open his mouth, the rain started to pour. Rollie looked up at the sky while Drake sought refuge under a canopy that housed the dock canoes and inflatable boats.

"It never rains in California," Rollie mumbled as he joined Drake beneath the small shelter. The wind picked up, and the rain came in sheets.

"Yeah, you said that already."

"Drake?"

"What?"

Rollie's eyes traveled to the sky. "We're getting wet."

CHAPTER 30

The Watcher moved with the rain, from one boat ramp to another. She watched several cars arrive, and immediately deducted everyone was accounted for. All she had to do was pick them off one at a time. The need to remain unseen was aided by the rain. Rollie was still down by the boats with the big guy. She had time to do Rollie because Pataglia would go after the actors, and would run into trouble with her people. All she needed was one clean shot at Rollie, and she would move on to Pataglia. With both out of the way, she'd be able to buy her way back to a trusting relationship. Business was looking up.

She stood in the shadows of the restrooms next to older boats that had been hauled out for repair. Quietly she moved among old smelly craft now designated for shore duty. Every vessel she passed was in need of repair, or they weren't sea worthy. Nothing in the whole yard was as impressive as what she and Sonny Harris owned. Tears swell up. She genuinely missed him. He was lucky to have had her when the time came. Damn him! She missed his smile, and the way he looked at her after she mastered a kill. The Watcher refused to be bothered by any setback. Sonny convinced her, it was the cost of doing business.

The Watcher circled the yard. She came in from the other side. Rollie was pinned down, and the only way out was to walk up the ramp or swim in fifty-degree water. He wasn't stupid and knew hyperthermia would begin quickly. He'd stay put. She looked over her position and knew the rain would protect her. She crossed over the parking lot to a chain-link fence, climbed over, and dropped to the other side. The rain picked up, impregnating everything to the core. She continued around more land-yachts, and finally came in from the side of the marina.

When she peered down to where he was holed up, she saw he was still there, crouching down in front of a big yacht. Problem for her now was he was too far away for her to get a decent shot. Damn! The rain was pounding her, and the harder it fell the more frustrated she became. She glanced around for a place to get the shot off, found one, and ran off.

The Watcher planned to put two bullets in Rollie and make it quick. Time was running out for her to get Pataglia, and it had taken much longer than anticipated. The wind picked up, and cold ocean breeze was coming to shore with vengeance. She hated working in the rain, and the chill worked over her body. If she failed this time, her sudden death was inevitable.

The Watcher didn't see it, stubbed her toe into a steep cement step, and went down face first. Her knees hit first, tearing chunks of skin. She dropped her gun. It slid across the boat yard and stopped beneath a huge boat-trailer. She scrambled up and tried to get the gun, but couldn't reach it. Suddenly everything was going wrong. She looked around. Found a board that would extend under the trailer, but she had to lie on her stomach to fish for it. Her knees stung like hell when the wet pavement came in contact with the scraped skin. Her breasts felt as if they would explode from her bodyweight smashing down against them. A diet sounded like a good idea. She was getting too fat anyway. She'd address it later. Now all she cared about was getting the gun back and taking Rollie Kemp out cleanly.

CHAPTER 31

Fabrio opened the car door and helped Pataglia. Archie opened the back door and tried not to embarrass Gi Carlo, so he let the man struggle on his own. A glance at Fabrio assured he did the right thing. Fabrio led them all into the deserted building.

"How many are there?" Pataglia asked.

"Maybe a dozen." Fabrio answered.

Inside, the old building was being used for storage. Stacked everywhere, desks, chairs, and cabinets cluttered the room. The only light came from two low-watt fixtures hanging precariously from the ceiling. Fabrio cleared a chair and helped Pataglia sink into it. Gi Carlo refused help from anyone and stood off in the corner. Outside the rain pounded mercilessly.

"Where's Sammy?" Pataglia said.

"They took him out." Fabrio's voice low with anger.

"Someone has to pay for that." Gi Carlo spoke softly.

Pataglia agreed. "You a good shot, Roland?"

"Better'n most."

"Why don't you three go? Find out who's down here. See who is leading their troops."

Fabrio shook his head. "Archie, stay with Roland. Gi Carlo and me will go. Move someplace where you can see what's goin' on. We'll be right back."

Fabrio followed Gi Carlo out. They huddled against the building. Fabrio watched his old friend. Watched body chemistry. The older man was wounded, but he was getting a second wind.

"You okay?" Fabrio whispered.

"If you wanna worry, spend time on those we're gonna kill." Gi Carlo dashed away from Fabrio, crossed the courtyard, and dropped down a staircase. Fabrio followed. They climbed down the stairs, and found the door unlocked. Quietly, they entered the building. The hallway was in shadows. Outside, the rain came in buckets, and lightening irradiated the darkness every few moments. The bedazzling energy bolts created radiant daylight, and booming claps of thunder followed most. In-between the noises nature created, Fabrio heard voices. He motioned to Gi Carlo to remain silent, and inched closer toward the sounds. Down a short hallway, Fabrio saw a group of men. He froze. They were heavily armed.

The dim lights provided enough illumination for Fabrio and Gi Carlo to see. There were six men, and they recognized three. Drew Lipesky, Bobby Manners a local union worker and colleague a few years ago, and another collaborator, Detective John Miller. He was the same John Miller on William Drone's payroll -- so much for loyalty. The other three, two black men and a tall, lanky kid with a bald head. The two black kids were standing guard, armed to the hilt with shotguns and Uzi's. There was no music playing and yet the two black guys danced to vapors in the air. Fabrio knew both were high on something, and that made them all the more dangerous. Their eyes were glazed over, wild and reckless.

The first black man said, "Why don't we just go in blasting and take 'em all out?" He checked the load in his guns, and was satisfied he was ready to go.

The second black man nodded. He too, couldn't keep both feet on the ground at the same time, "That's a plan. We'll catch 'em off guard."

Fabrio saw the look on Drew Lipesky's face. He had his hands full with a bunch of crazies, and that might help them.

Drew snarled. "Shut up and listen to me. We ain't goin' in there blasting anyone. Hell, we don't even know how many are in there. We need to slow down, and you two need to listen, or you'll end up six-feet under."

Fabrio could see dozens of antique autos and a series of busted out monitor screens, long out of service. Above the monitors were several panels with lots of switches and electronic buttons. The rest of the room was typical office furniture. There was no way they could get all of them. He saw Detective Miller and Bobby Manners exchange looks. They stood behind Drew, looking as though they'd run if the opportunity presented itself.

The tall lanky kid was checking the electronic panel. It had no power. "I'll check the power in the other building. If there is any, you want me to cut it off?"

"Yeah, Nicky. Go check it out, and stay low." Drew said.

Nicky edged himself out through a narrow doorway and vanished.

"You two. What were your names again?" Drew Lipesky said, pointing at the black guys.

"I'm Shark," the taller one said.

"Name's Wade," the shorter man answered.

"We're ready." Shark said.

Drew gave them a look. "That's good. I want you two to go outside, and carefully circle the building behind us."

Shark protested. "It's raining, dude."

"I need you outside." Drew snapped.

Wade's face registered confusion, "What for?"

"The windows are low to the ground and easy to see through. Count how many men they have, and make sure you count right."

"We can count, man." Shark was insulted.

"I'm sure you can." Drew said quickly. Fabrio could see the questions on his face. "That's why I'm sending you two out there. If it wasn't important, I'd send someone else. We need to know exactly how many they have, and where they are." Drew looked the two over, "You can do that, right?"

"Sure," Wade looked at Shark.

Shark nodded.

The two gangbangers went out into the rain and started around the massive building. Fabrio was about to wave Gi Carlo back when Drew spoke again.

"Stupid assholes." Drew said. "Let's hope they get back before someone kills 'em, or we'll never know how many Pataglia brought with him." He turned to Detective Miller, "When this is all done, either bust those two or take 'em on a one way ride outta town."

Fabrio backed up. Gi Carlo followed. When they got back to the door, Fabrio checked outside, and both ducked through the doorway. Standing in the alcove, sheltered from the pounding rain, they watched Shark and Wade split up and walk off.

Fabrio whispered. "Let's get rid of two guys."

Gi Carlo nodded. "I'll take the tall one."

CHAPTER 32

Rollie, followed closely by Drake, watched from the dock ramp as the two gangbangers made their way around the building next to the one with the stripe. When the two dark figures stood next to it, the building took on a whole new dimension. It was much longer than first thought, and looked like a football field could fit inside -- and still have room. The two goons separated. Both were dressed in black. They trudged through the rain and stopped.

"Your call," Rollie said.

"It's a big payday."

"We can either watch it all slip away, or go get the actors before they get hurt."

Drake protruded his lower lip, "We don't know how many are out there."

"Yeah. There's probably six."

Drake curled his lip while the rain soaked them. "You gonna help here?"

"We asking for more money?"

"You bet."

"And I'm getting part of it?" Rollie asked.

"Don't push me."

"Hey, if they're shooting at me, I should receive a bonus of sorts."

"Okay, I can do of sorts." Drake snapped.

"Drake?"

Exasperated, Drake raised his shoulders. "If we go there, and if we survive and if we get the actors out, we'll be partners."

"Cool." Partners! They watched the two human shapes, standing still, in the same place they were. Then, they saw two more figures move in on the first two. "What the hell goin' on?"

"My bet, they're trying to stay dry." Drake offered.

"Out in the rain?" Over Drake's broad shoulders, Rollie saw a person run from one boat shed to another, and disappear. "Let's move over to the Chris Craft to your right."

"As one?"

"Why not? I'm kinda getting used to it."

They hunched together and moved from the shelter of the canopy, out into the open. Rollie glanced over his shoulder and saw the dark figure running and ducking. They stepped across the dock and got up close and personal with a thirty-eight foot Chris Craft.

"One in black, over your left shoulder." Rollie whispered,

"We can't stay here." Drake looked around for shelter.

"You think?" Rollie searched with Drake. Everything was too far away.

The dock was sparse on shelter, one boat lift, two small storage sheds, and a bunch of dinghies. Basically, there was no place to hide, except at the side of the powerboat they were standing next to. The closest other shelter was a visitor's landing fifty-feet away. Rollie gestured with his head, and Drake looked.

"Too far," Drake answered.

"We're sitting ducks." Rollie didn't get nervous, but invisible little varmints were busy crawling beneath the skin.

"Maybe he didn't see us?" Drake said thoughtfully.

"Yeah, I guess he could be blind."

"Let's just stay wait here, and see if he comes back."

Rollie scanned the marina, and saw lots of places to hide up at street level. He turned back to Drake and hit his head on a surfboard protruding from the Chris Craft. The board was loose, so Rollie pulled it down. "We can use this to extricate ourselves to another location."

Drake whispered. "Extricate?"

Rollie shook his head. "You know, free us from entanglement."

"Entanglement?" Drake repeated.

"What would you call our situation?"

"Screwed." Drake answered.

"Okay, but either way if we don't get outta here..."

Drake stared down at the surfboard, "Both of us on that tiny little board?"

"Or we could stay here, and get shot."

"I need a minute." Drake stared at the small surfboard.

"Take all the time you want, Drake."

They heard movement, footsteps in the rain. Both dropped to their knees. Rollie saw the dark image cross above them. Drake saw it too.

"There's only one," Drake whispered.

"You sure?" Rollie whispered back, inching closer to the Chris Craft.

"No," Drake said, following the inch-by-inch movement. "There could be more."

CHAPTER 33

The Watcher had them out in the open and couldn't reach her damn gun. She scrambled around on her knees, crawled beneath the gigantic boat trailer, and found it. She rose and bashed her head on the trailer axel. Standing up, the rain came down in sheets and washed the grit from her body. See across the marina was near impossible. The Watcher made her way back to the edge overlooking the boats. One in the chest, and one in the head she thought. She wouldn't miss, not even in a torrential downpour.

Where the hell did they go? Her eyes scanned down each slip. They had to be hiding, but what were they hiding behind?

She wasn't about to screw it up now. She dropped to her knees and peered down into the marina. Had they moved in those few seconds? Her eyes danced nervously over the platform. Was she looking down on the wrong dock? They were next to an enormous Chris Craft, but she couldn't see that boat either. Where was it? She moved to the next dock.

She crawled along the edge and moved from dock to dock. She spotted a large man getting into a smaller boat. It wasn't Rollie. They had split up. She was looking at Drake Fargo. Damn! She watched Drake try to crawl on board the small craft, and was convinced it wasn't Rollie. She had no issues with Fargo. He could live.

Rollie thought he was shrewd. She smiled at his stupidity. She couldn't be fooled that easily. Rollie was still down there, and now he was alone. She searched over the marina and finally found the monstrous Chris Craft. It was about three hundred feet away, three or four docks over. The rain was relentless, and started to mix with a thickening fog that was rolling in. It was now or never. Rollie, and then Pataglia. She couldn't wait to see the look on Pataglia's face when she shot him. She moved slowly, carefully. She knew Rollie was armed, as was Drake. They wouldn't hesitate to kill her if she gave them a chance.

Draft Fargo disappeared on the small craft.

A car drove through the marina. The Watcher ducked, and froze. The car slowed. She tried to melt into the pavement. The car stopped. This wasn't expected. She had Rollie pinned down, but now someone had her right out in the open. She scrambled behind a trashcan, heard a car door open and close. The footsteps she heard over the wet pavement were heavy sounding, indicating the approaching person was large, and undeniably a man.

CHAPTER 34

Fabrio crouched down and moved to a guard shack window. The rain slashed, without compassion, against the glass. Fabrio stood back in the shadows, and watched Wade peer through the window. Wade couldn't see much. The rain blurred his vision. Fabrio looked beyond Wade. He was alone. Fabrio pulled out a long-barrel twenty-two, with a silencer attached, and fired one shot through the glass. The bullet pierced the center of Wade's forehead. He flailed for a moment eyes wide open, and fell forward, through the window where he stayed. Fabrio waited. Gi Carlo came around and cast a glance at Wade's body.

Fabrio stepped out from the shadows. "Did you get the other one?"

"He went back inside before I could get him. "Gi Carlo whispered.

They crossed the courtyard as Archie stepped out behind them.

"Where you guys been?"

"Eliminating a problem." Fabrio whispered.

"Where's mister Pataglia?" Gi Carlo asked.

"Upstairs with Roland and Santino." Archie gestured with his head to an alcove behind him. "Did you see how many they have?"

Gi Carlo shook his head. "Lots, and heavily armed."

Fabrio saw a bright flash of light. A flashlight. It was at the other end of the striped building. He gestured to the others. "C'mon." Fabrio led the way, followed closely by Archie. Gi Carlo lagged behind them. They walked slowly, in a semi-circle. Archie watched their backs until they entered the striped building.

Once inside, Fabrio moved quietly to a short staircase that led to the first floor. He gestured with his hands, and Archie moved to the other side of the stairs. Gi Carlo stayed back in the shadows. He wanted to make sure they weren't followed.

Fabrio moved down a hallway to the only doorway there. With Archie at his side, Fabrio quietly opened the door. The room was dark. They waited. Fabrio took out a penlight, and found Ben Parker tied to a chair. His mouth was taped. Fabrio searched the area. No one else there.

"He goes with us." Fabrio said to Archie. He turned to Ben Parker. "Where's your buddy?" Fabrio ripped the tape off his mouth.

"They took him." Ben Parker winced. He had been severely beaten.

"How many men do they have?" Fabrio asked.

"I don't know. They pounded on me, killed Raymond, and took Andre away." Tears flushed Ben's eyes and raced over flustered cheeks. "They're gonna kill him, and then come for me."

Fabrio glanced at Archie. "Let's get outta here."

Archie led Ben from the room. "Say a word and it'll be your last. Understand me?"

Ben Parker nodded and went willingly with them. Fabrio raised a thumb to Gi Carlo. They left the building and cross over the courtyard.

Fabrio brought Ben Parker into the room where Pataglia waited. Drego Santino was sitting with Roland. Pataglia rose to his feet when he saw Ben Parker.

Santino smiled, giving Fabrio a hug, "Am I glad to see you guys,"

Fabrio gesticulated, and Roland Wynan crossed the room and stood behind Ben. The color had left Ben Parker's face. He stood like a statue, terrified. Gi Carlo joined Roland by the door while Archie moved to Pataglia's side.

Pataglia studied Ben Parker. "Why don't you tell me what happened to Tawny?"

Ben shook his bleeding head. "I didn't have --"

Roland hit Parker hard in the kidneys. Parker plummeted to the floor. His face slammed into the concrete before he could break his fall. His nose broke, and bled heavily. Roland jerked Ben to his feet and held him up.

Pataglia smiled. "Let's try again." He concentrated on Ben Parker's eyes.

Ben held out his hands in self-defense. "Tawny liked to party."

Roland hit him, and Ben dropped to his knees. Roland was about to pounce on him when Pataglia put up his hand. Roland stepped back.

"What happened to her?" Pataglia whispered.

Ben Parker wiped at his bleeding nose to no avail. It dripped freely down the front of his shirt. "Arnie Aronjelovich took her down the hall to another bedroom."

Pataglia nodded. "Before he took her, what did you do to her?"

He flinched. "We partied is all." Expecting more punishment, Ben cowered.

Pataglia glared at him. "Tell me?"

"We smoked some weed," Parker started slowly, looking at the floor, "took down a few lines, and made love."

239

Pataglia felt the pain in his stomach. "Who gave her the drugs?"

"I gave her some coke," Parker pleaded, "but she had her own weed."

Pataglia asked like a kindly old grandfather, "You give all the girls you fuck around with drugs?" His voice was calm and rational, like a friend talking to a buddy.

"It's what we all do," Ben said. When Archie stepped toward him, Ben felt threatened and blurted, "Yes, yes, the drugs make it easier to score." Then he closed his eyes and waited to get hit.

Archie whispered something into Fabrio's ear, and Fabrio nodded. They walked to the stairwell and stopped. In the window behind Roland, a black man peered through the rain soaked glass. He took several quick looks, and then he was gone.

Pataglia took a deep breath, his eyes tearing up. "So tell me something? Did you intend to help Tawny with her career, or was she just a punching bag you used to get your rocks off?"

Fabrio disappeared down the stairwell, and Archie followed after him.

In the rain, Fabrio and Archie crossed the courtyard. Archie tripped and fell over a dead body. Fabrio helped him up, and Archie rolled the body over.

"Who the hell is that?" Archie whispered.

The man's left eye had been shot out.

"I came down here with him." Fabrio said looking at the body. "That's Sammy."

"An eye for an eye," Archie whispered angrily. "Let go take out a few eyes."

CHAPTER 35

The Van Nuys Police Station was located just east of Van Nuys Boulevard, a couple of blocks south of Victory in the San Fernando Valley. Rader came over the 405, headed east on the Ventura Freeway and exited at Van Nuys Boulevard. The drive took less than fifteen minutes. Rader knew during the day, the trip would take half hour to an hour thirty. Time lost was part of traveling in Los Angeles -- you either accepted traffic delays or moved to another state. The destination didn't matter where you were going, you waited, you fought traffic, breathed smog, put up with graffiti, crime, rudeness, and a whole lot of other inconveniences just to say you lived here. The weather was fantastic, when you could see the sky. The ocean was spectacular without the fog and mist. Problem in California was there weren't many clear days, but you lived for the good ones, and enjoyed them to the max. Rader hated and loved the city. Smog usually hung over everything, and along the coast you had June gloom, clouds, and fog. He loved to walk on the beach in the fog, even when he got soaked from the constant mist. Another reason to put up with the California landscape.

Rader parked in the back area with other police vehicles. The neighborhood had gone downhill over the years as white-collar workers moved to Valencia, Orange County, and Simi Valley. Those who could afford it, moved to West Lake Village or beyond to Camarillo, Oxnard, and Ventura. No one moved to Santa Barbara. Those who lived there couldn't afford to sell, and those who wanted that madness couldn't afford a fixer-upper. Santa Barbara was exclusively for the wealthy. Here in Van Nuys, immigrants moved into homes and apartments with several other families, and they shared everything. The valley had become a monster commune.

Rader showed his ID to the Desk Sergeant. His nametag identified him as Sergeant Moriarty. Mid-thirties, thin as a post, black-hair buzzed to a unusually short crew cut, and dark piercing eyes that silently stated -- don't mess with me.

"What can I do for you?" Moriarty more or less demanded an answer.

"Detective Rader from Santa Monica Division. I'm looking for Detective Mullwood?"

The Desk Sergeant nodded, picked up the phone, and dialed. "This is Moriarty at the desk. You have a Detective Rader out here to see you?" He nodded, "I'll send him back." He hung up and pointed to the door. "Through the door, second hall on your left, third door down. I'll buzz you in."

Two Patrolmen half dragged a teenage Hispanic kid in. The kid fought them with every ounce of strength he possessed. The kid wiggled all over the place to no avail. The main reason Rader transferred to the beach area. They had problems in Santa Monica, but not like Hollywood or the valley. In town, cops lost their humanity. Patience didn't exist.

The kid bellowed, "I didn't do nothin', man. You got the wrong guy."

The patrolmen ignored the kid. Rader had seen it before. Old news.

The kid screamed in their face. "You guys fucking deaf? You hear what I'm sayin'?"

One of the Patrolmen looked at Rader. "He was loading cases of beer from a closed liquor store into his pickup, and thinks we got the wrong guy."

Rader nodded. "Maybe he thought he owned the liquor store?"

The two patrolmen laughed.

The kid didn't think it was funny, and threw Rader the finger. "Fuck you too!"

The locked door gave out a unpleasant buzzing sound; more like a screech as it unlocked. Rader nodded to Moriarty, pushed his way through, and went down the hallway.

Bill Mullwood sat in a small, depressing cubical. He got to his feet when Rader tapped on his door. In his fifties, working on a solid beer-belly, and rapidly losing his hair, Mullwood's cheeks were flushed. Either too much sun or he had a penchant for booze. His suit was dark brown and badly wrinkled. Rader didn't care. He wanted to get this over and go home.

"John Rader."

"Bill Mullwood."

They shook hands. Mullwood came around the desk and led Rader down the hall. As he walked, he talked over his shoulder. "You should'a seen the look on those porn guys faces when we got to their office. It was great. Sick bastards. Their storeroom was wall to wall with cases of that shit. A few less on the street thanks to you." They turned down another hallway. "This chick is another story, a real whacko. When she first called, we didn't take her seriously. Our fault, but we get so many crack heads you don't have enough time in the day to deal with all of them."

"I know what you mean." Rader knew only too well. Hollywood had been so full of the creepy side of life that regardless of how many jails were built, there still wasn't room for all the crazies, pimps, robbers and killers. The jails were so over-crowded -- they'd make arrests, have quick court appearances, and send them to county jail where they'd be released back into the population – circular, revolving door police protection. Delay the inevitable was all the cops were doing. Rader managed as long as tolerated and then transferred out. No regrets.

"I have her in the interrogation room. You wanna see her through the glass before you have the pleasure?"

Rader shook his head. "No, I'll go straight at her."

"You got guts, Rader. She's a real nut case."

Mullwood unlocked the door, and Rader entered.

"I'll knock when I'm finished." Rader said.

"You got it." Mullwood closed the door.

Kali sat with her long, shapely legs drawn up to her chest. Her face carried bruises, a cut lip, a gash on her chin, and a black half-moon bruise under her right eye. She ignored Rader. Her hands shook, so she wrapped her arms around her legs. "You won't believe me either, will you?"

"Why don't you tell me what you know, and I'll tell you what I believe? Okay?"

"Whatever. Nicky Henderson, the guy I thought was my boyfriend is a creep liar. He's a drug dealer and been holding me prisoner for over a year."

"You couldn't run away?" Rader looked skeptical.

"The bastard chained me to the bed when he went out." She flashed her ankle in his direction, showing him the abrasions.

"Okay so far." Rader said. The ankle bruises looked legit. He also noticed her wrists had purple blemishes from being bound too tightly.

"This guy, he walks into our house as if he owned it."

"Did the guy have a name?" Rader took out his little notebook.

"Drew something or other, I don't remember." Kali glared at him.

"Where was the house?"

"What the fuck difference does that make?" Rader didn't answer. "Up Laurel Canyon somewhere. I don't know, up in the hills." She narrowed her gaze, "You wanna hear this?"

"Absolutely." Rader sat back and waited. He knew if he pushed her, she'd clam up.

Kali stared into space. "The place was a dump. Nobody cleaned it. Crap everywhere. Drew, the guy who just walked in, he had these two black guys over, Shark whoever, and Wade something, asshole gangbangers. Anyway, this guy named Drew asked about some electronic stuff Nicky was supposed to have planted somewhere. Then he gets all upset about some woman getting the shit beat out of her, and wants to know what the woman told Nicky, and Nicky says some actors are hiding in a warehouse down at the marina."

Rader sat up. "Did he say what marina?"

"What?" Kali looked at him as though it was the first time she'd seen him. "Marina, you know, a place they keep boats and stuff. Like dah, how many marinas are there?"

"What else did the woman tell him?" Rader needed to keep the story going, and it didn't help asking stupid questions with someone so strung out. Kali was on

245

her way down, and in a few minutes he'd get nothing out of her.

Kali tried to remember. "Some detectives found the electronic stuff Nicky had planted, and ripped it out. Then Nicky tells him about the shootout in a dark house. With bullets flying' all over the place, it was impossible for him to get back inside and remove the electronic stuff." Kali started crying. "Drew was furious they lost the electronics mumbling about how much it cost. That's when he asked where he was."

"Who asked?" Rader said.

"This Drew guy. He said something to Nicky, and then he came into the bedroom, and beat the shit outta me. I was tied up, man." She held up her wrists to verify the rope marks. "I couldn't defend myself." She angrily curled her lip. "He kept asking me, over and over."

Rader shook his head, "I don't understand. What did he ask you?"

"If I was Rollie Kempinelli's wife, and then he wanted to know where Rollie was."

"Do you know where Rollie is?"

"He's driving to the marina, to look for the actors! What part of this don't you understand?" Kali glared at him.

"I'm sorry." Rader closed his notebook. "Please, continue."

"I told him," she stopped, sucking air over her tears, "I said I was married to Rollie Kemp that he changed his name, and this Drew guy shouts, whatever! He lifted up my skirt and stared at my panties, you know as if he could see through them? The creep then looked inside my blouse, at my tits. It was disgusting, the look on his face when he cut the rope." She sobbed.

Rader felt helpless. He ran fingers through his hair, sat back in the chair and waited.

Kali caught her breath. She played with her lips for a moment, then pulled her ratty hair back behind her shoulders, and sat up. "He asked me about my marriage. Wanted to know if I still talked to Rollie. Wanted his cell phone number, then wanted to know where he was right at that moment." Tears streamed down her cheeks, "I said I didn't know and he punched me. He asked about Rollie's accident, how his legs were, and how much money he had. Then," Kali hesitated, stared up at the ceiling, a steady stream of tears rolling over her cheeks, dripping onto her chest, "This Drew guy then said I was lucky."

Rader lifted his shoulders, "Lucky?"

"Yeah, how ironic is that?" Kali snapped. "He said if I was still married to Rollie, he would've killed me. So I ask him if he's gonna, you know, kill Rollie, and he nods and says yes. Said he was going to kill Rollie tonight." She tried to fight more tears from departing her bloodshot eyes. "Then he put his gun under my chin, like this," she uses her finger to lift her chin up, "and says, inches from my face, not tonight doll." The sobs came back, and Kali fought to regain her breathing. "He looked down at me with pity in his eyes and said I'd be killin' myself soon enough with the drugs. That piece of shit sells me the stuff, and then said I'm killin' myself." She glared at the floor instead of looking at Rader.

Rader remained silent and waited her out.

Kali twisted her hair with her fingers, her lower lip protruding in a pout. "The bastard tossed drugs on the floor by my feet. I heard him asked if Shark and Wade were carryin' and they said yes and showed him their guns, so he hired them, took Nicky, and they all headed to the marina."

"Is that it?" Rader asked.

Kali thought some more. "Nicky said he'd be back in a couple of hours as if I was gonna wait for him. He forgot to tie me back up before they left. When they were gone, I called Rollie and told him they were comin' to kill 'im."

Rader watched Kali. There was no doubt, clean and sober, she'd be a ten -- a real looker. "Did this Drew guy, aside from the gangbangers and Nicky, come to the house alone?"

Kali shook her head, "No, I told you, didn't I? Whatever, no he had two other guys with him." She put a finger to her mouth. "One looked like he'd cut your throat for a nickel, and the other one looked like a cop."

Rader perked. "A cop? You've seen the guy before?"

Kali shook her head, "No, I don't think so, he just had that look." She wiped the tears away. "After a while, you learn to spot 'em, ya know?"

Rader knew only too well. "Anything else?"

Kali got a blank look on her face. "Drew said he was from Philly. Told Shark that."

Rader walked to the door. Before he could knock, she blurted, "Do you believe me?"

Rader turned back to her. "Yeah, I believe you."

"They're gonna kill Rollie unless you stop it." She brushed her hair back and wiped the tears from her eyes. "I'm gonna try to get it together. I still love Rollie. I made a big mistake, but it's not too late. You are going to help him, right?" She gauged Rader's face.

"Rollie's my friend. I'm gonna help him." Rader answered her. He hesitated at the door, studied her for a long beat, and felt a pang of guilt. She was pathetic, and yet the eyes held purity, innocence he didn't understand. When she smiled, in spite of the beating, she had a vulnerable demeanor. She worked her pout, the curl of her lips, the body posture, the feminine moves, the eye movements, they all but made Rader feel sorry for her. He asked, "You have someplace to go?"

"No, I need to get in a program. I'm ready. I'm really ready this time. Can you help me?"

"The drugs this Drew guy tossed at you. Where are they?"

Kali sneered. "Still on the floor where I left them. I'd rather die than take his drugs."

Rader turned to the door. "I'll see what I can do for you."

"These guys?" Kali said. "They have lots of guns. I think they might kill anyone who gets in their way. The guy sounded like he was, you know, on a mission?"

Rader tapped on the door. It opened, and without looking back he walked down the hall with Mullwood.

"This case out of Santa Monica?" Mullwood asked.

"Yeah." Rader answered. His mind was racing.

"If we can help, let us know. It sounds as though you got a handful."

"Appreciate the offer. The girl, will you check around and see if you can find a place for her?"

Mullwood was surprised. "You wanna help her?"

"Yeah, she's the ex-wife of a colleague."

"My friend runs a battered woman's facility." Mullwood said. "I'll check availability and see if she can squeeze your ex-wife in. She'll get her some help."

"Thanks."

Rader had to make a few calls before he got to his car. He wanted everyone in his office within the hour. He called the organized crime unit at L.A.'s Metro division and talked to O'Rowrk. They had the resources to narrow down the search for which marina might be the best choice. There were several marinas in the area, Marina Del Rey, Huntington Beach, Long Beach, and San Pedro. If only he had listened to his old buddy. Both Rollie and Drake had suspicions, and now Rader wished he'd have paid more attention to them. The real Rollie Kemp, or Kempinelli was confusing. Where the hell did his friend go? What else didn't he know about his academy buddy? He wondered, as he drove off, if he'd ever get the chance to ask Rollie about it?

CHAPTER 36

Rollie rose up and spotted someone running. The rain was so intense he couldn't determine how many were out there. He hugged Drake.

"What are you doing?" Drake protested.

"Just move." Rollie answered.

Rollie pushed Drake further down the landing to a double slip. He carried the long surfboard under his arm. The board was wrapped in a black zipper canvas bag. On one side of the slip was an even larger boat than the first one, and in the other slip was an inflatable dingy that was out of the water. He could see a boathouse several slips away on the next dock over.

"Let's take the dingy and the board over to the boathouse." Rollie suggested.

"I'll take the dingy,"

"Let's hope it will hold you."

"Very funny."

Rollie struggled with the dingy and finally got it into the water. It needed air, had no motor and he couldn't find oars. He looked around for a way to paddle it. The soft rubber boat started to drift off with the current, when a silent bullet pierced the material and the whole boat deflated.

Piffff, piffff was the only sounds heard as two more shots came, one hit Drake in the back, the other penetrated through his ankle. They were standing together, and both men fell.

Rollie scrambled for the dingy when he first heard Drake moan, and then repeat the groan a second time. Instinctively he pulled Drake back, and then threw the surfboard into the water. It made an enormous splash. He covered Drake with his body as two more silent bullets tore chunks out of the landing and the surfboard.

"If you're still breathing, don't move a muscle." Rollie whispered.

"It hurts like hell," Drake mumbled through his teeth.

Rollie strained to see where the shots came from. He spotted movement, and then he heard the unmistakable sound of a gun being reloaded. A magazine sliding out, being replaced, a distinctive clicking sound. The image hesitated, standing up in the parking lot, waiting, and then he ducked down, and disappeared.

Rollie held Drake tightly, and finally heard him moan. He peered over the bow and saw a person moving in the shadows above them. He was obviously watching, pacing, waiting for movement, and finally he turned and walked away.

"Talk to me?" Rollie whispered.

"Back hurts like hell and my foot feels as though it's gonna explode."

Rollie checked his back first. He found a bullet hole in the center of the jacket material. It didn't go through. He moved down to Drake's shoes and even in the darkness he saw the blood. He ran his hand over the wound. Bone was exposed, and the pain had to be beyond excruciating.

"Damn!" Rollie whispered.

"What?" Drake tried to see, but Rollie was in the way.

"You need a doctor." Rollie tried not to sound panicked.

"Why?" Drake went into a panic mode.

"I told you your feet were too big. You took one just below the ankle."

Drake bit his lower lip. "The whole thing is numb. I can't feel it."

"I gotta stop the bleeding."

Rollie found some rags in the dingy. He lay as much pressure over the wound as Drake would allow. Rollie realized the bullet had passed through the leg, making a mess of skin and tissue on both sides. To stop the bleeding, he tore the rags into strips and tied them tightly around Drake's ankle. Drake finally sat up against the dock post and watched Rollie.

"I think I stopped the bleeding. It should hold for a while."

"Where'd you learn to do that?" Drake grimaced.

"At the police academy." Rollie never thought he'd use that information, but was grateful he paid attention. The only way to get help without a cell phone service was to cross the parking lot to the payphones on the other side. If he had to cross the parking lot, he had time to get the guy who shot Drake.

"I'm not sure if I can walk."

Rollie pushed Drake up against the post. "You're not gonna try. The bone is shattered, so you're staying right here until I come back."

"Where you going?" Drake searched over Rollie's face.

"They assume you were shot in the head and chest, and I think it was meant for me. A contract hit.

The rain and your jacket saved your ass, but I'm not gonna let 'em shoot my partner and get away with it." Rollie pulled out the biggest gun he carried, and brought a bullet into the chamber.

"Kid, listen --"

"Save it. They were after me and got you instead. Now it's personal."

"There's too many of 'em."

Rollie placed a solid bright orange plastic flotation under Drake's foot to lift it up off the ground. He looked at Drake. "I'm sorry they got you instead of me."

"You can't do this alone, Rollie. You're not ready. They'll kill you!"

"I'll get back as soon as I can. Stay where you are."

"Rollie?"

Rollie got up close and personal. "Promise you'll stay right here. If you move, you might not ever walk again, so promise me!"

Drake caved in. "I promise. Just be careful."

Rollie turned and dashed up the ramp to the parking lot. He looked back at Drake, sitting on the dock in the rain. Drake was his family, and he loved the oversized moose. Hurting Drake was unacceptable, and someone was going to answer for it. He looked through the rain at the building with the bright band around it. They'd have to make room for one more. He had no idea who was shooting at him or why they wanted him dead, but it was time to find out.

CHAPTER 37

Fabrio and Archie dashed across the courtyard and made it to the edge of the striped building just before two men came from the stairwell they had come from earlier. They turned in the opposite direction and trudged off in the rain. Fabrio moved along the edge with Archie. He glanced over the yard and watched Gi Carlo leaving the abandoned building and follow two men. The pounding rain limited his vision, and there was no way Fabrio could warn Gi Carlo. The two men were joined by another man wearing dark clothing. Fabrio held his position, making sure they weren't seen. He watched Gi Carlo walk around the edge of the building and duck down. Fabrio waited until the three men went inside. The moment they entered he waved Archie to follow them.

"Where you going?" Archie asked.

"To help Gi Carlo. He's not in any condition to fight. I'll catch up with you."

Archie moved off, and Fabrio ran in the direction Gi Carlo had gone. When he got to the end of the building, Gi Carlo was gone.

Fabrio turned around and saw a tall black man a millisecond before he was shot in the chest. The power of the bullet knocked Fabrio backwards, lodging in his protective vest. He played dead and felt a heavy, wet boot kick him in the ribs. He didn't move.

Someone stood over him, "Tough guy my ass!"

Fabrio felt a hand remove his gun, and then heard footsteps, walking away. His chest hurt like hell. Adding that to the pain from his shoulder, ribs, and the back of his head, he was lucky to be alive. He felt his chest and looked for blood. No blood, but the distressed tissue gnawed at him from everywhere beneath his hairline. Rolling over, he used the side of the building for support and rose to his feet. Wiping the rain from his eyes, he lumbered on, rounding the building after Gi Carlo. Where the hell did he go?

A few yards away, Gi Carlo's body lay face down. Fabrio ran to him, and slowly turned the burly man over. Blood gushed from a serious head laceration and blood seeped from a chest wound. Fabrio couldn't find a pulse, or a weapon. He moved on. Two men crossed in front of him, walking from the parking lot to the building at his side. They entered a darkened doorway less than fifty feet from where he stood. Fabrio inched on. If he survived, he had no idea how he was going to tell Pataglia about Gi Carlo. It would break the old man's heart.

Through a broken out window, obviously the way they had entered the building, Fabrio saw Drew Lipesky. The angry young man was once a friend. They grew up together. Fabrio hadn't seen him in years, but Drew looked the same. The actor, Andre Garrison was sitting on a chair. Fabrio wanted to rush in and kill them all, but he had no weapon, and there were at least five or six armed guys inside who would gladly blow his head off.

A young, tall, pimply-faced kid who was drenched to the bone, moved over to Drew. "Damn it's wet out there. The building they're in has no power. The box must be wired to the street 'cause the only source of light is the low-voltage security floodlights on each floor."

"Can you cut them?" Drew asked.

"No, they're coming from somewhere else and connectors are underground."

Fabrio watched the same black man who shot him, jerk open a side door and enter. He scared the hell out of everyone, soaked and looking like the devil reincarnated. His curly, black hair hung down over his face. "There were nine, but I got rid of two."

Lipesky was surprised. "So there's only seven left? You sure?"

"Yeah, man, I can count, but it looks as if only five might be a problem."

"Why do you say that?" the tall kid asked.

"Cause two are hurt, and they're beatin' the shit outta another one, that's why."

Fabrio pressed himself against the building. The rain felt good on his wounds. He searched for a weapon but found nothing. He returned his gaze back to the men.

"Where are they?" Drew asked.

The black guy pointed out the window, "On the first floor in that building over there."

The longer Fabrio watched, the more he realized he not only knew Drew Lipesky, but a union worker who worked for them named Bobby Manners was in there. The other guy was their cop, John Miller. Damn!

The tall kid looked out the window, right next to where Fabrio stood. "Where's Wade?" he asked. If he turned his head, he'd look directly into Fabrio's face. Fabrio ducked back.

"He'll catch up with us," The black man answered sharply.

The tall kid withdrew from the window. Drew snapped, "Let's go surprise 'em."

Fabrio saw the cop look at the union worker and get a nod.

John Miller looked serious. "We'll stay here and watch your back."

One of the other guys Fabrio couldn't see, said, "No, I don't think so."

Another unseen voice spoke. "Then we have a problem."

Drew talked between his teeth. "Shark, take a look outside. If anything moves, kill it."

"Gladly," a voice answered.

Fabrio had to go. He ducked down and ran back along the side of the building.

CHAPTER 38

The wind changed the course of the rain as Rollie crossed the parking lot and approached the buildings. He decided to come in from the side furthest away from the marina. If he met someone out here, the striped building would be less pronounced than the deserted one with the broken windows. He headed for the courtyard in-between the buildings. Dim light was all he could see through the windows. Shadows moved on the first floor at the end of the building. Rollie watched the shadow of a man's head moving in the striped building, and knew he had people in both. The light totally sucked, and the rain forced the glow from the streetlights to darken.

The sudden movement from the abandoned building stunned Rollie. Six men, all in shadow ran across the courtyard, just yards from where he was hiding. Discretely they entered the striped building at the dark end. Rollie heard the door open and then close.

Rollie followed and moved to a darkened window. The minimal light was enough to summarize Pataglia and his men were inside. Rollie caught a glimpse of Ben Parker and Santino. He couldn't see the other men. It didn't, however, look like a party. Rollie waited behind a row of dumpsters, trying to figure out the best way to get inside, use another door, and get in without being detected. In a film, he had a bit part in, Psycho Revenge, a stuntman buddy, Chuy Burnette, taught him how to open any locked door quietly. Uncle Charlie's teaching was different. It was straightforward and to the point. Just break in any way you can. If it made a little noise, oh well, that's what guns were for. Chuy's lesson was better. It made little or no sound whatsoever. This wasn't a movie, however, and how the hell Rollie was going to get the two actors away from everyone was a mystery. He remembered Chuy using his knife, and on the movie set it worked perfectly. Here, a mistake could be fatal. Whoever shot Drake was inside one of these buildings, and Rollie was ready to take them all down.

Ducking low to the ground, Rollie moved from the dumpsters to the striped structure and hurried down the side of the building where the men had gone. Somewhere along the side of the property he had seen, several service doors or the trash dumpsters wouldn't be there. He glanced over the grounds, the parking lot and off toward the harbor. No one in his or her right mind would be out in this. He'd lived in California a long time and had never seen rain this hard. He remembered his old man talking about how they would surround a building before entering and that he was one of the guys they always left outside as a guard. Rollie froze, melting into the side of the building when he saw them. A group of men came from the other end of the striped building. There were all carrying guns. Rollie dropped to the ground. The rain thrashed so heavily all he saw were dancing shadows. As he inched along the stucco, he came to a small alcove with a door leading inside. He propelled himself into the recess and withdrew the knife from the sheath along his leg. He had men with guns on one side, and on the other a locked door and a knife. Inside was yet another group of armed guys. Not optimal choices. He peered out. They were coming straight to where he stood. If luck were with him, he might get several with his gun. He could also miss in the rain, and they'd shoot him dead. Not a good option. He turned back to the door. What did Chuy say? Use the tip, and slide it into the doorjamb. The only thing that would stop him was a deadbolt. One little deadbolt and he was screwed. Chuy said to hold the knife steady, and when you hear the metal slide, push the door open. He looked out. They were thirty feet away. Three were coming right at him, and two were drifting away. Lightning lit up the sky over the distant ocean. Rollie turned back to the door, slid the blade up into the doorjamb, and when the thunder boomed he lifted the knife and pushed on the door. At first it didn't budge. Then it caved in and opened. Rollie quietly entered into an intensely dark corridor, closed the door as quickly as possible and relocked it, and ducked beneath the meshed window in the door. Shadows filled the window as the men gathered outside the door. The doorknob turned. The lock held. He envisioned the door lock being cut off or smashed from the knife, but it had slipped back to the position he first found it. With luck, it would hold a few minutes longer.

He glanced up and christened the knife as a gift from God. He slid it back into the sheath, careful not to cut his leg, and moved down the passageway toward the only door he could make out in the dark. He held his breath. Maybe he could reason with his uncle? Maybe he could find the Rollie Kemp sense of humor, and charm all of them? Then again, maybe they had no sense of humor. He checked his gun. The safety was off. The chamber was loaded. Then he heard voices.

"You don't understand." It was a man speaking. His voice sounded weak.

"What don't I understand?" This voice was strong and bitter.

Rollie tried the doorknob, turning it slowly. Unlocked. A hollow sounding thud came from inside. Someone was hitting another. Gut wrenching gasps followed.

"How could you be so stupid?" Another voice said.

Rollie turned the knob all the way and edged the door in. Through the crack, he could see Andre Garrison sitting in a chair. A man holding a gun stood behind Andre. By the door stood a bald headed man. Rollie could get the drop on one, maybe two, but the guy behind the actor was a real problem. He couldn't see how many others were in the room. He didn't know where the guys outside went, but he'd only get one chance to do this right. He braced himself, building up the courage to step into the room, and put his life on the line. Ready. Now!

CHAPTER 39

Before Rollie could move, the door behind him opened. He froze. Melting back into the shadows gun in hand.

He heard a man's voice, somewhere, seething. "They killed my little brother!" The voice had crazy written all over it.

Rollie held his position and could only watch as a kid with bright red hair burst through, followed by two large men, Ben Parker, his uncle Anthony Pataglia, and Drego Santino. They trained together through the door Rollie was about to open, and all hell broke loose.

"Fuck all of you," A black kid spit out, firing his Uzi wildly.

Drew Lipesky followed suit, as did the tall skinny kid, all shooting at the same time. Rollie ducked, and bullets flew everywhere – missing everything except the wall. Rollie sprung like a cat, grabbing the tall skinny baldheaded kid. They grappled, tumbled to the floor, fists flying and then Rollie was able to pull the kids head back. He did it so quickly, just as the kid turned. His neck snapped, and he dropped to the floor.

The guy with red-hair yelled, "Oh, shit!"

The black kid continued to spew bullets at everything and anything. He hit Ben Parker in the hip, put several holes in the chest of the person standing next to Andre, put two in the wall just above Santino's head, and then he spun on Pataglia. Andre Garrison dropped to the floor and covered his head with both hands. Rollie saw two men run outside. They didn't come back.

The redhead grabbed Drew and threw him to the floor. Drew fired off several shots, missed, and they tumbled over each other, with Drew's gun exploding several wild shots. He managed to hit the redhead in the side of the head with the butt of his handgun.

Rollie couldn't tell who was on which side. Men were punching and shooting at each other, but no one seemed to go down. The black kid missed Pataglia, ran out of bullets, and pulled an enormous pistol from beneath his shirt. Rollie jerked Pataglia's arm, pulling the older man to the floor, just as the black kid got off another round. Rollie returned the gunfire, hitting the black kid in the shoulder. He spun around, and then took aim at Rollie, but Rollie's second shot tore a hole above the black kids left temple. Drew got the upper hand on the redhead, bashing him over and over with his gun. About to kill the redhead, Fabrio fired twice, both into Drew Lipesky's chest.

Rollie lowered his gun, walked to Andre Garrison, and helped him up. Andre surprised Rollie. He stood up, grabbed Rollie's hair, and jerked his head back. Andre slammed a gun in Rollie's back. He glared at Pataglia.

"You're a stupid man, Anthony. I knew if we had Tawny killed, you'd crawl out of your hole."

"You killed Tawny?" Pataglia asked.

"No, I don't touch whores." He pulled Rollie closer. "I had one of her girlfriends take her out. Tawny had a thing for pretty girls."

"How dare you..." Pataglia tried to get up.

"What?" Andre cut him off and pushed Pataglia back to the floor with his foot. "Call her a whore? Anthony, she was a lesbian whore. She slept with anyone, and she did it all in the name of hatred for you. That's how she died, old man, she was in bed with a woman. Problem for her was the woman was hired to enjoy her first, then kill her."

"Why?" Pataglia blubbered, the tears drowned out his anger.

"When they killed my great uncle, they spoiled the plan to consolidate family business, but now we have the men, the money and the know how to do it right. Your way is out dated."

"I don't know what you're talking about." Pataglia said.

"My great uncle, Joe Masseria, he was the Boss of New York's lower East Side, but the likes of your family got rid of him." Andre Garrison sneered.

"You have it wrong, son. We had nothing to do with his death." Pataglia rose to his feet and winced from his wounds. Fabrio moved in behind him and held him up.

"It doesn't matter, Anthony. We're taking over." Andre Garrison said. "We can make more money selling one little shoe box bomb then you can earn in a year. We got buyers all over the world, and they pay in cash. No more garment, trucking or shipping problems. No way to attract the tax boys, and best of all, no need for racketeering reluctant parties."

"What?" Pataglia screamed. "Now you turn on everybody and blow 'em up? Is that what we've become, terrorists?"

Andre Garrison laughed. "It's the new way of doing business. You set off a little disturbance, a few people die, and then you ask for the big bucks. They pay, you move on, they refuse, and we blow their office building and everyone in it. The entire company and all their records go bye-bye. Amazing how few follow in their footsteps."

"Where'd you get the seed money? Where'd you get the bombs?" Pataglia was beside himself with rage.

"It would've been easy, had this traitor," he kicked Ben Parker in the ribs, "joined us. But no, mister goody-two-shoes here would rather party than do serious business."

"I thought you two were inseparable?" Rollie said. His head hurt like hell. Felt like Andre Garrison was pulling his hair out, one strand at a time. He needed to buy time.

"We grew up together. Everyone thought, because of his name, he was related – was family. He's nothing!" He stared down at Ben Parker. "Our names became an E Ticket. Moe Brayden took us in, funded our films and introduced us to Mark and Drew. We grew, but stupid Ben and Brayden didn't want to go along."

Rollie felt the barrel of the gun press harder into his spine.

"Why didn't you go out on your own?" Pataglia asked.

"You still don't get it, Anthony." Andre Garrison said. "Louis Baxter skimmed off millions for us but got greedy. Your close friend, Ronnie Mauten wanted more money, so he stepped in to help us, but his insistence to bring you into the deal got to be too much. We'll take care of Moe Brayden later." Andre Garrison paced the room, pulling Rollie with him. The gunman helping him, kept his weapon trained on everyone.

"Where'd the bombs come from?' Rollie asked to try his best to keep Andre talking.

"Everyone's using them. Where do you think the Palestinian's or the opposing Iraqi's get 'em? Are you all dumb, deaf and blind? Look around you, Iran, China, and Russia all have nuke capabilities. They've mastered using the little bomb to make big statements. So, a few of us figured there was big money to be made." Andre looked down at Ben Parker. "Ben here made all the money but didn't want to share or participate." He kicked Ben Parker again. Ben Parker groaned, almost blacked out. "It took more than I had saved, but then Louis suggested pension money. They had lots of it. Why not use it to better our cause? But Anthony kept getting in the way with all this legitimate crap. The only way to draw you out was Tawny. Man how she hated your guts. Girl would've done anything to drop you. It was easy. She was trash, so she went the way garbage goes."

"And you don't think the cops will put this all together?" Rollie asked. The gun was hurting like hell, pressing against his spine. Remarkably he still held onto the gun in his hand. Andre Garrison had forgotten about it, and the other gunman hadn't noticed. Rollie gripped it tightly, and hoped he'd get a chance to use it. Rollie looked at the stocky guy holding Pataglia up. Their eyes locked. Both acknowledged a move had to be made, and soon.

Andre snickered. "Cops? Nah, they're still in the dark ages, searching for ways to put crime families down. I'm not on their radar. We have guys inside. We watched Homeland Security, but there was nothing there. They're like the CIA, all on their way out. And you, Anthony Pataglia, you too are in the way. Like my old man said -- you have to go!"

Andre Garrison aimed his gun at Pataglia, and Rollie made his move. He sent a heel into Andre's chin, stepped to the side, and fired his gun into Andre's head. The blunt impact killed him instantly. Andre's gangster froze, giving Fabrio time to shoot him.

Archie jumped up, about to blow Rollie's head off.

"Hold it." Pataglia yelled

Rollie stood in the middle of the room, still holding a smoking gun. Rain smacked the windows with such force it felt as though they would shatter at any moment. Lightening lit everything and must have struck something mighty close. When the clap of thunder rumbled, the whole building shook. Ben Parker rolled around on the floor, grasping at his hip. Santino huddled in the corner, half out of his mind. Roland was dead.

"He just saved my life." Pataglia said.

Rollie lowered his gun, as did the fiery redhead. Rollie stepped forward to check the pulse of the man lying on the floor next to Ben. He was dead.

The redhead stared at Rollie. He still held a gun in his hand, but it was pointing down. His eyes were burning. "And who the hell are you?"

"Rollie Kemp."

Pataglia stared silently at Rollie, his eyes roaming over him with mixed feelings of hatred and love all rolled into a strange expression. "You've grown up, Rollie." He looked at the others. "Rollie's my nephew." He turned back to Rollie. "And now I owe you."

"You owe me nothing." Rollie said.

Pataglia crossed over to Rollie and offered his hand. Rollie hesitated before shaking it, and that's when the window shattered. The explosion of a muffled gunshot broke the silence. Pataglia went down. Rollie spun toward the window, firing three quick rounds through the broken glass. Though the rain continued to pulverize everything, they all heard the thud of a fallen body outside. The redhead ran to the aid of Pataglia, and Rollie raced outside.

CHAPTER 40

The Watcher was mortally wounded. She crawled, with frantic gestures, toward her gun. When Rollie got outside he kicked the gun away, and pulled the hood on her jacket off to reveal Shelly Bufko, his accountant! Shot just above the neck protector, she was bleeding profusely.

"Shelly! What the --" Rollie couldn't believe his eyes. He'd known Shelly for years.

The redhead came out next to Rollie and stood over Shelly. They watched blood flow from the gunshot. "Who is she?" The redhead asked.

"My accountant." Rollie bent down next to her. "Shelly?"

"Why won't you die Rollie? I tried to run you down, shot you twice, and you're still here." She gurgled in her own blood. "You're supposed to be dead! I saw you fall into the water." She coughed, strangling in her own fluids. "Why didn't you die? You were floating in the marina." Her eyes drifted up. "This is a joke, right? We're both dead, aren't we?"

"You missed, Shelly. You shot a surfboard." Rollie watched her struggle trying desperately to stay alive. Shelly grimaced refusing the accept the conflict between life and death. The helplessness of it all.

"No, I never miss." She strained to see past him. "What about Pataglia?" Her eyes blinked rapidly. The Grim Reaper was waiting to collect her miserable soul. "Pataglia is as dead as his daughter, right? I got them both, didn't I?"

"You missed him, too," Rollie lied. "Put a big hole in the wall."

"No, no, no, no!" She gasp, her breathing sporadic, "I can't go out like this."

She coughed, shackled by the constraints of a body closing shop. She reached out and grabbed Rollie's collar, pulling him down close to her face. Her eyes danced nervously, piercing his vision, trying to keep his face in focus. "It was nothing personal, Rollie. You're a nice guy. It was a contract, like Tawny, and I honor all my contracts. You're so lucky to be alive. I can't believe I missed you three times. You're --" The words caught in Shelly's throat. Her eyes got wide as the last breath seeped from her lungs.

Rollie stood up and stared at her.

"Now I recognize her," the redhead said. "That's The Watcher. She was one of the best contract players in the country. Damn."

Rollie lifted his eyes to the redhead. "She was the hit man who killed Tawny?"

"Hit woman, friend. Guess we never know who's comin' after us, do we?"

"Guess not." The hair on Rollie's arms stood up. He'd made love to Shelly. His eyes traveled back to her. She always appeared to be so naive, and sexy. The Watcher. Rollie felt sick.

Archie patted Rollie on the back, "By the way, my name's Archie."

Rollie shook his hand, still numb from the impact of what Shelly had done – of what she was.

They went back inside and found Pataglia back on his feet. The top of his shoulder was very bloody. Fabrio had gone outside and collected Gi Carlo. He was still alive, but not doing well. Gi Carlo was in tremendous pain. Covered in blood, his face was a mess. He said nothing when Fabrio brought him in. Off in the night, sirens and approaching helicopters could be heard.

Pataglia came over to Rollie. "Can you handle this?"

Rollie looked at the carnage and nodded. "Yeah, you better go." He'd have a hard time turning his uncle in. The man wanted to bury his daughter and go home. Had he managed to kill anyone decent, Rollie might've thought differently. Instead, Pataglia was a lonely old man. His punishment was the memories he'd have to live with.

"Now Tawny can rest." Pataglia stood before Rollie, studying his features. "Lipesky wanted you dead. One of the men your father killed was Mark's older brother Jake. You remember your father comin' home all bloody?"

"I remember."

"Lipesky didn't know where you were. He's been lookin' a long time – ever since your old man killed Jake. He's carried the vendetta against you for years."

"My mother said that's why they killed pop. Revenge. I had nothing to do with it."

"No, you didn't, but Lipesky didn't care. He needed revenge to get closure, and getting rid of all the Kempinelli's was his goal. It's over now, Rollie. Anytime you want to come back to New York, please call me? I could use someone like you to help run my company."

"We live in two different worlds, Mr. Pataglia."

"Uncle. Please call me uncle. We are flesh and blood."

Anxiety was crushing Rollie's chest. "Yeah, okay, Uncle, but I won't be coming back to New York. Am I safe, or do I continue to look over my shoulder?"

"You're safe. You have no beef with Moe Brayden or me." Pataglia's eyes flushed, a single tear rolled down his cheek. "Thank you, Rollie, for saving my life."

Rollie's head moved slightly. He wasn't sure of anything. How could he be pleased? Even if Pataglia was his uncle he was still a crime boss.

The bloodied, heavy-set man came up behind Pataglia as the sounds from the sirens grew louder. He stared at Rollie. "I'm Fabrio. Sorry I shot at you. You're a bad shot, and still managed to hit my shoulder, so we're even. He glanced at Pataglia. "We have to go."

Pataglia bowed his head. "I know, Fabrio," He took one more look at Rollie, then his eyes traveled down to Ben Parker writhing in pain. "Our apologies Ben Parker. Your connection with Moe Brayden sent us in the wrong direction."

Ben Parker was sitting on the floor staring at Andre Garrison. His stare glazed into a black hole only he saw. The spirit and sarcasm was long gone. Rollie was wrong about him too. His connection was as a child. He and Rollie had something in common.

"When his head clears," Rollie said, "I'll make sure he knows."

Fabrio leaned in close to Rollie. "If he has anything to say, remind him what he's doing to young girls is sick. Who knows, maybe he'll wake up?"

Rollie glanced at the Ben Parker. "I doubt it."

"Me either." Fabrio said.

Fabrio helped Pataglia to the door. They walked out without looking back. Archie stooped over, placed a dead man on his shoulder, and disappeared behind them. Rollie looked around the room. Blood and bodies were everywhere. He turned to

Santino. "Can you help me get my partner out of the rain?"

"Who's your partner?"

"Drake Fargo."

"I know Drake, he's done work for me." Santino's face was ashen. "Where is he?"

"Down on a landing in the marina. Foot got shot up pretty bad."

Santino put his hand out, and Rollie shook it. The helicopters and sirens were getting closer, louder.

"Thanks," Santino said. "I wouldn't be alive if you hadn't intervene."

"Good thing I'm getting the hang of it." Rollie said as the two men walked out the door.

CHAPTER 41

LAPD swarmed over the marina, racing every which way in search of evidence. The Organized Crime and Vice guys were everywhere. The parking lot was littered with various detective and patrol cars. Helicopters hovered overhead, some news media, some law enforcement. The Harbor Patrol had the waters covered, and somehow Pataglia and his men had slipped through the cracks. There was no evidence they'd ever been there. Drake lay in the back of one ambulance and Ben Parker was being attended to in another. John Rader and his team of detectives spread out making notes and taking pictures. Rollie watched FBI agents invade the docks and buildings like hungry termites. Rollie sat on the ground with Drego Santino. The rain had stopped, but the fog was thick, and the chill factor crept like a sneak into the center of their bones.

Rader came over, leaned against the building and lit a cigarette.

"Those things will kill you," Rollie said without looking up.

"I'll quit when I grow up." Rader looked out at the ambulances, and the EMT's who worked over both men. "This is a mess, Rollie."

"Yeah." It was the only thing Rollie could think to say. Nothing he could say would explain what happened. Hell, he had a hard time believing it.

Rader waited. "That's all you got to say?"

"Lots of blood." Rollie mumbled.

Rader raised his eyebrows, brushing back his hair, "And it went down just like you said?"

"Bodies," Rollie mumbled.

"Dead bodies," Rader added. "Let's go over it one more time so I can get a clear picture in my mind 'cause I don't get it, and LAPD has asked me to wrap it up for them – since we seem to have started the whole mess." He glared at Rollie. "They don't get it either."

Rollie stared out, "Shelly."

Santino said nothing.

"Okay," Rader started. "These guys were after you, and you were looking for the actors, whom you were told, incorrectly, were on Mr. Santino's boat."

Rollie corrected him, "Yacht."

"Right, yacht." Rader's hair fell over his forehead. He left it there. "So these guys, along with that actor, Andre Garrison, came to kill you. You don't know why, they just came, right?"

"Right out of the dark," Rollie said.

"Yeah, right, it was dark. So let me get this straight. They came in shooting, missed you, got one of the actors, a few others, and that's when you shot 'em? Is that how it went down?"

"Something like that." Rollie wanted a warm bed.

Rader read from his notebook. "Then, you said there was some lightening..."

"And thunder," Rollie added.

"Oh yeah, let's not forget the thunder. Then, the ah, the window shatters and that dead broad over there..."

Rollie nodded thoughtfully, "The Watcher. Shelly Bufko. She killed Tawny."

Rader looked at him, his eyes squinting like he didn't hear what was just said. "She killed the girl at the party?"

"And ran the guy off the road in Malibu Canyon."

"Anything else?" Rader got testy.

"Yep," Rollie answered, "right before she died, she confessed to shooting the guy at the airport and leaving his body in a trunk of a Rolls Royce." Rollie moved his head a fraction of an inch. His clenched fists went deeper into his pockets. "Yeah, she shot the surfboard, the dinghy, and Drake's foot before she tried to kill me. Shelly."

Rader got more and more annoyed. "Shelly. Right." He took out his little black notebook, flipped it open and made a few notes. "So, she comes down here to kill you, hits the dinghy, the surfboard, and Drake." He stopped writing. "She tries again, misses again, and that's when you shoot her in the throat." He waited for another smartass remark but didn't get one. "Part of what I don't understand is why Andre Garrison is laying up-side-down on top of those other guys?

"They all worked for him." Rollie said.

"What?" Rader was exasperated.

"He was trying to start a crime family." Rollie tried to explain it. "Had 'em all killed."

"Oh, come on, Rollie. You don't expect me to believe this crap, do you?"

"Suit yourself. Drake believes it, and so does Ben Parker."

"Was Andre Garrison coming, or going?"

Rollie shrugged. "I don't remember that part."

Rader looked at Santino, and he shook his head. Rader closed his notebook, reopened it, read a few things, made some notes, and slammed it shut. "Great. I'll have to face the D.A. in Los Angeles with this bullshit, you know? He'll love this one."

"Love is good," Rollie mumbled. He was tuning everything out.

"Oh, Damn Rollie, c'mon. What really happened here?"

Rollie looked out at the marina. The sky was starting to do its morning tricks, turning from dark gray, to lighter shades, and then the pink started to dance in. Without looking at Rader, he mumbled, "Check the guns. It's all right there."

"Oh, we'll check 'em," Rader said with a big nod, "and I'll be talking to your ex-wife again."

"Good." Rollie got up, and Santino joined him. "Can we go home?"

"Rollie, listen, there's --"

"They tried to kill us, John. A guy needs some sleep after someone tries to kill you."

"The crime unit will want to talk to you again." Rader persisted.

"You can handle that for me, right?" Rollie knew Rader would do just that. Rader would deal with it all. Drake would play dumb if questioned, and Santino wouldn't say anything.

"This is serious stuff, Rollie." Rader walked in a little circle.

"First, I have to go to the hospital. Ben needs surgery, and I'll never get rest until I know how Drake is.

Mr. Santino here feels so lucky to be alive, he'll probably sleep on his boat, right?"

Santino nodded without looking at anyone in particular. "It might be the first time I really enjoy that damn boat. You're both welcome to drop by for a drink." Santino walked off toward his yacht. No one stopped him.

Rollie turned to Rader. "Now all I need to do is find our car so I can get to the hospital."

Rader pointed. "It's over there."

"No problem." Rollie sort of collected himself and dropped his head into the morning breeze. His hair separated in a million directions. The rain was gone. The gentle breeze felt good, he looked like crap, and the best part was he didn't care.

Rader put up a hand, "Is that it?"

Rollie bounced his head once, "Yep."

Rader started to say something, but gave up. He opened the little black notebook, slammed it shut, and tucked it into a pocket. "Damn actors!"

"I'm not an actor, John, I'm a private eye."

"Bullshit," Rader shot back, "you just gave the best performance of your life."

Rollie, with his back to Rader, waved over his shoulder. His mood elevated with each step. He walked into the lifting fog, in the general direction of his car. Being alive was a good thing.

CHAPTER 42

Rollie slept in the corner of room 230 at St. John's Hospital in Santa Monica. His tall lanky body was curled up on a chair in a remarkably uncomfortable position. A nurse covered him with a blanket, disrupting an awful dream. He woke with a start, jumped to his feet and yelled, "No!"

"Okay," the nurse said indignantly, gathering up the blanket, "I was just trying to help."

Rollie's eyes traveled around the room. Drake was smiling, the nurse frowning, her thin lips all curled and drawn inward. Rollie knew she wanted to get nasty and say something she might regret. Only a consummate understanding of professional composure prevented her from dumping all over him.

"Oh wow, I'm sorry." Rollie said. "I was, ah, well, never mind."

The nurse tossed him a look that said drop dead you jerk, and left the room.

Drake clapped. "That was nice."

Rollie crossed to the bed. His neck was tied in a knot, and his back felt like a herd of buffalo had stomped on him. "You're awake and sarcastic. Good, now I can go home."

"You've been here all night?"

"Yep." Rollie was embarrassed. Drake's injury scared him.

"I didn't know you cared that much." Drake teased.

"Well, now you do." Rollie avoided his eyes, "Don't let it go to your head."

"How's my foot?" Drake tried to look down the bed.

"Bigger than it was." Rollie covered the foot with an extra blanket.

Drake laughed. "How bad? The doc said was it might eventually heal. What the hell does that mean?"

"It was a big bullet." Rollie could see the damage even though it was covered with a mile of bandages. The image tossed his stomach.

"I can't feel anything." Drake said, still trying to see his foot.

"They did a spinal. You're numb from the waist down."

"Oh. Did I hear you tell the cops she thought she shot me in the head?"

Rollie nodded and laughed. "Yeah." He looked at the foot, and then Drake's head. "I can see the resemblance."

"Wait 'til I get out of this bed!" Drake faked movement and paid for it.

"If I told you once, I told you a hundred times, you need a foot reduction." Rollie was glad to see Drake kidding around. It made a lot of crummy feel good.

"Get out of my room." Drake pointed to the door.

"Okay," Rollie walked to the door.

"Rollie?"

Rollie turned off, wearing his usual smile. "Yeah?"

"Thanks, partner."

"It's a bitch being humble, isn't it?" Rollie enjoyed pushing him. Make him want to get back on his feet sooner.

"Get out of here." Drake pointed again.

Rollie was shopping to replace the groceries that had spoiled from neglect and absence, when his cell phone started vibrating and ringing at the same time. A man on the other side of the fruit counter took out his cell phone at the same time Rollie did. He shrugged at Rollie and moved on. Rollie looked at the text message on the tiny cell phone screen, and stepped outside to call. He went back inside, paid for groceries, and got it his car. A dark maroon car followed after him. He drove west down to Pacific Coast Highway and headed north to Malibu Canyon Road. The maroon car went south. Rollie pushed paranoia out of his head.

The Dakota House was located on the south side of the canyon, up a private road that was buried beneath over-hanging trees and greenery. The house itself was an old rustic mansion that had been donated to the Dakota Society. The association's sole purpose was to help those less-fortunate individuals who could no longer cope with society's ills and peer pressure. Most residents had relented to a life of drug and alcohol addiction. Such was the existence of Kali. He paid to have her relocated from the San Fernando Valley halfway house the cops had arranged for her. He was grateful his investments allowed him to accept the Dakota House expenditure without creating a long-term financial burden on his portfolio.

Rollie marveled at the large living room that now served as the waiting and recreation area. A giant screen TV stood against one wall and small couches and lots of chairs clustered from one end to the other. All the furniture looked donated. Nothing matched. Some pieces were expensive, and others were a bargain-basement variety. The house had a smell to it, something like lemon disinfectant used in hospitals, only a bit stronger.

An elderly woman with white hair sat at the small desk near the front door. No window bars, or restrictive devices appeared anywhere. The residents could come and go to their will.

Rollie approached the white-haired lady. "Hi, I'm Rollie Kemp. I came to visit Kali Rocha?"

The white-haired lady smiled. "You can wait over there. I'll go fetch Kali."

"Do you ever lock things down?"

"Heavens, no. If someone wants help they stay. When they choose to go back down the hill, we seldom try to stop them. When you come to the Dakota House, dear one, you've already traveled down that one-way road. Most of us have hit bottom several times before arriving here." Her smile faded, eyes blinking shameful memories. "The waiting list is long, the screening process painful, but it is here we all discover, we can fly. Baby birds, stepping from the nest for the first time." She brightened, the sparkle in her eyes returning, "Dependence on others, becomes secondary. We know we can soar solo. I'll be right back."

When she walked off, Rollie's chest tightened, a tug at the heartstrings, a hope that Kali had hit bottom for the last time. A few women were sitting around the huge room, some had guests others were alone. Most, if not all, had the look of hunger and anticipation on faces -- younger than they're aged appearance. Their eyes were shallow, full of promise, bodies thin from years of punishment, yet smiles groped in an effort to find solace. Life was right in front of them, and they had somehow missed it. Rollie noticed all of their clothing was crisp, clean, and colorful.

Kali came out wearing a bright blue dress and white tennis shoes. She had been cleaned up a bit. In spite of the bruises, black eye, and cut lip, she held her head up high. The blond hair was pulled back in a ponytail, and even without makeup, the hint of extraordinary beauty was still there. A year or so back, she could stop a man, any man dead in his tracks. When she spotted Rollie, she broke into a huge smile. Rollie got up, and she hugged him. It was a careful embrace that came from her. He was the reluctant recipient. She had crushed their relationship -- broke their marriage vows, committed adultery and intrinsically destroyed their life together. She carried lots of baggage -- guilt and far more regret than most people could deal with. Proudly, she held her shoulders up, took his hand, and led him outside into a beautiful garden. A waterfall spilled into a large fishpond, flowers reached the sky with colorful blooms, and comfortable benches and wooden swing-sets adorned the yard. Fresh ocean salt air wafted in. Down at the base of the evergreen-covered canyon, ocean waves rolled gently to shore.

Kali didn't even attempt to sit next to him and took a seat in the middle of a two-person swing. They were quiet for a long spell. He didn't know how to talk to her anymore, and spent his time to looked around the grounds.

Kali whispered, "I don't deserve this."

"You asked for help."

Her big, saucy, blue eyes teared up. "Why do you still help me?"

Rollie shrugged. "I don't know."

"We both know it's over between us. You could never forgive me, and I'm not sure I will ever forgive myself." Her gaze drifted off.

"If you can get past the drugs maybe that will help." He said.

She nodded, wiping at her eyes. "Forgive me for saying this, but I will always love you."

Rollie chilled, like someone punched him in the gut. He didn't know how he felt about her. He probably hated her and loved her at the same time. He had a bitter taste in his mouth when he thought about what she had done. Anger and frustration had broken his heart, and yet he had no earthly idea why he kept coming back -- or why he wanted to help her again. She almost got him killed twice. He watched her swing back and forth. She nervously avoided his eyes, in an effort to preserve what little dignity she had left. Tears ran in a steady stream over Kali's sunken cheeks. She ignored the stream that slowly dripped to her breasts and down the front of her dress. He loved this woman at one time. This kind of feelings were gone, for her and most likely any woman. He was convinced a part of him had been sliced out. He was committed to helping her, to do whatever it took to make her happy. Maybe that was still there, and he'd always allow himself to return to her aid. Perhaps that was a way of admitting he still had feelings for her. Maybe it was a cruel kind of love that would always be in his heart. The forgiving part, the forgetting all the heartache she brought him was the black subject he couldn't get away from. Rollie, finally had to say something, "I'd like to see you beat your demons."

She nodded. More tears fell, and she hung her head down. "You can't say it can you?"

Rollie lifted his gaze up into her eyes. "Say it?"

They watched each other, and Rollie's stomach rolled.

"It's okay, Rollie. Down deep inside, I know you still love me. I know you do. You just can't say it. If you didn't, you wouldn't help me or do all the things you do. This place must cost a fortune." She brushed a single strand of blond hair away from her eyes. "Can we be friends? Can we try that?"

"We are friends, Kali."

"Thank you." She smiled, again wiping the tears with the back of her hand. "Can I call you once in a while if I need that friend?"

"Yes, you can." He didn't care. Inside, the need to be around her was still there. She emitted warmth he hadn't found in anyone.

"You won't get angry at me?" Kali persisted.

Rollie shook his head. "No."

"Even if I stumble?"

"Even then."

Kali stood up and reached for his hand. Rollie got up, took hold of her hand, and just held it. She inched toward him but stopped short of kissing. Their eyes locked.

"I want to hold you in my arms," she whispered, "but I'm afraid if I do it will be the last time it ever happens." She was trembling.

He opened his arms. "It won't be the last time." He felt a warmth pass over him.

"Promise?" She whispered.

"Yep." Then he smiled, and it came from the heart.

She walked into his arms, and he held her tightly against him. Her whole body shuddered as she laid her head deep into his chest. He could feel her heart pounding against him. Perhaps, in a tiny corner of his heart, there was an attachment -- but they'd never be a couple again. The damage far out-numbered the feelings. As strong as he felt he was at times, she brought out a flaw in him, a weakness he despised. He didn't have enough strength to deal with her on a constant basis. Being a good friend would be easier. That he could do, and have no regrets.

"Can I show you around, since you're paying for all this?" She asked.

"Sure." They continued to hold each other, but it wasn't a clinging feeling.

"Rollie?" She looked up at him, the back of her hand brushing over his cheek.

"I'm right here."

"I won't embarrass you again, I promise. I know I've said that before, but this time I mean it. This time, I want to get better, and I'm looking forward to being normal again."

"Okay." He'd heard it so many times it made him numb inside. Now she'd have to prove it, more to herself than anyone else. Words were meaningless. Actually doing it was the hard part. Hearing her say the words were a relief. It allowed him to withdraw. She'd cried wolf too many times.

CHAPTER 43

The DA in Los Angeles wasn't happy with Rollie. He backed off and gave Rollie time to work with various justice agencies and clear the case off the books. Miraculously Pataglia's name stayed out of the mix. Moe Brayden's name came up, but there was no connection the Feds could tie him in. Rollie sanitized a few pages in the ledger and together with Rader, turned it over to O'Rowrk. Arrests were made in New York, Philadelphia, Nevada and California. Homeland Security was all over the place. The FBI worked, albeit at arm's length, with the CIA. The bomb maker came from Argentina. He bought bits and pieces from different countries and learned his trade in a terrorist camp in Afghanistan. A CIA agent killed the bomb maker as he attempted to blow up Global Semi-Con, one of the world's largest suppliers of technical computer chips. John Rader stayed in the mix, and was invited to work with Deputy Chief O'Rowrk of the Organized Crime and Vice Division out of the Metropolitan Division in Los Angeles. Rader was given a commendation from both Los Angeles and Santa Monica for breaking a case most law enforcement agencies had been watching for some time. Rollie's name was mentioned a few times by the press, but he was, after all, a private detective, and not a public servant.

Rollie essentially took over the agency. The caseload was light and mixed with deadbeat and cheating husbands. The most compelling case was following an executive's wife because she was spending too much money. The guy wanted to know what she was spending it on. It only took a few days to realize she had a boyfriend, and liked to hang with young guys -- lots and lots of young guys. In between, Rollie was compelled to check on Ben Parker. Ben continued to recover and promised Rollie the sex games, and drug use was over.

Rollie hadn't been to the gym since he started working with Drake. Now that, the case was over, and Eddy Rosewell had paid them, along with their receiving an enormous bonus from the studio, Rollie started working out at the gym again. The gym was in Malibu, and the bay windows that overlooked the Pacific Ocean gave members something to look at while they punished themselves. Three times a week Rollie vigorously worked out, and it slowly started getting him back in shape. Times varied with his schedule, and when he didn't bring a buddy he worked out alone. His stunt buddy, Chuy Burnette was his usual workout partner. At thirty-two, Chuy Burnette was one of those guys who could pass for twenty or forty-five. He stood five-ten, zero body fat and weighed in at one seventy-five. His short cut bushy brown hair was cut short. He worked out five or six times a week when he wasn't doing stunts, and two or three times a week even when he worked long hours. Rollie loved to hang out with Chuy. He was a talented guy, honest, didn't use drugs, had a wicked sense of humor, and knew everyone. He'd been a stunt double for just about every major star in town, so Rollie got to meet lots of stars. Chuy looked like the guy next door and thus worked all the time. If not for Chuy, Rollie thought he'd never meet anyone in the business. Rollie was looking forward to doing the job Mildred had lined up for him, and couldn't stop from wondering if that would be his big break.

Rollie and Chuy started bringing Drake to the gym a week after the shooting. Chuy told Drake he was getting fat and lazy, so Drake forced himself to join them even though he rode around in a wheelchair. They put a steel plate in his foot, and did a bone-graft to correct all the damage. The prognosis was good, and the doctor said Drake would be up and walking within three to four months. Rollie or Chuy pushed Drake from one machine to the next. Drake worked his upper body savagely while Rollie and Chuy did their thing. They took turns spotting for one another on the weights. They laughed and had a great time together. It felt good to get back with the living. Rollie didn't say much about his uncle, and Drake didn't ask. No one else knew about it. All the other witnesses there that night were dead.

After they had showered, Chuy volunteered to take Drake to dinner. Rollie was tired and wanted to go home. He had a deadline with the Tabloid for Robin May's next story, and this one was all about the case they just wrapped up – only a fictionalized version. The names would be hinted at, and nothing fully exposed. Robin was such a crafty person. The paper loved him, and whenever he had the opportunity to write a story, they relished it. The power-players in town hated Robin May. Before the group left the gym, Chuy had taken Rollie aside.

"How's your love life, dude?" Chuy asked.

Rollie smiled, "Dead in the water."

"You gotta get back in circulation."

Rollie shook his head, "Maybe next week."

"Or the week after. C'mon, let's plan a night out, and we'll hit the spots, say this coming Friday night?"

"I don't know…"

"Rollie, in case you haven't looked in the mirror lately, you ain't getting any younger, dude. You gotta hit on the chicks while the looks are still there."

"Okay, Friday night it is." It was the only way to get Chuy off his back.

"Cool, see ya on Friday. Let's meet here first, workout, and then the night is ours."

"Right." Rollie said without conviction.

"A man of few words. See ya,"

Chuy rolled Drake from the gym. Rollie turned and walked right into a stocky man with bulging arms and legs -- a likely candidate for Mr. America.

Rollie held out his hands, "Sorry."

"No problem," the guy smiled, offering his hand, "I see you in here all the time. Name's Bobby, Bobby Manners."

They shook hands.

"How ya doin', Bobby, I'm Rollie Kemp."

"The detective guy that's all over the news?"

"Yeah." Rollie looked around, embarrassed, hoping no one heard him.

"Cool. I understand. You need to stay under the radar, right?"

"Something like that."

"Well, anyway, it's nice to meet you. We seem to come at the same time, so if you ever need someone to spot for you, give me a holler."

Rollie watched closely, the man was smiling, but the eyes were saying something else. "Yeah, I'll, ah, I'll do that."

"I didn't mean to eavesdrop, but I think I overheard your friend say he was a stuntman?"

So that was it. Damn if everyone didn't want something from you. Rollie turned, but Chuy had already wheeled Drake from the building. "Yeah he does stunts."

"Next time I see you guys, maybe you could introduce me? I promise not to be one of those pushy pains in the ass. I'd love to give that a try, ya know?" One side of his lip curled. "I'm one of those crazy bastards who will try anything, and so far, I've been lucky. Maybe your friend can help or, you know, introduce me to someone that can?"

"Next time we come in, I'll look for you." Rollie said, gathering up his gym bag.

Bobby Manners twisted his neck to loosen up. "That would be great, thanks."

Bobby Manners sauntered off. He didn't look back, but Rollie felt a chill. Bobby Manners wanted more than stunt work. Were the Fed's following him?

Rollie took a shower and looked for a hairbrush in his gym bag. What he found was a note with a name and phone number. He laughed.

"Tiler Adams," he read out loud. "So that's where I put your number." Every time he talked to Tiler Adams, she didn't sound interested. She was always busy, and yet she kept asking him to call again. He had seen her a few times after he worked on the TV show Over the Cloud, but that was a long time ago. That damn movie left another bitter taste. Getting fired from one studio job cost him. No one would hire him, he lost his theatrical agent, and yet, that was the movie responsible for his meeting Drake Fargo so maybe the bitter taste wasn't so bad?

At the gym juice bar, Rollie pulled out his cell phone. Tiler would never remember him. He thought he lost her number, and there it was in his bag all that time. He dialed, sitting at the juice bar. As it started to ring in his ear, a cell phone started ringing behind him. The rings stopped at the same time, and an extremely sexy voice answered.

"So who has a private line that's not in my phonebook?" The woman's voice asked.

Her voice in stereo from the phone in one ear, and live in the other. Rollie turned around. She was standing right there with her back to him. She had a cell phone to her ear. A different girl than he remembered meeting. Blond hair cut short, and from the side she was cute as hell. She took a sip of her juice drink, and Rollie caught the intense blue eyes that danced when she spoke. Her body was sensational and not in his memory. No way could he forget a body like hers, course he'd never seen her in tight workout clothes either.

"You probably don't remember me," Rollie said quietly.

"Try me?"

"We met a few months ago."

"Not a good pickup line." She said softly.

"I'm not picking you up, yet."

"No, you're not."

She closed the cell phone, dropped it into her purse, sipped the last of her drink, and headed for the door. Rollie got up and followed. When they got outside, half way into the parking lot, he started closing in behind her.

"You always that tough on strangers?" he asked.

Without looking, she said, "You should spend more time talking to someone else."

"Tiler?"

She stopped walking, and turned around. "How do you know my name?"

"You gave me your phone number, and told me to call you." Rollie could tell she didn't recognize him. The puzzled look spoke volumes.

"No way!" She shook her head while her eyes examined Rollie.

"Yes, way." Rollie said with a smile.

"Where's the note?" She demanded. "Show me."

"Right here." He dug it out and handed it to her.

"Did you just call me?"

"Uh, huh."

"Oh my God." Now she looked straight into his eyes. "Rollie Kemp."

"Yep."

"Why didn't you say something and why didn't you call back?"

"You sort of, hung up on me." Rollie stepped forward and took his note back.

"My grandmother was ill."

"Is she better?"

Tiler shook her head, "No, she passed." Her eyes avoided his, "She was ninety-eight. A great influence in my life." She took a deep breath.

Rollie watched her body movements. "I'm sorry for your loss."

"Me too," her eyes glistened, her face flushed a light pink, "She had a wonderful life, solid marriage, kids, grandkids, the whole nine yards. The last year was tough, but it was time."

It was awkward. Rollie's hands sunk into his pockets. "So?"

Tiler raised one delicate eyebrow, her eyes inquisitive, "Why didn't you call again?"

"Lost the note, couldn't remember your last name, my agent fired me, and things, well they sort of fell apart after that."

She chewed on a finger. "When did you find the note?"

"Five minutes ago. It was in my gym bag." He looked around the parking lot, and then turned back to her. "Can I buy you a drink or something?"

She laughed.

Rollie enjoyed the sound. "How about a cup of coffee?"

"Starbucks should work, they don't care how you're dressed as long as you can pay the bill. It's right down the street." She pointed.

"I know where Starbucks is."

"You going to follow me?"

"Yep. Won't let you outta my sight."

Several others from the gym were in Starbucks having lattes or some other exotic mix. Rollie followed her in. He ordered and brought their coffees to a table. In the dim lights of the coffee shop, Tiler took on a whole new meaning for the word sexy.

"You were laughing?" He watched her.

"Okay," she finally said, "I've forgotten what we talked about, the last time you called. It's embarrassing, but I might as well get it out in the open. I can't have an entire conversation without --"

"It's okay, we didn't have much of a conversation."

"Right," she said, taking in a breath and letting it out slowly, "I'm sorry."

"You still working at the studio?"

She shook her head, the blond ends bounced and took flight, "Oh, no. They're just a bunch of liars and hypocrites. It was temporary. I'm in Veterinary school. What about you?"

"I've become a private detective."

"Whew," she said under her breath. "You certainly know how to find people."

"Very funny." He toyed with his drink, trying not to overwhelm her in one gulp.

Suddenly she frowned, and raised one eyebrow into a perfect arch, "You're, not the one I read about in the newspapers are you?"

Rollie was embarrassed. "Something like that."

"That woman was really trying to kill you?"

His meddlesome eyes sparkled, and a tiny grin formed on his lips, "Imagine that?"

"Let's not go there." She quipped.

"Ouch." He feigned getting stabbed.

She watched him toy with his drink. "Is it always dangerous?"

"No, it's mostly following people and protecting movie stars. It's a good paying line of work."

"Then you can afford to buy me dinner Saturday night?"

He found her eyes and held them. "I can do that."

They finished their coffee, and he walked her back to her car. Rollie thought he saw a maroon car drive by, but he didn't want to spoil the moment. She stuffed her gym bag in the trunk, and they stood by her car for a long time. She still drove the silver Infiniti coupe. The sunroof was open.

"It's funny," she said.

"My jokes are pretty good when I tell 'em." The banter was alive and well.

"When I first met you, picking you up from the wardrobe department, you were so occupied, scared and innocent, and later you punched that actor. I thought you would frighten me. The sudden temper, and all that determination."

"Did I frighten you?" Rollie was sorry the moment he asked the question.

"No," she shook her head. "That wasn't whom you were."

"Is that why you gave me your number?"

Her smile made Rollie feel alive.

"You were different."

"Okay." Rollie already knew that. There was only one Rollie Kemp.

"You were nice as you are now. I hate a guy who's phony or so full of himself he can't talk about anything but himself."

"I'll try to remember that."

"You won't have to." She leaned forward and kissed him -- a light, quick kiss.

He held his arms at his side. He was a gentleman, and he wanted her to know it. "I'll see you on Saturday?"

Tiler smiled. A flirtatious gesture full of mischief, "Seven works for me."

"Me too. Should I just drive around at 7 and look for a building where you might live?"

"You're the detective. Find me." She got in her car and drove off.

Cute Rollie thought. Now he'd have to call in a favor to John Rader and ask him to run her plates. He'd find out why they put a tail on him while he had him on the phone.

CHAPTER 44

Rollie put on the only suit he owned, but had trouble remembering how to tie the necktie. He never wore a suit except to a funeral or wedding. His grandmother always said he looked good in blue, so when he shopped for a suit, the only color he'd buy was blue. Light blue, regardless of the material, looked Polyester. Dark blue was for funerals and weddings, so he chose a shade in-between, a shirt the same color, and a tie in mixed darker blue shades. The black shoes were only worn with the suit. They were new. Drake told him the meeting was no big deal. Drake chose, however, to stay home and recuperate. On his own, Rollie was essentially a fish out of water.

The drive downtown in morning traffic would make anyone crazy -- smog, fog and lots of crazy drivers. He left the damp semi-fresh air of the ocean, drove south on Pacific Coast Highway and then entered the wall-to-wall traffic jam of the Santa Monica freeway – where half of the population of Los Angeles County inched along in their cars. Four and then five lanes of bumper-to-bumper vehicles, people talking on cell phones, tooting horns, and drivers throwing the finger at anyone dumb enough to look at them. Motorists zigzagged from one lane to another in hopes of getting to destinations quicker. Changing lanes never worked, and generally created one fender-bender after another. Rollie came to a complete stop, looked at the empty passenger seat, and imagined the mischievous look only Drake could offer – bushy eyebrows, eyes sparkling and that dumb, stupid grim. Drake laughed with pure enjoyment when he sent Rollie off to get castrated by the District Attorney. Drake's character hung in the air.

"What can they do?" Drake had asked.

"Take my license away, pull my gun permits, put me in jail and destroy me, Drake."

"Yeah," he agreed, "they could do that or worse."

"Will you help me here?" Rollie begged.

"Can't do that, kid. When you fall in the mud, the only choice is to get up. Oh, I take that back, you could stay there and wallow in it."

"You're not helping me."

Drake nodded. "Yeah, it's sort of like the time you left me bleeding on the docks in the worst rain storm to hit Los Angeles in decades. I remember how lonely I felt."

"You're gonna keep rubbing that in, aren't you?"

"Yep."

"The woman tried to kill me, Drake."

"And shot me by mistake. Damn near shot my foot off."

Rollie couldn't pass on the opportunity. "That's cause they're too big."

"See?" Drake smiled. "That's another reason for you to go off alone today."

"Will you bail me out after they arrest me?"

"Maybe."

Drake's smile stayed on his lips until Rollie walked out the door. Rollie's cell phone rang, jarring him back to the gridlock.

"Hey, you almost there?" Drake asked.

"Yeah." He glanced in the rearview mirror and saw the maroon car behind him several lengths back. "You think the DA would put a tail on me?"

"Doubt it, why?"

"I keep seeing the same car, lingering behind me. It's been following me for days."

"You're a big boy, don't worry about it."

"Okay," Rollie said, still gazing in his mirror. The maroon car disappeared. "You didn't call for the heck of it, whaddya want?"

"On your way back, pick up some Chinese, enough for the three of us."

"Three of us?"

"Yeah, Erinn just stopped by to pamper me, and brought along a copy of the rag paper you write for. It seems Robin May's story about us is on the front page. Looks like it might be some good reading. Erinn is giggling her head off. I've only started reading it, but from the first few lines you better hope the DA doesn't see this. Robin Mays is one cruel bastard. It almost reads as if the guy was right there. He must have some mighty good sources."

"Yeah, so I'm told."

"Don't forget the Chinese."

Drake hung up on him again. Rollie was happy his Robin May's story hit the front page. He'd been writing for a long time and this was the first front-page story they'd ever given him. How weird was that? Write a story about yourself, and actually have the damn thing make the front page? Rollie circled the downtown area, heading south on the 101 Freeway where he exited, and turned right on Spring Street. Downtown Los Angeles was sectioned off into enormous square blocks, old and modern architectural designs mixed unimaginative concrete slabs with tinted, state-of-the-art glassed walls. They would never become historical landmarks. Lots of one-way streets, traffic, no parking spaces, trucks unloading packages, and people. Rollie had no idea where everyone was going, and they probably didn't either. The United States District Court stood off to his left. If you were in trouble, this was where you ended up. The Federal Building was a couple of blocks to the south, Los Angeles City Hall stood like a massive ship in the next block, and Los Angeles County Criminal Court was across the street from the Los Angeles County District Attorney's office. Rollie turned on Temple Street and drove into the underground parking structure. The meeting was for 8:30. His watch read 8:28. He was late.

The DA's Office was a maze of cubicles, private meeting rooms, hallways that were abundant, and waiting rooms. They had a staff of nineteen hundred and sixty-two bodies, of which 948 were Deputy DA's, 239 were investigators, and a support staff of 775. Rollie felt like a little speck of dust about to be stepped on. His heart pummeled wildly in his chest while nerves raced in various directions, and, to make matters worse, his palms were perspiring profusely.

In the waiting room John Rader sat. The detective wasn't smiling as he glanced at his watch when Rollie strolled in. "You're late."

"Sorry. Traffic."

"Lame excuse," Rader said. "It's a good way to piss everyone off. Why is it every time someone is late they blame traffic?"

Rader walked over to a receptionist and whispered something. She nodded and got up. She glanced at Rollie, frowned, and then disappeared behind large doors – the entrance to a fortress. A few moments later she returned, and held the door open. Rollie trailed Rader as they walked down a long hallway, finally stopping at a doorway marked Peter S. Haskoff Deputy District Attorney. Detective Rader tapped on the door and opened it. Rollie recognized the two FBI agents, the smiling face from Homeland Security, and Deputy Chief O'Rowrk. They all gave him the look when they walked out of the office.

Peter Haskoff sat behind his desk. His eyes narrowed at the sight of Rollie. He wore a perpetual frown, shook his head when he glanced at his watch, and angrily opened a file – one of many on his desk. Rollie guessed him to be in the mid-fifties. His brown suit was already wrinkled, his tie askew, and his reading glasses had scotch tape holding the left arm in place. His glasses tilted sideways on his nose, and he was used to them being there. Haskoff's desk was littered with case files, and on the floor were more files neatly stacked on top of one another. His comb-over didn't really help cover his shiny head.

Haskoff gestured for them to enter and sit without looking up from the file. "I'm expected in court this morning, so we don't have much time."

Rader cleared his throat. "This is Rollie Kemp."

"I know who he is." Now Haskoff looked up, and the frown grew. He glanced at his watch, just to rub it in. "When I looked over your file, I recommended we prosecute."

"Prosecute? I, ah…" Heat reached Rollie's face as he stumbled for words.

Haskoff continued, "The DA said it looked like a clean shoot, as clean as killing three or four people can be, and said I should move on. He said you did us all a favor."

Rollie took a real deep breath. "Thank God."

"Do more than thank him, Mr. Kemp because I didn't see it that way. Your next shooting will be examined with a fine-tooth comb under a microscope. If so many hadn't already been arrested on this case, I'd personally brush your bones into a cell." Haskoff pushed a file over to Rader. "You can release his weapons." The frown expanded creating itsy-bitsy eyes that zeroed in on Rollie. "You can go, Mr. Kemp. There's a copy of our investigative report in the file. You've been cleared of charges, but we'd like you to think about calling the police next time you feel there might be a shootout, or someone carrying bombs that are about to bring great harm to our country. Perhaps a call to Detective Rader would work. If he's not available, try nine one-one."

"I'll do that." Rollie was relieved, blowing a breath out between his closed lips.

"Impressive shooting." Haskoff said, glancing over the file, "I see you attended LAPD's academy."

"I did, a long time ago."

"You're too young for it to be that long ago." Haskoff said. "How are the legs?"

"I can usually tell when it's going to rain."

Haskoff turned away from the file. His eyes studied Rollie's face. He nodded, trying to get a read on him. "The group before you thought you did one hell of a good job. Because of you, a lot of arrests have been made. So now I'm hearing you would've made a good cop."

"Maybe I'll be just as good a PI?"

"Let me ask you something?" Haskoff dropped his eyes back on the file. "Did you know any of those people before this went down?"

Rollie shook his head. "I do now, but we were originally hired to watch two actors. The studio thought their life might be in danger because of the girl dying at a party they were attending. All we knew is when we got to the marina, there was a group of men and one of them went nuts. Said he was starting a new kind of crime family. They started shooting When we tried to stop it all hell broke loose. Ben Parker is lucky to be alive."

The room fell into a deafening silence that seemed to last forever. Haskoff continued to read through the file. When he closed it, he kept his eyes on Rollie without saying anything.

Rader ran a hand through his hair, moving his body nervously. "Do you need anything else, Pete?"

Still scrutinizing Rollie, Haskoff placed both pudgy hands on top of the desk and clasped his fingers around closed fists. "Two known gang members, a film star, drug dealer, recognizable son of a notorious gangster suspected hit man, and a woman who was identified as a wannabe actress who did accounting and was under suspicion of being a contract killer. Interesting that any of them had enough intelligence to buy and sell mini nukes, but more interesting is the fact you were hired to protect them, don't you think?"

"You're kidding me?" Rollie looked from Haskoff to Rader, and then back to the Deputy D A, "I'm lucky to be alive." He glared at Haskoff. "Wow."

"Yeah, I bet." Haskoff waited, watching body language.

Rollie stood his ground, almost looking casual. He purposely held one hand at his side, and then gestured with the other hand, a simple gesture of innocence. "I did the best I could."

Haskoff twisted his neck, uncomfortably, in deep thought. He turned his chair around and stared out the tiny window behind him. "I guess you did."

Rollie glanced at Rader. Rader shook his head, like he didn't know what to think. Rollie looked at Haskoff's back. "You mentioned something about being in court this morning. I would hate to think it was me that made you late. Are we good here?"

"Sure," Haskoff answered spinning his chair around for one more take of Rollie. "Keep your nose clean." He pulled out a large file and started thumbing through it.

Rader pointed at the door, and Rollie followed him out.

In the hallway, Rollie stopped Rader. "What's with the tail?"

"Tail? What tail?"

"Don't give me that crap, Johnny. "Whoever it is, tell 'em to cool it before I get mad."

"Well, we all know what happens when you get mad."

The elevator doors opened. It was empty.

Rollie held the door open. "Just call 'em off, okay?"

"I'll see what I can do." Rader brushed the hair from his forehead, "Rollie?"

Rollie stepped into the elevator and glanced back, "Yeah?"

"Thanks, the ledger, everything." Rader was being genuine.

"Don't mention it. Glad I could help."

"I'll check, but I don't think anyone has a tail on you." The look of concern filled his face. "Be careful."

CHAPTER 45

For the first time in days, Rollie could look out over the ocean as he drove, and enjoy the view. Girls ran in tiny bikinis, guys had their surfboards, seagulls scrounged trash containers, waves crashed, and Pelicans soared. The atmosphere was majestic, and food for Rollie's soul.

Erinn's new Lexus was in Drake's driveway. The smell of the ocean touched his nostrils, freeing his lungs from the God-awful smog found in the city. The beach gave Rollie a rush, like a kid who won his first Little League baseball game, striking out twelve, and hitting a home run to score the winning run. He was free from the threats and danger.

He carried a large box full of Chinese food in one hand, and clear plastic evidence bags with his guns in the other. He also bought a copy of the rag newspaper, Tell All, when he bought the food, and had already read half of his story by the time he got to Drake's house. He took a small box from within the large one and set it on the floor.

Drake and Erinn were out on the patio. They were sharing a lounge chair, with Erinn sitting in his lap. Drake's foot was stretched out and raised over a pile of pillows. He wore an unsightly cast with wire bars running straight through the foot and out the other side. The

305

doctors called it an external-fixator. The couple looked like the recovery team from a bad accident. Both had a copy of Tell All, read the story out loud, and laughed their heads off.

Drake was in tears. "He crawled up the boat ramp, bullets flying everywhere and grabbed hold of his ankle."

Then Erinn read, "She smacked the window, and shot the wall."

They both roared, tears storming from their eyes.

Drake waved his hand to stop her laughing. "Wait. Listen to this one. Slowly, with shots ringing out all around him, he pulled the huge forty-five from his belt and fired. They stood toe-to-toe, shooting at one another, and when the gangster ran out of bullets the detective's last round struck him in the forehead before he could reload his gun. He cried out..."

They became hysterical. Rollie didn't think it was that funny.

Erinn was so out of breath she could hardly speak. "He's shot dead in the head and still he was able to cry out, Oh no, before his limp body fell at the feet of the detective."

Drake read on. "They were a couple of feet from each other when they were shooting."

Rollie sat down at the table next to them and dished out the Chinese. How ridiculous the story sounded. How did it make the front page? Both Drake and Erinn looked at Rollie and burst with more tears and laughter. Rollie found it contagious and laughed with them. They kept reading the story over and over, and the more they read the more hysterical they became. All shared a bottle of wine, ate Chinese, read more of the story, and laughed until there were no more tears left.

Their stomachs were killing them, as though a bunch of old boxers had punched them.

Drake, finally able to say a few words, glanced at Rollie. "Man you should be a comedy writer. This is great stuff."

Erinn nodded. "Not to mention he should be full of holes."

They went off again, with dry laughter.

Tears flooded Erinn's eyes as she read further. "As he crawled out of the room, his gun still smoking from the flying bullets, his body ached. The detective had taken a merciless beating. He stood up tall ready to face another day against the bad elements of the world. The life of a PI was more than he had expected, but he and his partner were the best, and only the best would have survived."

Drake finally spotted the evidence bag. "They gave you back your weapons?"

"They said I was a hero."

Both Drake and Erinn looked at him with wide eyes and open mouths. "Really?" They spoke simultaneously.

"Well, yeah," Rollie said earnestly. "I did shoot the bad guys, remember?"

Erinn glanced at Drake with the hint of a smile. She turned back to Rollie. "So, they actually used the word hero?"

"Yep." Rollie's response had a certain ring to it, even though he struggled to maintain a zealous face. He avoided Drake's groping eyes.

Drake asked one question. "Are you full of crap?"

"Yep." Rollie answered without missing a beat.

They all laughed again.

"I had both of you."

"Only for a second," Erinn said.

Drake frowned. "What about their investigators?"

Rollie took a mouthful of Chinese. "The D.A. told me to call nine one-one next time."

Drake and Erinn glanced at each other and chuckled.

"Deputy DA must be a sharp guy." Drake said.

"One or LA's finest," Rollie added.

Rollie's cell phone rang. He looked at the caller ID display and flipped open the phone. "This is Rollie Kemp."

"You haven't called me lately. Are you too busy?" It was a throaty woman's voice.

Rollie joked. "Who is this?"

"Who do you think it is hot shot?" The gravel voice coughed.

"My God!" Rollie exclaimed.

"No, but I hope to meet him some day." She said.

"Mildred? Is that really you, Mildred Wanamaker, my agent?"

"Let's not go overboard, funny man. And it's still Miss Wanamaker to you, hot shot."

"What's wrong?" Rollie braced himself for grim news.

"Listen, I'm busy so let's cut to the chase. You own a blue suit?"

"Of course." Rollie looked down at the suit he wore and couldn't suppress his smile.

"Your audition has been moved up to next Monday. You're goin' for the role of the wise guy, and the script says he wears a blue suit." It sounded like she didn't believe he owned a blue suit and was making a big deal out of it.

"I got it covered. You wanna have lunch or something?"

"No hot shot, I wanna see if you can actually get a job. TV show's called Walmandon's Journey. Have you heard about it?"

"Yeah, of course, it got great reviews." Rollie perked up. Damn this old broad was good.

Both Drake and Erinn sat up and watched him.

"You think you can look like a gangster type?" Mildred asked.

Rollie sat down, grinning at Drake and Erinn, "I'll do my best."

"Part is good. The guy has a twin brother who's a cop, so you might get more than a couple days work if you play your cards right." Mildred hesitated. "And don't hit anyone."

"This is great, Mildred." Rollie said cheerfully. "I'll be a good boy."

"Be at the Universal lot at 6 Monday morning. I'll get you a drive-on pass, and you can get directions to the set from the guard at the gate. Don't be late." Mildred waited.

"I won't. Thanks, Mildred, you're the best."

"That's nice to hear. Oh... and hot shot?"

"Yeah?" It was Rollie's turn to wait.

"I don't know who Robin Mays is, but I'll bet you a ten spot he was writing about you in the front-page story today?" Mildred snickered.

"Why would you say that?" Rollie asked.

"Because you're the only guy I know dumb enough to do something like that. Come see me on Wednesday, and I'll tell you what the director thought of you. Oh, and Rollie?"

"What now?"

"Don't hit anybody."

Mildred hung up on him. Rollie closed the phone and looked at Drake and Erinn. "Damn! They want me to star in a big-budget film."

Drake and Erinn spoke simultaneously. "Really?"

Rollie nodded, his back to them, "Wow, I don't know if I can do this."

Drake glanced at Rollie and got serious, "Of course you can do it. This is great, kid."

"Yeah," Rollie said looking out at the ocean. A hint of a smile touched his lips.

Erinn blurted, "I didn't think he was that talented."

Drake kissed her. "Didn't I tell you he was good."

Rollie turned back to them. "Gotcha." They both pointed fingers at him. "Wait, I forgot something." He dashed into the house and carried out the small box he placed on the floor earlier. Rollie set the box on the table next to Drake and carefully opened it. He lifted out a small Golden Retriever puppy and handed it to Drake. Drake came within inches of crying.

"What's this?" Drake asked as the puppy kissed him.

"It's your dog, Ralph. You know, the greeting you've been missing?"

CHAPTER 46

The horror of the shooting slowly crept into Rollie's mind, and replayed itself in dreams that came and went during the night -- bullets, blood and dead bodies. He worked out at the gym, took long walks on the beach, and sat on the sand trying to clear his head. None worked to eliminate the guilt of taking a life. During his tenure at LAPD's police academy, they talked extensively about the after effects of a shooting. Most officers involved in taking a life sought counseling, or it was given to them as part of the mandatory recovery. Rollie had counseled himself his whole life. This was different. He heard his father and Uncle Charlie talk about death and destruction, but that was bullshit talk about things that may or may not have happened. Rollie wasn't there and couldn't relate to their activities. Back then Rollie was a kid, and thank God he was never with his father. He was grateful not to have that kind of baggage in his head. Everyone he overheard his parents talk about were strangers who died, or committed crimes he knew nothing about.

It was strange how quickly everything changed. One minute he and Drake were laughing about watching two stupid actors, and then it took a nosedive. Without time to prepare or think, he took the lives of four people. He could rationalize all day that those he eliminated were scum of the earth, but that wouldn't change the guilt, the gut wrenching remorse of ending a life. The worst part was the constant juggling around in his head. The replays. Over the years he knew Shelly, he adored her, fantasized about her, and finally made love to her. She was, he thought, a friend. As she lay on the ground, strangling in her own blood, Rollie felt the remorse, but she didn't. Her only regret was the failure to honor a contract. Rollie could still see the look in her eye when she shot at him and at his uncle Anthony. Shelly was cold, calculated, and evil. No doubt she would have shot him dead and gone about the following day as if nothing happened.

Rollie drove to the Claw of the Lobster Seafood Restaurant. He'd never been there and had to check the ambiance of the place at night. Tiler was remarkable, and the environment for their date implied how much thought he gave to their rendezvous. The eatery overlooked the ocean and the marina. The view was perfect. Driving on, he took the long way back to his house, driving north on Pacific, which turned into Ocean Avenue. Tiler lived in Santa Monica. She was within walking distance to the oceanfront park and the pier. He drove by the address Rader had given him, not for any particular reason other than to check out her neighborhood. Santa Monica was beautiful, day or night. Lazy trees tumbled over pristine streets, providing shade and beauty. Quiet surroundings, with well-lit driveways, and manicured yards, spread over rolling hills with little or no traffic. It was homey, a great place to raise a family.

Like all bachelors, the need to shop for essentials was always pushed back until you actually ran out of things. The all-night market on Olympic solved most problems and could invariably be counted on for last minute needs. Although it was in an intensely unbridled neighborhood, next to the industrial area of Santa

Monica, it was well lit and essentially considered a safe place to shop. Alongside the store, buried at the back of deep lots, stood dark warehouses, vacant lots, and rolling hills sparse of traffic.

Rollie parked in the crowed lot and couldn't help notice the maroon sedan pulling in behind him. He felt like strolling over and jerking the surveillance team out of their car. Then he rationalized he was in enough trouble, and entered the grocery store. His distaste for shopping never changed – grab the essentials and get out. Like most men, he shopped quickly.

Rollie came from the store bag in hand, when a man's voice called out, "Rollie?"

Without thinking, Rollie dropped the grocery bag, spun toward the voice, grabbed the guy and poked him. Two lightening fast jabs dropped the man. He held up his hand, and Rollie froze. It was the guy from the gym. His nose was bleeding, but he was smiling.

"It's cool, man," the guy said, "I'm Bobby Manners, from the gym?"

Rollie felt foolish. He helped Bobby Manners get up. Other customers walked around them, giving opinionated stares, shaking heads and staying away from trouble. "I'm sorry, dude, I guess I'm a little edgy. You okay?" Rollie rubbed over the pain in his knuckles.

Bobby wiped the blood from his nostrils with the back of his hand. "You got one hell of a punch, but look," he held out his hands, "wouldn't I make a good stuntman?"

Rollie smiled. Over Bobby's shoulder, he watched a silver-haired woman climb behind the wheel of the maroon car, and drive out of the lot. The car triggered paranoia, replaced by crimson warmth washing over Rollie's face. He turned back to Bobby, "I'll say this, man, you can take a punch. Next time we're in the gym, I'll introduce you to Chuy." He studied Bobby's face. The guy still wore a friendly smile and a twinkle in his eyes. He looked excited and grateful. "If anyone can get you in the Stuntman's Association, Chuy can. The guy knows everyone."

Bobby grabbed Rollie's hand and shook it like a pumping oil well, "God that would be sensational. Thanks, I really appreciate it."

Rollie sucked on his lips, the embarrassment lingering. "So I guess we're okay here?"

"What about the punch?" Bobby asked.

"Yeah, I'm really, ah, oh, crap, can I buy you a drink?" He was so humiliated it kind of blanked out all his troubles.

"Absolutely." He helped Rollie pick up his groceries, and then wrapped his muscular arm around Rollie's shoulders. They walked out to the parking lot.

"You wanna follow me down to Q's on Ocean Boulevard?" Rollie asked.

"Yeah, sure. What are you driving?"

Rollie turned, pointing to his SUV. "My wheels."

Rollie didn't see the punch coming. A blow to the base of his skull all but paralyzed him. His knees buckled, but Bobby Manners grabbed hold of him before he fell. Rollie tried to focus as the muscular giant carried him to the back of the store, and pushed him face-first over the hood of a different maroon sedan. Rollie tried to shake off the blow as his wrists were bound behind his back. Bobby worked quickly as Rollie forced his eyes open. They were in the back of the store, and the lot was void of cars. No one was around to rescue him. Bobby shoved him into the passenger seat, walked around the car, and slid in behind the wheel. Rollie tried to clear his vision. They drove out of the lot in silence.

North of Malibu, on the west side of Pacific Coast Highway, Bobby Manners maneuvered his car down an unpaved road that ended on the cliffs overlooking the ocean. In the dark, as his perception cleared, Rollie saw the lights bordering the coastline. They were for all practical purposes, out in the middle of nowhere.

Bobby Manners stopped the car, leaving the headlights on, and got out. He pulled Rollie out and slammed him against the car. "Let's get this over."

Rollie's head was still spinning. "Aren't they all dead?"

"A contract is an honorable agreement. If I don't complete my obligation, trusting me will no longer exist."

"Bobby, if that's your name, we don't even know each other." Rollie was trying to delay the inevitable. Death was waiting for him.

Bobby nodded, glaring at Rollie, "I didn't know the others I hit either."

Rollie blew a breath through clenched lips, "But why?"

"Something your old man did. He killed Lipesky's brother and Vince Masseria. I don't know all the details. Don't want to know. Sorry."

"You worked with Shelly?" Rollie needed time.

Bobby gave Rollie a strange grin. "Actually, I was hired to make sure all the loose ends were cleaned up, and then get rid of Shelly. You did that for me, thanks. She was one dangerous bitch."

Rollie struggled. "That's it, then, right?"

"Yeah,"

He grabbed Rollie's shirt, and Rollie slammed his knee at hard as possible, into Bobby's groin. Not once, but a series of short knee movements that doubled the thickset man over. Rollie bashed into Bobby, the binders on his wrists tearing the skin. He knocked the brawny Bobby onto his back. Rollie fell over him, ramming his shoulder into Bobby's face. They rolled over one another, inching toward the edge of the cliff. Bobby Manners was gasping for air, holding his crotch while Rollie pummeled his body against the guy with all the strength he could find. Rollie kicked at the dirt, losing his balance while the pain in Bobby's testicles subsided. Bobby suddenly growled, picking Rollie up, dragging him to the edge. Rollie fought, twisted, pulled and jerked to no avail. Bobby was stronger than he was. Bobby grabbed Rollie behind the neck and down between his crotch, and lifted him over his head as though he was a barbell. Bobby had Herculean strength. He screamed out, about to send Rollie over the cliff when several shots rang out, breaking the eerie silence. Bobby's knees buckled.

Bobby's grip eased and he fell backwards, dropping Rollie behind him.

Rollie spun around seeing Rader, Frank Mustio and several other cops holding flashlights. They surrounded him. Rader checked Bobby. He was dead.

"What took you so long?" Rollie blurted.

Rader untied Rollie's hands. "We couldn't just follow you up here and give our position away. Had to wait for him to show us what he was going to do, or we'd have no case."

"What if he tossed me over the cliff before you got here?" Rollie was angrily brushing the dirt and blood from his clothes and face.

Rader thought about it. "Well, we'd of still made the arrest. When we saw that old lady get in her maroon wheels, I didn't know what to think. Almost call the whole thing off, 'cause we didn't see his car."

"What stopped you?" Rollie wanted to know.

"We saw Bobby at the gym. Seeing him at the grocery store was too much of a coincidence." Rader laughed. "I don't believe in coincidences."

Rollie walked around in tiny circles, nodding, shaking his head, waving his arms wildly, and attempted to come up with the appropriate thing to say. He clenched both fists into solid balls, and then thought better of hitting Rader. "Thanks for getting her address"

"Ah, there's the man with the romantic heart. I thought you were going to hit me."

"Why would I hit you?" Rollie inched closer to Rader's face.

"Because we let that big moose tie you up?" Rader said.

"He gave me a sucker punch." Rollie admitted.

"Yeah, but before that you did hit him a couple of times. Why didn't you hit him again? All of us thought you had a potent punch."

Rollie's eyes narrowed, "I would've taken him."

"On the way down?" Frank Mustio asked from a few feet away.

Rollie smirked, "If that's what it took, we'd have gone over that cliff together."

"Right." Mustio said. He walked back to the patrol car to avoid Rollie.

Rader sniffed, backing away. "Damn, you stink." He shined the flashlight over the ground, locating the source of the stench. Cow patties. "You need a shower, dude."

Rollie took a slow, hot shower, played a Chris Botti CD, and while the soft, melodic jazz wafted through the air, he opened the slider and sat outside sipping Jack Daniels over crushed ice. Gentle rolling waves danced when they capped, causing golden-tongued, angelic songs over the rocks along the shoreline. He felt his knuckles tighten, creating fisted balls, as the ghost of his pop smacking his mother's face came back. For years, he wanted to hit his old man, punch for punch, whacking him for taking out his failures on Rollie's ma. Even though, he was only thirteen, he practiced throwing the short jab that scored, the one that would hurt his old man, the coward who took everything out on his wife and son. When they killed his pop, Rollie felt short-changed. He never got to punish him for hurting a woman half his size. Rollie glanced at his curled fists, and for the first time understood part of his stored up anger. His old man – the punch he never got to throw. He smiled at the irony. Perhaps now, he could put a dark shadow from his past to bed. He sucked at the crisp night air, and it responded, bringing a tranquil peace to his heart. Tired, beat and bloody, he still got a few laughs from the cops when he filled out the report. He thought about Kali, and how truly messed up her life had become. He didn't know a relationship with her was possible after all she had done to him. They had a tumultuous bond, a connection he couldn't explain. Once upon a time he loved her so much, he even thought about suicide when he caught her in bed with another man. Suicide wasn't a real consideration, just another inconvenience she dumped on him. Drugs had taken Kali away and slowly destroyed what they had. He missed Kali's laughter and hated the damn drugs had chewed her into tiny little pieces. After all she had done, she still had the courage to beg for his forgiveness. The funniest part of that -- he gave it to her.

Rollie glanced up at the sky, closed his eyes, and hoped for an answer from the Angels. They had to be present; otherwise, there was no earthly reason for his survival. If they weren't there, he would certainly be dead, wouldn't he? A warm feeling gushed over him, his skin tingling from the sensation. Every once in a while, whenever he questioned his faith, he felt a presence. There was always hope. It warmed his heart knowing the Angels hadn't given up on him. He would find time to help Kali, not with money and certainly not with a relationship, but if she could be helped and wanted it badly enough to keep asking, he would continue to be there for her. He needed to move on, away from the love that had collected so many misgivings. He had no idea what Tiler could bring to his life, but she was the first woman, after the divorce from Kali, to uncover feelings he didn't think he was capable of encountering again.

The phone rang. Rollie jumped up and caught it on the second ring.

"This is Rollie,"

"Turn on your video phone!" Millie Jefferson demanded.

"Grandma?"

"Don't you grandma, me. Turn on your phone."

Rollie glanced at his watch. It was after 11, which meant it was 2A.M. in South Carolina. He plugged in the videophone and waited for it to warm up. Finally, there was a close up of Millie, waiting. She was angry, pursed lips, squinting eyes, and a demanding stare she shared when wanting something.

"Okay," Rollie said, "What now?"

"I had a dream Rollie. It was an awful dream, and you didn't do well in it."

"Oh, yeah?" Rollie put his face close to the camera. "See my kisser?"

"Yes, and I also see cuts and bruises. Someone beat the stuffing's outta ya, didn't they?"

Rollie stammered. "You haven't seen the other guy."

"Did you hurt him?" She was getting too close to the camera. Her image blurred.

"The police did."

"You promised to be a good boy."

"I have been, ah, most of the time." Rollie forced a smile and his lips hurt like hell. "Listen, remember when I said I was thinking about coming back down to see you and Beanie in the next week or two?"

"Yep, and I gave up on that idea." He watched her smirk.

"All right, let's start over. Hi grandma, how are you?"

"Oh, you wanna play that game again?"

"Yep." Rollie smiled, and his bruised lip cracked.

"Oh, my goodness, is that really you, Rollie?"

"Very funny. How's my favorite girl been?"

"Just fine, sittin' here all day waitin', fussing' over my grandson's well been', and waitin' for him to call me. Huh! He must still be too busy for an old lady like me."

"Hey, Grandma?"

"I must've dialed the wrong number. Doesn't even sound like you."

"I love you. I was sitting here looking at the ocean, and the first thing I thought about was you, and how much I miss you."

Millie started to sniffle. "Oh, Rollie. You always know what to say when I scold you."

"I do, ya know, love you very much."

"I love you too, Rollie. So, big shot, when exactly are you gonna get on that big bird and fly back to see me?"

"I might have an acting job next week so how does the following week sound?"

"If you don't get the job, you still comin'?"

"It works for me if you promise to cook some biscuits and fried chicken?"

"Comin' alone?"

Rollie thought about it. "Don't know, we'll see. Take care. I'll call in a few days with my travel plans, okay?"

"Yep. By the way, do you have the time?"

"Yes, ma'am, I do and it runs as good as always."

"Hold it up."

Rollie raised his wrist to show her the watch. His ribs were on fire. "It's past your bedtime, Grandma. You need your beauty sleep."

"God bless you, Rollie. I can't wait to see you." She hung up like she always did. Never said goodbye to anyone.

CHAPTER 47

From a block away, she strode toward him with a small dog attached to a leash. Tiler, without trying, strolled with an innocent saunter, like a teenaged girl walking in high-heels for the first time. The closer she got the better the view became. There was no false pretense in Tiler's body. Tiler was feminine from head to toe, not cheap or flirtatious, and yet honestly unsophisticated and naive. Rollie's stomach flipped, and heat rose into his cheekbones. She wore black slacks, and a powder-blue turtleneck blouse with matching earrings. Her black flats were soft crushed leather. The only jewelry she wore was a tasteful wristwatch. The leash on the dog matched the color of her blouse. Her blond hair was flipped out in the back, with just enough bangs to drift gently over her forehead. The dog was a little Papillion. His oversized ears made his head look like a fluffy butterfly. He pranced proudly.

Rollie got out of the car and watched her approach.

When she spotted Rollie, she broke into a huge smile. "You found me?"

"Said I was good."

"Bet you followed me?"

"Nope, I didn't have to." And that was the truth.

"Really?" She raised an eyebrow and waited.

"Uh huh." He looked down. "Who's your friend?"

"This is Pappy."

"Pappy? An Interesting name." Rollie could see how attached she was to the little guy.

"I couldn't think of something cute to name him, kept repeating he was a Papillion and found myself abbreviating it to Pappy. His ears stood up, and that was it. Pappy."

The little dog looked up at her and barked.

Rollie glanced down at the dog. "A French butterfly. I see he likes his name."

The dog moved over to Rollie, stood on his hind legs, did a dance in a circle, and checked Rollie over from the knee down.

"I think he likes you too."

Rollie knelt down, and Pappy came to him. Rollie picked him up and got his face licked.

"That's a first," Rollie said

"I'll bet. Pappy never does that, not to anyone, especially men."

They caught each other's eyes and held the exchange for a long beat.

Rollie finally broke the spell. "You ready to have a great dinner?"

"Let me put his food down and freshen up. Why don't you come in for a minute while I get ready?" She skipped up the stairs and entered her apartment.

Rollie followed, holding Pappy and watching the sensual movement of her body. He couldn't imagine her getting any fresher than she was.

The moment they entered her apartment, Rollie knew Tiler was going to be a part of his life. He wasn't sure how it would happen, he just knew. The apartment was fresh, alive with color, tastefully decorated in natural earth tones, leathers, and luxurious materials. It looked like a model home, with elegant figurines in a lighted cabinet, artwork of which every painting told a story, and flowers arranged in a crystal vase. A small entry table was clustered with family pictures -- her mother, father, grandparents, and what looked to be two sisters and one brother. In the hallway was a religious picture with a shelf-table beneath it. The only thing on the small shelf was a bible.

Tiler went into the kitchen, filled the dog's bowl, and set it on the floor. She came back into the room as Rollie was unhooking Pappy's leash.

"That goes in the utility closet, in the kitchen. If you don't mind, I'll be right out?"

"No problem."

She disappeared down the hallway. Rollie went into the kitchen and hung the leash in the pantry. Rollie was impressed at how clean, and in place everything was. No dirty dishes or signs of laziness. Pappy went to his bowl and ate happily. Rollie returned to the living room and was looking over the family pictures when Tiler came up behind him. He held up one picture of Tiler playing in a snow-covered setting.

"That was taken in Rocky Bottom where I grew up." The pictures brought fond memories to Tiler, and Rollie enjoyed watching her light up just looking at them.

"Where is Rocky Bottom?"

"South Carolina. That was the day after I graduated from Clemson." She was embarrassed and turned away.

"Smarty pants, huh?"

"More determination than brain power."

"How come I don't hear a Southern accent?"

"Oh, it comes out when I go back home." She answered with a touch of the south.

Rollie set the picture down and admired the others -- photos of what looked to be the rest of her family. "And who are these good looking people?"

"Mom, dad, grandparents, two sisters, and one big brother who never stops watching over all that I do. Butch is always there when I need someone to lean on."

"Lucky you." Rollie was jealous. He never had a family. How neat it would have been to enjoy brothers and sisters? He felt his cheeks sting grateful he had Millie.

"Are you an only child, Rollie?"

"Yeah. It must be fun coming from a big family?"

Tiler laughed. "At times."

He looked into her lusty blue eyes. His heart rate increased, and while she did nothing to encourage his feelings one way or the other, the heat coming from her -- a raw sensual desire he had only experienced once before with Kali, was provocative.

Instantly, Rollie had sweaty palms while his stomach did valiant flip-flops. Nervous feelings raced. "Dinner?" He barely got the words off his tongue.

Her voice was so incredibly soft when she took a breath. Her breasts rose up against the silk material of her blouse and fell away when she exhaled. "Rollie..."

He took her hand and felt her whole body shudder. He moved closer and she started breathing irregularly. She took cute little gulps of air as if it were running out. Rollie felt like a kid on his first date. He wanted to kiss her and hold back at the same time. He didn't want to rush this, to scare her off, and yet she was like a giant magnet pulling him toward her. Their bodies gently came together.

"Not too fast?" He whispered.

"I don't know," she whispered back

"I'd like to hold you," he continued to whisper as he looked deep into her eyes.

"Okay." She murmured.

Rollie took her into his arms, bent over and gave her a kiss. "I think we should go to dinner, and see if this feeling is still there on a full stomach."

She giggled, and wiped the lipstick from his lips "It will still be there."

"Then I have something to look forward to."

That's when Tiler took his hand and led him into the bedroom. "I don't think we should wait."

Rollie had forgotten how gratifying it was to hold a woman, kiss her deeply and make uninterrupted love without worrying about someone jumping out to ruin it all. No one was there to beat him up or attack unexpectedly. No one came. He held Tiler, and she held him back. Their bodies became one, and it felt right.

Claw of the Lobster Seafood Restaurant turned out to be a good choice. They ate outside on the patio overlooking the marina, where a zillion boats bobbed in a giant parking lot on water. The warm weather brought out people from all walks of life, strolling along the walkways, holding hands, creating a romantic setting -- a living Norman Rockwell painting. As daylight faded, the sky changed into a gigantic canvas of orange, pink and gray as it covered the horizon. Lights glittered from the multi-storied apartment buildings, and yachts roamed with the current. It was captivating. Rollie sat across from Tiler. Dinner was scrumptious. They shared a bottle of wine and held hands like two teenagers. He told her about his childhood, leaving a bunch of stuff out, and she told him about hers. They had nothing in common, but the electricity between them was alive and well.

Rollie's cell phone rang. He frowned because he thought he had turned it off. It rang again.

"Answer it," she said.

"I'm sorry, I thought I turned it off."

"It's okay. I have to go to the ladies room anyway."

Rollie opened his cell phone as she walked off. His eyes drifted, watching her walk, looking so hot without trying. The girl had a fantastic stride. Knowing she knew his eyes were on her with every step, made it all the more fun to watch.

"This is Rollie."

"It's Uncle Anthony."

The hair on Rollie's arm stood up. He looked around to see if anyone might be listening. "What did I forget?"

"Nothing. Everyone is home and okay, thanks to you." There was a pause. "Can I ask you something?"

"Sure." Rollie didn't know what to expect.

"Why did you let us go?" Pataglia asked.

Rollie thought about the question. He'd ask himself the same thing over and over. His eyes traveled out into the marina. "From what I could see, you didn't come out here looking for trouble. You wanted to know about Tawny, find out what happened to her, resolve that issue and make peace with the troublemakers. You didn't come here to kill innocent people."

"I'm glad you understand." Pataglia whispered. "Thank you." He again hesitated. "You do know the man wasn't sent by us?"

He abruptly hung up. Finally, Rollie spoke up." He almost killed me."

"Won't happen again. We've talked to everyone. An apology is on the table."

327

"Accepted." More silence. "You must want something else, right?" Rollie thought about the ledger. Did they know he turned it in?

"Just wanted to thank you. Fabby, Gi Carlo and me, owe our lives to you."

Obviously they didn't. "You owe me nothing."

"Sure we do. Fabby is sorry he messed up your office."

"It can be fixed," Rollie said. "Besides, I shot the guy."

"That's forgotten. Next time you're in New York, I'd like you to have dinner with me."

"Why?"

"Why not?" Pataglia shot back.

"We're strangers."

"Tawny loved you. If you weren't blood, you would've been the only man in her life. She never stopped talking about you, so if you were good enough for her, there has to be room in both of our hearts for one another. We don't have to be strangers, Rollie. It's my fault we never got to know one another, but it's not too late."

"We live different lives and have nothing in common."

"The commonality is your mother and I were siblings. We made lots of mistakes, Rollie, a lifetime full of errors and a clock that can never be turned back. That's not what I'm asking from you. I want you to live your life the way you want. I admire your honesty and determination to make a better life for you, I really do. You have no idea how proud you make me. You got out, and I need you to stay out because I can see the smile on your mother's face. She would have been very proud to say you were her son as I am to say you are my nephew."

Quiet sobs came over the line. "I hope you can forgive me?"

Rollie had never heard his uncle cry. "There is nothing to forgive."

"You keep saying that, but yes there is way too much. You need to forgive so you can go on and leave all the rubbish behind. You won't forget, but you can forgive."

Rollie thought about it as Tiler walked back to their table. Uncle Anthony was right. He needed to forgive them all. Perhaps it was ignorance, or self-indulgence that made them function through horrible times. He didn't want to know about the past; about the misgivings or unfathomable deeds his family had done to survive their upbringing. He didn't want to hear excuses, and so he was left with forgiveness. He wasn't one of them and never could be.

"You're right, Uncle Anthony. I need to forgive you, and I do from the bottom of my heart. I'm sorry things aren't different but, such as they are, we can move on. Next time I come to New York, I will look forward to sitting down and having dinner with you."

Tiler rejoined him at their table.

"Thank you." Pataglia blew his nose. "We gave Tawny a private service. I hope you will remember her as a child."

"I'll never forget her," Rollie answered.

"It may be inappropriate to say, but I love you and will always be here if you ever need anything. Sometimes we can easily turn over rocks you can't lift."

Rollie didn't say anything but was sure that was true. He hoped that day would never come. He didn't want to be in debt to anyone.

"Goodbye, Rollie." Pataglia sounded somber.

"Goodbye, sir." Rollie closed the phone. His eyes flushed over.

"A hard conversation?" Tiler asked.

"Yeah. A stranger calling to tell me one of my childhood friends died." Rollie felt guilty telling a little white lie, but it was easier than the truth.

"I'm sorry."

"Me too."

She took his hands and held them between hers. "When I walked by the bar I couldn't help notice the basketball game. Do you follow basketball?"

He cleared his throat, pushing the phone conversation far away. "I do. You saying you're a fan?"

"Avid."

"What team keeps your attention?" Almost everyone in L.A. was a Laker fan.

"You're gonna hate me. I know when you live in Los Angeles your supposed to be a Laker's fan, but I've been following the Clipper's ever since I moved here." Tiler was gushing with excitement just mentioning her team. "I love an underdog, and now they're as exciting as any team in the NBA."

Rollie laughed. He couldn't believe this girl. "Me too. So much so I have season tickets."

"To the Clippers?" She howled with delight.

"Yep, two seats, middle section, three rows up. I love the game."

She laughed, a euphoric giggle, like small children often do when they get tickled. Rollie liked the sound. It was contagious. Maybe she would like to go with him to Charleston and visit Grandma on spring break? Maybe she was a keeper? She continued to show happiness, and it brought Rollie out from beneath the dark clouds of his past. Childhood memories spoiled too much in Rollie's life. It was time to let the past slip off into the night. The ugly that had kept a vise-like grip on his life for too long was finally over. It felt good. Rollie Kemp was on a roll. He had survived a wild shootout, just got an acting job on a TV show, wrote a silly tabloid story that hit the front page, received an apology from a notorious crime family boss, created a partnership with one of the best PIs in the country, and met a girl -- a girl named Tiler. Oh, and the topper was the girl loved the Clippers. Imagine the possibilities? He joined her raucous exuberance, and people all around them started laughing too – even though they had no earthly idea why.

AUTHOR'S NOTE

Law enforcement comes in many flavors, cops, private detectives, Federal Agents and those serving their country in various entities. As a filmmaker and actor, I have had the pleasure of working with most. Many retire to private practice in one form of security or another. I based the character Rollie Kemp after several men I knew and worked closely with. I wanted a man fueled by a past, and yet unfulfilled in just about every aspect of life. Rollie Kemp is confused, dangerous, honest, and trustworthy; and would still give you the shirt off his back. He has the proverbial short tempter, the guts to face death with both feet on the ground and continues the quest to find a woman who will recapture his heart. The heart his ex-wife stomped on. The fun of Rollie is, he's been through hell and back again. He survived a terrible accident, ragged divorce, tried law school, acting and a few other things before meeting legendary Drake Fargo. They partnered and do things most others have already turned down. Both men are incredible movie-star handsome irresistible teddy bears, but you never want them angry or after you.

ABOUT THE AUTHOR

William Byron Hillman is an actor, filmmaker, novelist and public speaker.

A published author of ten novels

Bill is also an actor with many films and television credits. He did a two-year stint on "Days of our Lives," appeared in films like Ice Station Zebra, has been a motivational speaker at college campuses nationwide, sold numerous screenplays and produced, directed and wrote a series of well-known movies. As an actor/filmmaker/novelist, Bill has a international following and appreciates all of his fans.

Bill currently lives in South Carolina with his wife and 16 paws where he is putting the finishing touches on Bad Rap, the fourth Rollie Kemp thriller.

Author Web Site: http://www.williamhillman.com

Author Amazon Page
http://www.amazon.com/author/williamhillman

Author's Blog: http://williambyronhillman.blogspot.com

PREVIEW OF

"APRIL"

A new Rollie Kemp novel

"APRIL" CHAPTER 1

These two guys dressed as janitors got off the elevator. They looked like Big John and Sparky. The sizable one was ugly, pot marks covered his face; his hair was black and unruly, and his body was well hidden beneath the coveralls. The short guy's head was shaved and shined like a bowling ball. He was both dangerous and nasty looking. The bigger one pushed a cleaning cart with stacked towels, a bucket of water, several mops and brooms and other cleaning material. The small guy, the one with a bald-head followed. The hallway was upscale, rich carpet, expensive wallpaper, framed artwork behind glass, and light fixtures that cost a bundle. The two guys ambled to the end unit. Nice entrance and decorative doorbell button with a light draped around the F on the door.

The bald guy opened a small book to verify, put the book back in his pocket and then both men put rubber gloves on, took out handguns and screwed silencers on them. They positioned the cart in front of the door, and both stood aside to avoid being seen through the peephole. The tall guy rang the bell. Footsteps were heard shuffling across carpet and then a hard floor. Both men stood still, knowing whoever was inside was peering through the peephole. The only thing visible was the cart.

They heard the deadbolt slide, the chain was easily unhooked, and then cautiously the door opened.

"Hello, is anyone there?"

The tall guy stepped out, hiding the gun behind him.

"Are you William Bradberry?"

"Yes, who are you? I didn't call maintenance."

"Sure you did."

Without hesitation, he pumped two muffled shots at Bradberry, hitting him directly in the middle of his chest. William Bradberry backed up a few feet with a stunned look on his face and then collapsed to the floor. He was dead before the thud was heard.

The two acted quickly. The short guy grabbed the body and pulled it out of the way. The tall one rolled the cart inside and closed the door. Methodically, they searched the upscale condo. They pulled drawers out and dumped the contents. They emptied the closets, looked behind the artwork, and dropped every book on every shelf. They turned the beds up-side-down and sliced open all the pillows. They removed everything from the refrigerator and freezer and pulled all the pots, pans and dishes out. They turned the place apart but didn't find what they were looking for.

The short guy came out of a bedroom and joined the tall one.

"No safe, no computer and no briefcase."

The tall one pulled his unruly hair back and tied it into a ponytail. He eyes roamed around the condo as if seeing through the walls. They had been given false information, or they killed Bradberry too fast and would pay for that mistake later. Their info said Bradberry wouldn't go quietly and would scream like a little boy. It was too dangerous to keep him alive, and as it turned out too stupid to kill him. He glanced at his watch and shook his head.

"We have to go."

The short guy wanted to continue looking.

"What about..."

"No, let's go."

"We can't go back empty handed. What are we gonna do?"

"Plan B." The tall guy glanced at his watch again and headed for the door. "We've been in here too long. Leave the cart. Let's get out of here."

The tall guy looked out the door. The hallway was empty. The two men closed the door to unit F and hustled down the stairway.

"APRIL" CHAPTER 2

So this guy came into the office as if he owned it. He loomed over Rollie and challenged him to get up. Rollie leaned back and smiled. The guy had this look and was built like some square bodied football player. His frown was a reflection of being constipated or making a feeble attempt to look tough. Rollie guessed him to be around fifty years old and was unimpressed. If it came to pasting him in the chops, Rollie was sure he could drop him.

"You obviously have something on your mind."

"Get up."

"That's not how it works."

"Not how what works?"

"You're telling me to get up. If I get up when I don't want to get up, I get mad. Do you really want to see me mad?"

The guy stood there like someone just stole his memory. The look on his face told Rollie he was no longer able to think. He put his hands on his hips, dropped them to his side, raised one arm and almost pointed at Rollie and finally thought better of doing anything. He turned around and left the office. A moment later he came back in and tried to smile.

"Are you Drake Fargo?"

"No," Rollie answered without looking up.

"Will he be coming back soon?"

"Don't think so."

"Okay this isn't working out as I hoped. Can I ask who you are?"

"Sure."

The guy didn't know what to do next. He became an instant statue.

"Okay, I'll start over. Drake Fargo worked on a case last year. He helped William Bradberry solve a mystery. Someone was stealing his diamonds, and Drake Fargo figured out it was the janitorial crew that came late at night to clean his building. Saved Bradberry a ton of dough."

"I remember the case."

"Then you do know Drake Fargo?"

"He's my partner."

The guy came closer and glared down at Rollie.

"You're Rollie Kemp? I was told Rollie Kemp was this huge dude who asked questions after he punched someone's lights out. That Rollie Kemp, according to what Drake said, is legendary."

That did it. Rollie stood up, all six feet five inches of him. He towered over the guy with the slippery tongue who quickly stepped a pace or two backwards.

"My God you are huge!"

"Does he owe you money?"

"Who?"

"Drake, remember? You came in to see him."

"No, I ah, maybe this is nothing."

"What's nothing?"

"Look, sit back down, please. You're making me nervous."

Rollie nodded and sat.

"Drake is in Hawaii recovering from a gunshot wound. Is there something I can do for you?"

"William Bradberry was murdered last week. We live in the same condo units. The cops were all over the place asking questions. I must've been awake when it happened because I didn't sleep much last night. I would have noticed gun shots had I not been wearing my iPod all night. I love to listen to jazz, it's a weakness I have. The poor devil had two bullets in his chest, and there I was right down the hallway. I heard nothing, and that seems impossible. I should have heard them and done something."

Rollie thought the shooter probably had a silencer on his gun. "What do you think you might have been able to do?"

"I don't know something. Damn, they just shot him and let him bleed out."

"And you think Drake can help do what while the cops are working the case?"

"That's the whole point of my visit. I think they took his daughter April."

"The cops?"

"No, whoever shot Bill."

"For the diamonds?"

"Diamonds?" His face had that glazed stare again. He shook it off. "No, April came back from a dinner meeting, got all hysterical. She stayed in my spare bedroom that night, met with the detectives who checked her alibi and confirmed she was with a group of people at the time of death. She had old Bradberry cremated two days later, had someone clear out his condo and put the place on the market."

"So why are you thinking someone took her?"

"Because she's disappeared."

"What exactly does she do for a living? Did she work in diamonds like her father?"

"No, she's some big-shot chemical person who works in the food industry. She's like the daughter I never had. I told the cops she was visiting, staying with me and then the day before yesterday, she went back home."

"And now you can't find her?"

"She's disappeared, but all the cops said I was overreacting. Her cell phone goes right to voice mail."

"Maybe she's mourning her losses?"

"Are you a detective like Drake?"

"Drake is my partner, and yes we own this private detective agency together. Guys who own a detective agency are usually detectives."

"I see," the guy said and just stood there. His eyes roamed around the converted house Rollie, and Drake liked to call "the office" and noticed the bullet holes in the walls, cabinets and desk front. "April called me Uncle Lenny."

"Is that your name?"

"Yeah, oh damn I didn't introduce myself. I'm Leonard O'Lander the architect." He said it as though everyone should know whom he was.

Rollie didn't, but nodded as if he did anyway.

"So Leonard, or should I call you Lenny?"

"Lenny is good."

"Okay, Lenny. I'm Rollie Kemp, and I'm still not sure how I can help you?"

They shook hands and then Leonard O'Lander found a chair and sat down. He ran a hand through his wavy full-head of graying hair and stared at nothing. He glanced at Rollie but didn't see him. He frowned and tried to focus. Rollie Kemp watched him and waited. After a bit Lenny stood up again. His eyes glossed over, and tears were about to spill out. "Why do you have bullet holes everywhere?"

"Got into a shootout and haven't had time to fix them. I'll get around to it."

"They're quite fear-inspiring."

"Sorry about that. Maybe you shouldn't look at them?"

"Yeah, that might help. I need to know April's okay. I'm hoping they didn't take her."

"They?"

"Whoever shot poor Bill?"

"What makes you think there was more than one person?"

"Bill was a careful guy, so it had to be two or more to take him down like that."

"Maybe it was a robbery gone bad? You said he was in the diamond business."

"He never brought the diamonds home. He was a wholesaler, kept things in a big vault, you know, like the safe they have in banks."

"I'm sure the cops will figure it all out as soon as possible."

"It's Rollie, right?"

"Yeah, Rollie Kemp, that's me."

"So if I wanted to hire you, to make sure April's okay, how does that work?"

"I think you should wait a few days, Lenny. Let's make sure she's actually missing and not like I said earlier, out there morning her father's death."

"How long you think I should wait?"

"Wait a day or two and then I think you should talk to the cops. If she doesn't come back by the day after tomorrow, you can file a missing persons report which will give them a reason to start looking into where she is.

By the way, how long was she going to be here visiting her father?"

"At least another month."

"So what, she lives across town or down at the beach?"

"She lives in Charleston South Carolina where the laboratory she works for is busy testing whatever she was working on. Her colleagues are doing some trial testing, and she just wanted to get away and visit with her dad for a while. Her phone in Charleston goes to voice mail, and her office hasn't seen or talked to her in days. We hadn't seen her in almost nine months before her visit. After Bill had been cremated, April wanted time to be alone, but this is not like her. She would have called me."

Rollie watched Lenny. The guy was a nervous wreck. Drake wouldn't like them getting involved in a case where the guy hiring them wasn't even related. On the other hand, going to Charleston would be refreshing. He could visit with his grandma Millie. Lenny kept looking at the bullet holes in the wall and cabinets, and this distracted him. He should have fixed the damn holes. Most were caused by his gun wildly shooting at an intruder who intended to kill him. Why was he thinking about the shootout? Then he noticed Lenny was writing a check. He tore the check from his book and slid it across Rollie's desk. Rollie looked up from the check.

"You said we? What does that mean?"

"Aside from Bill being my neighbor, he was my best friend. We went to school together. His wife died before mine, and when Carole got her breast cancer, that's what Bill's wife also had, so we bonded and grew closer. That was over twenty years ago. April was just a little girl, and we sort of raised her together. I've been to every school event, every dance and graduation ceremony that girl has had. I met all the boys she ever dated, helped her get through college without sacrificing her inner being, and she's turned out okay. We did a good job."

Rollie nodded and looked back at the check and this time, he took a closer look and focused on the numbers. All he saw was a inordinate number with lots of zeros. When he looked, Lenny was waiting, expecting questions.

"You wrote me a check for seventy-five thousand dollars?"

"I don't want to wait for two more days. Something is wrong. Drake Fargo is a legend, and if he partnered with you, you must be over-the-top good, and I want the best. I need you to promise you'll find April and bring her home. If, by chance, she's no longer alive, those responsible need to pay with their life. Can you do that?"

"I'll find April. What happens to those who grabbed her just happens."

Lenny gestured to the check.

"Is that enough?"

"Depends on how long it takes."

"Whatever you need Rollie. Just call and you'll have it. I don't care what it cost."